DOUBLE ESPRESSO

Forge Books by Anthony Bruno

Devil's Food
Double Espresso

ANTHONY BRUNO

A TOM DOHERTY ASSOCIATES BOOK / NEW YORK

This is a work of fiction. All the characters and events portrayed in this novel are either fictitious or are used fictitiously.

DOUBLE ESPRESSO

This book is printed on acid-free paper.

A Forge Book
Published by Tom Doherty Associates, Inc.
175 Fifth Avenue
New York, NY 10010

Forge® is a registered trademark of Tom Doherty Associates, Inc.

Library of Congress Cataloging-in-Publication Data

Bruno, Anthony.
Double espresso / Anthony Bruno.—1st ed.
p. cm.
"A Tom Doherty Associates book."
ISBN 0-312-86650-X (acid-free paper)
I. Title.
PS3552.R82D68 1998
813'.54—dc21 98-13570
CIP

First Edition: August 1998

Printed in the United States of America

0 9 8 7 6 5 4 3 2 1

For Harry Dawson,
the one teacher who made all the difference

DOUBLE ESPRESSO

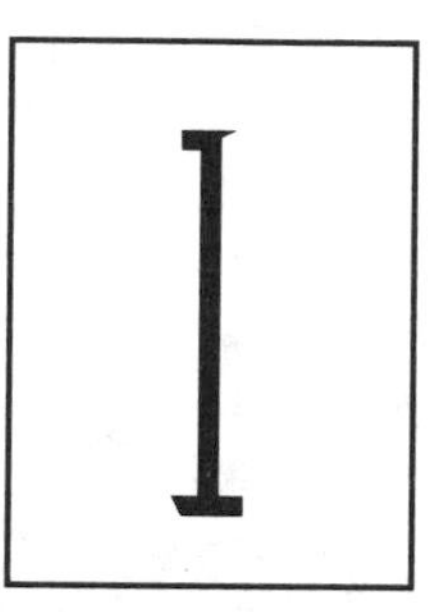

I won't die, Parole Officer Loretta Kovacs told herself for the fiftieth time that day, and it was only nine-fifteen in the morning. *A person can live perfectly well without it,* she kept thinking. *I don't need it. I won't die.*

She was sitting at her desk in the basement offices of the Jump Squad—more formally known as the State of New Jersey Parole Violators Search Unit—flipping through a law-school brochure that had come in the mail yesterday. But her mind wasn't on going to law school, and it wasn't on her job, which was tracking down parole violators. Her head was tilted down toward the brochure, but her eyes were glued to her partner, Frank Marvelli, who was standing over his desk with his back to her. *Nice butt,* she thought.

Marvelli was sipping a cup of hot coffee as he perused the sports section of the *Ledger.* His back showed a broad expanse of the black-and-white houndstooth sports jacket he was wearing. He was muscular with big hands but not terribly tall. The back of his head was as square as a cardboard box, but his hair was thick and dark. She just wished he wouldn't gunk it up with whatever goop he used to keep it combed straight back. A cheese Danish with one bite taken out of it sat on a napkin at the edge of his desk.

Yes, Marvelli did have a mighty fine butt, Loretta thought with a sigh, but at the moment she couldn't decide what she wanted more: his butt or his coffee. It was Monday morning, and today was her first caffeine-free workday. She'd decided over the weekend to give it up.

Loretta ran her fingers through her long wavy dirty-blond hair and squinted her lozenge-green eyes as she tried to focus on the print in the glossy law-school brochure. She felt woozy and disoriented, and she could feel a headache coming on. Her hands were shaking slightly. She'd never imagined that withdrawal from caffeine would be like this. It was only coffee she was giving up, for God's sake. What if she were hooked on crack or coke? Or diet pills, God forbid.

Without thinking, Loretta sucked in her gut and bloused out her ivory-colored shirt from the waistband of her black slacks, and instantly she hated herself for doing that. So what if she was a little overweight? There's nothing wrong with that, she thought defensively. She'd been trying to cool it with the self-deprecating attitude lately, but sometimes it just snuck up on her like a ninja. She was trying to think positively about herself. After all, it wasn't as if she were the fat lady in the circus. One hundred and seventy-eight pounds is not an outrageous weight, especially at five foot six. She wasn't built like a bowling ball. And besides, this was not something to obsess about, she told herself. Obsessing about weight only promotes negative mind.

But that cheese Danish on Marvelli's desk was calling out to her like a snake-charmer's flute. It would go so nice with a cup of coffee, she thought. Her head started whirling like a dervish on cold medication. She closed her eyes to make the room stop spinning. She didn't need coffee, she kept telling herself. Her doctor had told her that it was bad for her health, that among other things, caffeine worsens PMS attacks. And she certainly didn't need that cheese Danish either.

But Marvelli, on the other hand, was a habit she wouldn't mind getting into. He was a genuinely nice guy who really seemed to care about people. Unfortunately, in her heart of hearts, Loretta knew that the chemistry just wasn't right between them, and she had a feeling she'd be better off not thinking about him—not *that* way. She forced herself to concentrate on the law-school brochure.

Her phone rang, and she reached over to pick it up. "Parole Violators Search Unit," she said in deadpan voice. "Kovacs speaking."

"Loretta?" the voice on the other end said. "It's Bonnie."

"Hi," Loretta said, sitting up and changing her tone. Bonnie was her sister, who had her own law practice in Chicago. "What's up, Bon?"

"I can't talk long," Bonnie said. "I'm due in court in fifteen minutes, but I've been thinking. Why don't you apply to some law schools out here? You could work part-time with me while you go to school. God knows, I've got plenty of things you could do."

Loretta glanced at Marvelli's back and wondered about leaving Jersey. She hadn't considered that. "It's an idea, Bon. I'll have to think about it, though."

"What's to think about? It would be a perfect arrangement for you. Or don't you want to work for your little sister?"

"Don't be silly. I don't have a problem with that."

"Then do it. Look, Chicago is a great town, and we've always talked about going into practice together. You could do the criminal work, and I'll take the civil stuff. Kovacs and Kovacs. It'll be great."

"Yeah . . . maybe." Loretta was trying to adjust to the notion of moving to Chicago. She wasn't sure she was ready for that much change in her life. Of course, there was nothing holding her here.

"I took the liberty of calling a few law schools in the area for you," Bonnie said. "You'll be getting applications from Loyola, Northwestern—"

"Hang on a minute, Bonnie." Loretta covered the phone with her hand and frowned at the shouts coming from the long narrow hallway that lead to the holding cells out back.

"Jumper's wild! Head's up, people!" Loretta recognized the voice. It was her boss, Julius Monroe, the head of the Jump Squad.

A "jumper" suddenly emerged from the hallway and burst into the main office, a tall, dark-skinned black man. He was built like a running back and was good-looking despite the hardball expression, with a shaved head and a thin mustache outlining his upper lip. A pair of handcuffs dangled from one wrist. Marvelli had apprehended him that morning. When the jumper spotted Marvelli, he stopped dead in his tracks and gave some serious eyeballing to the man who had arrested him.

"I got him," Marvelli called out.

"The hell you do," the jumper said. He was gripping the open end of the handcuffs between his index and middle fingers like Captain Hook.

"Come on, Rashid," Marvelli said wearily. "Let's not be stupid." He walked toward the man with his arms extended, palms up. Rashid was more than a head taller than Marvelli.

"Get the hell away from me," Rashid warned, showing the whites of his eyes. The hook was poised over his head. "You crazy, man."

Marvelli kept moving toward him. "Don't make it any worse than it already is, Rashid. Put your hand down and I won't have to add resisting to your sheet."

Rashid frowned deeply. "What the hell you talking about, man? I resisted you all the way down Broad Street. I resisted you like *hell.*"

Marvelli shrugged it off. "You call that resisting? That wasn't resisting. Not really. I woke you up and got you out of bed. You were just mad."

Rashid scowled. "What do you mean, I wasn't resisting? We must've been going at it for a half hour at least. And that was just in my bedroom."

Marvelli shrugged. "I wasn't watching the clock, Rashid. Now just put that hand down."

"No way," Rashid said. "I'm out of here, man." He dashed for the door, but Marvelli quickly dove over a desk to block Rashid's path. The body block threw Rashid backward, and he banged his head on a file cabinet. Marvelli quickly sat on Rashid's stomach and pinned the wrist with the handcuffs to the floor. In the meantime Rashid got his free hand around Marvelli's thick neck, thumb on the Adam's apple.

"Don't make me mad, Rashid," Marvelli croaked. "It's bad for my biorhythms. You mess up my biorhythms, there's no telling what I might do."

Rashid gritted his teeth and struggled to get Marvelli off him while Marvelli hammered Rashid's hand against the nearest file cabinet, trying to break his grip on the loose handcuff. Their tussling on the floor was shaking the whole room, threatening to topple the stacks of case files that were perched on top of the row of file cabinets.

Loretta noticed Marvelli's coffee cup tottering on the edge of his desk next to the cheese Danish. She glanced down at the two men wrestling on the floor. If Marvelli wasn't going to eat it, she wouldn't mind having a little bite, but not if it was drenched in coffee. She was already two days into her break from caffeine, and she'd be damned if she was going to start this ordeal all over again.

"Bonnie?" Loretta said into the phone. "I'll have to call you back tonight. I've got a situation here." She hung up the phone.

"Hey!" she yelled, annoyed with the ruckus. "Break it up, you two." The three other POs in the room hardly took notice. This kind of stuff happened every day at the Jump Squad.

Rashid ignored Loretta's warning and kept trying to strangle Marvelli.

She raised her voice. "Hey, Rashid. *Rashid!*"

He curled his lip back and bared his teeth. "Get outta my face, woman, before I—"

That's when he saw the gun.

She was standing up in the triangle position—feet apart, knees bent, both hands on her weapon. The barrel of her .38 was leveled on his head.

Rashid smiled like a movie star. "Now, what're you gonna do with that thing, sugar pie?"

"Ventilate your skull if you don't settle down."

Rashid's eyes rolled toward Marvelli. "She serious, man?" he whispered.

Marvelli nodded. "Very."

"Who the hell is she?"

"My partner," Marvelli croaked.

"The new one?"

"Yup."

"The one who shot Bootsie Burnside through the bottom of his foot while he was running away from y'all?"

Marvelli nodded. "From fifty yards. She knows how to use that thing, Rashid."

"And she ain't afraid to use it, huh?"

"Does she look like she's afraid, Rashid?"

Rashid narrowed his eyes and looked her up and down, then focused on the muzzle staring down at him. "You the lady who took Moolie Jefferson while he was in bed with his woman?" he asked her.

Loretta nodded.

"He keeps a goddamn Uzi duct-taped under that bed. You know that? That boy is stone-cold. He could've killed you good."

"He didn't get the chance," she said.

"How's he doing?"

"Still in the hospital ward at East State as far as I know," Marvelli said. "He'll be all right . . . eventually."

Rashid looked at Marvelli, then looked at Loretta again, thinking it over.

"She really took down Moolie, huh?"

Marvelli nodded. "All by herself. I was downstairs."

Rashid thought about it some more, then after a while he let go of Marvelli's throat. "Sorry about your biorhythms, man," he apologized to Marvelli. Rashid clicked the open handcuff around his free wrist and got to his feet. "I know the way back to the pen. You don't have to take me."

Marvelli stood up and clapped the big man's shoulder as they walked back toward the hallway. "I'm proud of you, Rashid. You're doing the right thing. *And* you're showing some good judgment. That's very important. That means your energy is starting to flow in the right direction."

"Cool it with the spiritual stuff, man. You sound like a damn Muslim."

"Aren't *you* a Muslim?"

"Nah. I just like the name. Muslims got too many damn rules." He walked down the hallway. "I'm back, boss man," he called out. "And I'm not resisting neither."

Loretta put her gun back in her handbag, shaking her head. Marvelli certainly did have a way with people. Loretta envied him. He managed to stay relaxed in the most stressful of situations. Maybe when she kicked the caffeine habit, she'd learn how to relax, too.

Suddenly Marvelli's phone started to ring. He trotted back to his desk to get it. She watched him pick up the receiver and put it to his ear. There were wisps of dark hair on the back of his hand. She'd never noticed that before.

"Marvelli," he said, then his face relaxed. "Oh, hi, Annette. What's up?"

Annette was his mother-in-law, the Godmother. Loretta had met the woman only once, and she seemed nice enough. Just a little bit bossy and very Sicilian.

Loretta listened to Marvelli's voice as he spoke into the phone. It was a nice voice but a little on the high side.

Marvelli furrowed his brows. "Did you talk to the lawyer?" he asked his mother-in-law. "What did he say?"

Marvelli turned around and leaned against his desk, and Loretta quickly looked down at the brochure. Marvelli was stocky—just an inch or two taller than Loretta—but he was trim and muscular. He had small eyes—a little too close together—but they sparkled whenever he smiled, which was most of the time, especially when he was eating, which was also most of the time. The only thing she'd really like to change about him was his style. He was pure Guido, an Italian-American dinosaur from the age of Fabian. Dark slicked-back hair. Black knit sports shirt with white trim on the collar and down the front. Pegged forest green pants. Black pointy-toed imitation-alligator shoes. On most days he looked like an extra in a Martin Scorsese movie.

"No, Annette, that's not acceptable," he said into the phone, his voice getting higher and his face turning grim. "If the guy doesn't want to take our case, then we'll just get another lawyer. . . . No, Annette, that's not what I'm saying. The hospital didn't *kill* Rene. She was very sick—we all knew that. What I am saying is that the hospital could've done more for her at the end. They could've made her more comfortable, given her something else for the pain. Instead they just sent her home to die like a dog. These goddamn hospitals have to start treating people like people, for crying out loud. Someone's got to show them that they just can't get away with this kind of crap. So you just call up that shyster bastard and tell him he's fired. I'll find us another lawyer."

Loretta sighed. This was the real problem with Marvelli. He was still stuck on his wife. Rene Marvelli had died three months ago. Breast cancer. But he wouldn't let her go.

Marvelli didn't have a case against the hospital, and Loretta suspected that deep down he realized that. Mounting this crusade was just his way of keeping Rene's memory alive, convincing himself that he could still do something for her.

Loretta's gaze drifted to the cheese Danish on Marvelli's desk. Except for that one bite, he still hadn't touched it. That wasn't like him at all. Usually he'd eat a half dozen pastries in one sitting and still have room for more. When Marvelli didn't have an appetite, that meant something was radically wrong, and Loretta knew that it had to do with Rene. Loretta also knew that unless he could let her go, no other woman would ever stand a chance with him.

Not that Loretta ever thought *she* stood a chance with him. Not really.

But maybe this was all for the best, she thought. Even if she were serious about Marvelli—which she wasn't, not anymore—starting up something with him would be a terrible idea. She was still on probation with this job, so an office romance would not be very smart. Not that this job was all that great. To be honest, it pretty much sucked. The people who worked here were fine, and

Marvelli and Julius were great, but she just couldn't see herself hunting down parole violators and hauling them back to prison for the rest of her life. But since she'd managed to work her way *down* the ladder in the Department of Corrections from assistant warden in a women's correctional facility to just a regular old PO on the lowly Jump Squad, she figured no matter how horny she was, she'd better behave herself.

Loretta scanned the bull pen of Jump Squad's basement offices. Along one wall a series of grimy, iron-barred windows looked out on a Newark sidewalk where a lot of legs and feet walked by. On the opposite wall twenty-six jam-packed file cabinets stood shoulder to shoulder, each one balancing a precarious stack of case files on top. The eight metal desks in the big room each hosted a few more stacks, and there were even more stacks on the carpeted floor. Each case file represented a parolee who'd jumped, disappeared without notifying his or her PO. There were seventeen specially assigned parole officers in the Jump Squad, but only a handful of them were in the office this morning. The rest were out on the street looking for jumpers, which was normal for a weekday morning.

The overwhelming number of case files was enough to discourage anyone. Everyone on the Jump Squad knew that most of these jumpers would never be caught. Still, they had to try, particularly when it came to the dangerous ones, and Loretta was determined to have as perfect a record as she could. So far, she and Marvelli had brought in sixteen of the twenty-two jumpers they'd been sent out to find, which for the moment sort of made them the Mickey Mantle and Roger Maris of the office.

But Loretta realized that she hadn't been on the job all that long, and her streak could end in a flash. She was still pretty green compared to Marvelli, who'd been doing this for eleven years. He actually claimed that he liked it here, but she thought he was just stuck in a rut. This was the only real job he'd ever had.

Loretta tried to focus on the law-school brochure in front of her, but her eye kept going back to Marvelli's desk, the cheese Danish on the napkin, the steaming cardboard cup of coffee, the chrome-framed photo of Rene. That picture had been taken before the woman had been diagnosed. She was very pretty—even with the big hair and the raccoon mascara. Loretta had met Rene once, and even though she had been going through hell with radiation treatments, she still looked pretty good. Loretta stared at the photo and wondered what Rene had been like when she was well. According to Marvelli, she was his everything.

Loretta abruptly looked away, annoyed with herself for dwelling on Rene and Marvelli. She had other things to worry about. When she had first started this job, she'd made up her mind that she was going to overhaul her entire life—professionally, personally, and romantically. She was planning to apply to law school in the fall. She was also working out more, watching what she ate, and now she was giving up caffeine in the hope that it would alleviate her raging PMS. She was finally getting her act together.

Except in the romance department. She was still batting zero in that category.

Marvelli picked up his coffee cup and took a sip as he sat on top of his desk, feet on the chair. "So how was your weekend, Loretta?" he asked.

Crummy, she thought, but she held her tongue. *Think positive,* she reminded herself.

"Not bad," she said, but her voice gave her away. It always did. Sarcasm was encoded on her DNA.

"You do anything exciting?" he asked.

She shrugged. "I cleaned my gun."

He nodded as he took another sip. "That's good."

She wondered if he was even listening.

"*You* do anything exciting this weekend?" she asked.

"Well," he said, "I went to my daughter's lacrosse game on Saturday. Afterward the parents took the whole team out for pizza. On Sunday I stayed home and worked on our case against the hospital, sorting through all the paperwork and going through Rene's diary. She kept incredibly detailed notes about her treatment."

"I'll bet she did," Loretta said. She wanted to leave. She did not want to talk about his dead wife.

"Her notes are actually pretty interesting. If you'd like to read them sometime, I'll bring you some copies I've made. Not the personal stuff, just the parts about being sick."

Loretta forced a smile. "That's okay."

She wanted to grab him around the neck the way Rashid had and shake some sense into him. *Rene is dead!* she wanted to yell in his ear. *You're not! Stop beating yourself up. Get on with it.*

A long high bluesy note wafted out the hallway and into the bull pen. It sounded like Louis Armstrong playing an ensign's whistle.

Loretta rolled her eyes toward Marvelli. "I think we're wanted."

They got up and headed down the hallway to the first office on the right. Julius Monroe, the head of the Jump Squad, was sitting on top of his desk in his stocking feet with his legs crossed in the lotus position as he blew into a silver flute. What he was playing sounded like a jazz raga to Loretta, but she'd learned not to comment on the maestro's music because her observations were usually wrong and Julius wasn't shy about telling her so—at length.

Julius's eyes were closed in bliss as he played. He was wearing burgundy-colored pants, a white short-sleeved shirt, and a wide pink-and-black floral-print tie that lapped over his Buddha belly like a Saint Bernard's tongue. A white knit skullcap covered the top of his balding head, and his gray goatee quivered like a Geiger-counter needle whenever he held a note.

The small office was jammed with waist-high stacks of case files taking up most of the floor space. The walls were covered with posters of Julius's heroes, the masters of jazz—Miles, Dizzy, Monk, Trane, Bird, Mingus, and his all-time personal favorite and musical guru, Rahsaan Roland Kirk, the man who could play two saxophones at once and could also play a wooden flute through his nose as he hummed along. Julius had demonstrated this nasal technique for Loretta several times. Each time she'd lied and told him she was overwhelmed.

Marvelli plopped down into one of the imitation leather chairs opposite the desk. "What's up, Julius?"

Monroe ignored him and kept playing.

Loretta took the chair next to Marvelli. "I think we have to wait until the snake comes out of the basket," she muttered.

Monroe abruptly stopped playing, opened one eye, and cocked an eyebrow at Loretta. "I heard that, Mizz K."

"Sorry."

"Don't be sorry, Mizz K. I took it as a compliment no matter how you meant it. Any man who can use his music to keep the beast from biting is a true genius. If Adam had possessed such talent, he might have been able to turn the tables and seduce the serpent. He might have turned its Godzilla gaze into pea green goo and undermined the evil design. If ol' Adam had had the chops, we'd all be sitting pretty right now. Paradise on ice."

"What about Eve?" Loretta asked sharply. "Couldn't she have gotten the gig?"

"Possibly, yes. Yes, possibly." He rolled his eyes and flashed a sly grin. "But you just can't be sure about a woman's embouchure." Julius's eyes became slits as he howled at his own pun.

Loretta made a face. "Why do I always feel like I'm talking to the Cat in the Hat whenever I talk to you?" she asked.

Marvelli looked puzzled. "I don't get it," he said. "What's embouchure? Something to eat?"

"Embouchure is how the muscles of the mouth are held to play a wind instrument," Julius said. "Horn players, flute players, clarinet players—we all have to work on our embouchure."

Marvelli shrugged. "I still don't get it."

Julius picked up a thick file folder from his desk and tossed it into Marvelli's lap. "You may not get it, O marvelous one, but now you got it." He waved his flute over Marvelli and Loretta as if it were a magic wand. "I now pronounce you cowboy and cowgirl," he said. "Bring 'im back alive, cowpeople."

Marvelli opened the folder and winced as soon as he glanced at it. "Oh, man," he groaned. "Why me?"

"Why you!" Julius said, his eyes popping open. "I'm doing you a favor giving you this. I picked it out special for you as soon as it came in."

"Thanks a lot," Marvelli grumbled.

Loretta leaned over to see whose file it was, but she couldn't make out the name. "Who is it?" she asked.

Marvelli exhaled in disgust. "Sammy friggin' Teitelbaum."

The name meant nothing to her. "A repeat jumper?" she asked.

Marvelli nodded wearily. "Mob associate, small-time schnook, and supposed mad-genius hit man."

"That ain't all," Monroe said, grinning like a quarter moon.

Loretta looked from Monroe to Marvelli, waiting to be enlightened. "Well? What about this guy? Tell me."

Marvelli shook his head and sighed. "On top of everything else, Sammy Teitelbaum is my brother-in-law."

"Oh . . ." Loretta puckered her lips and nodded.

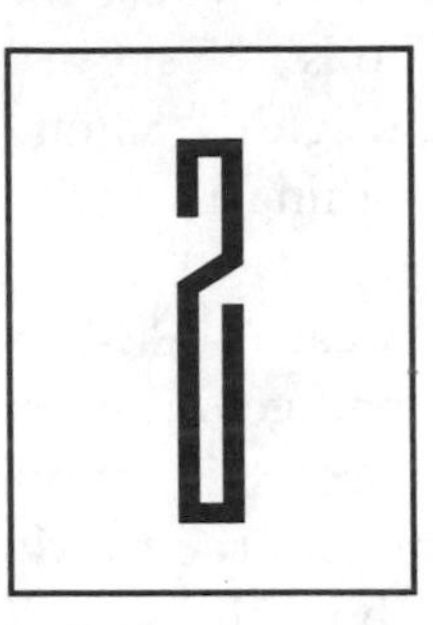

Loretta drove the white Bureau of Parole Chevy Cavalier into a muddy lot that looked like a World War I battlefield. It was crisscrossed with deep ruts, and trailer-truck tracks were flooded with oily brown water. A dirty gray cinder-block garage loomed at the far end of the mud field like a prehistoric creature that had just crawled out of the primordial ooze and paused to collect its preevolutionary thoughts. A peeling sign over the bay doors said Tino's Truck Repairs. The Chevy jolted and dipped as Loretta did her best to keep from breaking an axle, but there were so many potholes and craters it was useless to try to drive around them, so she just drove very slowly and took them as softly as she could.

She glanced over at Marvelli, who was sitting on the passenger side. He didn't look happy.

"So your brother-in-law's a hit man," she said, trying to make conversation. "That's pretty ironic."

Marvelli kept his eyes on the garage up ahead. "There's nothing ironic about it. Sammy's an asshole. Brother-in-laws usually are, aren't they?"

"Yeah, but not everybody's brother-in-law is a hit man."

Loretta winced as the car hit bottom, rattling the muffler. "Damn," she hissed.

"Sammy Teitelbaum is not a hit man," Marvelli said emphatically. "Why do you keep saying that?"

"Because that's what it says in Sammy's file."

"That's just a rumor. He was never convicted of murder."

"No, but he was convicted for assault. He beat the living crap out of some kid who'd gone to bed with a made guy's fifteen-year-old daughter. Six weeks later the kid's body was found floating in the river near the Statue of Liberty."

"Sammy wasn't charged with that murder. Only the assault."

A hard thunk rattled the car as they hit bottom again. Loretta cursed under her breath.

Marvelli was staring out the window, shaking his head. "He's a real piece of work, my brother-in-law. The guy's got a Ph.D. in English lit. Can you believe that?"

"What'd he do his dissertation on? *The Godfather?*" Loretta kept her eyes on the potholes.

"Sammy sort of even looks like an English teacher, the little dweeb, which is what he should be. But instead he wants to be a tough guy. Teaching is boring, he told me one time. He wants to *live* life, he said, not read about it."

"So he hangs out with mob guys to get his kicks?" Loretta asked.

"I don't think he actually hangs with them. It's more like he's their pet, I think. Once you meet him, you'll see what I mean. He's definitely not the wiseguy type."

"He did do some time, though. That must've toughened him up some."

Marvelli shrugged. "Maybe, but I doubt it. Sammy lives in his own world. He probably thought prison was a wonderful 'life experience.' "

Loretta laughed. "It's an experience, all right. I don't know about the wonderful part, though."

Marvelli shook his head. "You don't know Sammy. He's crazy."

"So why do you think he stopped reporting to his PO? Is he that crazy?"

Marvelli shrugged. "Who knows? Maybe he's trying to impress someone, prove that he's a real hard guy. Maybe he's just trying to be a pain in the butt."

Loretta steered around one of the smaller craters. "Tell me again. How's he related to you?"

"He's married to Rene's kid sister Jennifer, but they're separated now."

Rene again, Loretta thought. She kept her mouth shut and prayed this didn't get him started on that topic.

As they approached the garage, the car rumbled over a series of deep ruts, the tires bouncing like basketballs. Loretta hit the brakes to slow down, but when she pressed the accelerator again, the tires started to spin in the mud. She gradually gave it some gas, then a little more and a little more until she was revving the engine, but all that did was kick up a muddy cascade in her rearview mirror. Loretta peered out at the expanse of mud outside her door and made a face. She tried giving it gas again, then abruptly let up on the pedal, repeatedly giving it gas and letting up, trying to rock the car out of the mud, but all that did was dig her in deeper. "Dammit," she muttered.

Marvelli looked at her shoes, then at his. She was wearing black suede flats; he was wearing black leather ankle boots. He let out a sigh of resignation. "I'll go in and talk to Tino. Maybe he'll tow us out."

"Why would he do that?" Loretta said. "We came here to bust his chops."

"Yeah, but Tino's a decent guy. Just as long as you don't owe him money."

Marvelli opened the car door and hesitated before he finally extended his foot and eased himself out. Loretta heard the squoosh. She leaned over to see Marvelli up to the hem of his pants in mud. "Sit tight," he said with a frown. "I'll be back."

He shut the door and slogged toward the garage, holding his arms out for balance, having to yank each foot out of the muck before he could take another step. By the time he made it to the front door, he was muddy up to his knees.

He pounded on the door with his fist and let himself in. Knocking was just a formality. He knew that Tino wouldn't answer it.

Marvelli stomped his feet to shake off the mud as he walked between two truck tractors, both with their hoods open. They were both dusty relics that had been there since 1985 when Tino had stopped fixing trucks and started putting all of his efforts into illegal sports betting. They were just there for show.

"Tino!" Marvelli shouted as he gazed up at the array of spare parts hanging from the water-stained ceiling—dry-rotted fan belts, rusty muffler pipes, grimy air filters. "Tino!" he shouted again. "It's Frank Marvelli from the Bureau of Parole."

A muffled voice came from the back of the cavernous space. "Be right with you."

Marvelli headed back toward the office, a partitioned space set off in a corner. The office had picture windows that looked out on the garage, but they were covered with newspapers so no one could look in. Marvelli knocked twice on the door and opened it.

A little man with a potbelly and bushy eyebrows was sitting at a computer, his hands poised over the keyboard, a pair of tortoiseshell glasses perched on top of his hairless head. He was wearing slate blue mechanic coveralls, but they were immaculate.

"I said I'd be right with you," the man said hotly, glaring at Marvelli. "What is it with you, Marvelli? You some kind of premature ejaculator?" The man glanced at the computer screen, which suddenly went blank. After that he seemed to relax.

Marvelli coughed up a wry laugh. "Downloading sure beats having to burn slips, huh, Tino?"

The little man scowled. "What're you talking about, Marvelli? I'm doing my books here."

"You mean, *making* book. In the old days guys like you used to eat the betting slips when the cops came knocking. Then came quick-burn paper. But now computers make it easy for you. Where do you download to? Canada? Mexico? Bermuda?"

"I don't know what the hell you're talking about, Marvelli." Tino glanced at the screen again to make sure it was still blank.

Marvelli shrugged. "I don't care about the betting, Tino. I'm not a cop. I just came to ask you a few questions."

Tino contorted his bushy brows until they looked like a single crooked caterpillar. "Questions about what?"

"Sammy Teitelbaum."

"Who?"

Marvelli's smile faded. "My brother-in-law, Sammy. The Sammy who used to hang out here with your two *citrull'* nephews, Jerry and Larry. You know, the dum-dum twins who raped that poor retarded girl when they were in high school—"

"Now, wait a minute. They never raped anyone. They were acquitted on those charges."

Marvelli ignored him. "I'm looking for the Sammy Teitelbaum who used to do collections for you before he went away on an assault conviction. You know who I'm talking about now?"

Tino looked puzzled. "No. Not really."

Marvelli pulled up a chair and sat down backward on it. He stared Tino in the eye. "Just because I'm not a cop, that doesn't mean I don't talk to cops, Tino. You want your balls busted? I can have that arranged very easily."

"Come on, Marvelli—"

"The alternative is you can stop being a funny guy and just give me a few straight answers. It's your choice."

Tino sat back in his seat and rubbed the corners of his mouth. He looked at Marvelli, then looked at the computer. Marvelli knew what he was thinking. He was thinking how much of a hassle it would be if he got busted. A bookmaking charge he could beat—that wasn't the problem. What would hurt would be the cops confiscating his computer and bringing him downtown, maybe holding him overnight. The computer could always be replaced. It was the loss of business until he could get himself set up again that worried Tino.

Tino was a made man, and he had a reputation as a real moneymaker in the Luccarelli family. Marvelli's guess was that he was clearing about fifteen, twenty grand a day here, and better than half of that went to the family. But the big problem with being a moneymaker was that the bosses came to depend on your profits. It was their cash flow, and they tended not to be very sympathetic when a moneymaker had to take a few unexpected "sick days." The irony of mob logic was that a moneymaker who stops making money for whatever reason usually ends up getting whacked. Big dogs don't like anybody messing with their bowls.

"So what's it gonna be, Tino?" Marvelli said. "Shall we have a friendly exchange of ideas, or do I have to drop a dime on you? Enlighten me, Tino."

Tino's mouth was as crooked as his eyebrows, but he seemed resigned. "What exactly do you want to know, Marvelli?"

"Where's Sammy?"

"That I don't know."

"Come on, Tino. Don't get cute."

"I'm telling you the truth, Marvelli. I don't know where he is. I haven't seen him since he went away."

"He got out two months ago, Tino. You haven't seen him since then?"

Tino shook his head. "Nope."

"What have you heard about him?"

Tino furrowed his brow and shrugged as if he were insulted by the question. "What do I ever hear? Nothing. That's what I hear. I never leave this place. I'm too busy."

Marvelli just stared at him. "You're holding out on me, Tino. Sammy used to practically live here."

"That was a long time ago, Marvelli. I'm telling you. If I knew something, I'd tell you. Believe me."

Marvelli extended his leg and stared at the toe of his muddy boot as he rolled it slowly on his heel. "Cross your heart and hope to die, Tino?"

Loretta threw the transmission into reverse and hit the gas, then threw it into drive and gunned it again. She kept doing this over and over, trying to get the car to rock, but the mud was worse than snow. The wheels had no traction at all, and the car seemed to sink in deeper each time she tried to get it out. She scowled at the sea of mud outside her window, then looked down at her shoes—black suede sling-back flats. "Crap," she muttered.

"Hey, lady!"

Loretta jumped, startled by the voice and the sudden banging on the passenger-side window. Two male faces were looking in at her through the mud-speckled glass. "You stuck, lady?" one of the two men asked.

Loretta stared at them, speechless for a moment. Both men were wearing the same face, and it wasn't the kind of face you'd want to have two of—perfectly round, no neck, thin flyaway hair, bad skin, chubby cheeks, and slits for eyes. They looked like Italian-American Okies.

"You want us to help you get out?" one of them said as he opened the door and stuck his head in.

"Yeah, we're good at this," the other one said. "My name is Jerry. This is my brother Larry." They were perfectly identical.

"How you doing?" Larry said with a big smile. "We work here at the garage. We have to get cars out of the mud all the time."

"Why don't you just pave the lot?" Loretta asked. "Wouldn't that be easier?"

The brothers looked at each other, dumbfounded by the entire concept.

"Gee, I dunno," Jerry eventually said.

Larry just shrugged.

A couple of brain surgeons, these two, Loretta thought.

"Can you really get me out?" she asked.

"Sure," Larry said eagerly.

"Okay, you push," she said, "and I'll—"

The brothers were both shaking their heads.

"Don't have to push," Jerry said.

"We can drive it out. It's easy. You just have to know how."

"All right. Tell me what to do."

"Don't worry. We'll show you," Larry said as he ran around to the driver's side. Jerry hopped into the passenger seat and shut the door.

"Hey, wait a minute," Loretta objected.

But Larry was already opening the driver's-side door. "You just shove over, lady," he said. "I'll show you how to do it."

"No, wait—"

But Larry was already getting in, nudging her over with his big butt. He slammed the door shut, and suddenly the three of them were packed in tight, love handle to love handle. Loretta was sitting on the parking brake, her shoulders getting crunched, but she'd be damned if she was going to put her arms over the seat backs to give herself more room. She didn't want to give these two idiots the wrong idea. Not that they couldn't get the wrong idea on their own.

"Okay, here we go," Larry said. He threw the transmission into low gear and gunned the engine, turning the wheel all the way to the right. The tires whined and spun. Larry let up on the gas, turned the wheel all the way to the left, and gunned it again. The tires were still spinning, but the car was gliding sideways.

"All right!" Jerry shouted in triumph.

Loretta could smell beer on his breath, and it wasn't even noon yet.

The engine was screaming for mercy, but Larry was unaffected, keeping his foot to the pedal as the car continued to drift sideways. "See?" Larry said. "You gotta be tough with mud."

"Yeah, you gotta ride it *hard,*" Jerry added.

"I see," Loretta said. They both smelled, and it was getting hot inside the car, fogging up the windows. She wanted them out.

Suddenly Larry spun the wheel to the right again, and the car fishtailed 180 degrees. The brothers whooped as Larry kept his foot on the gas and spun the steering wheel left and right, jolting over ruts and kicking up a muddy arc behind them.

Loretta didn't like this at all. "Pull up to the garage doors," she ordered.

But they ignored her, whooping it up as Larry kept fishtailing around the yard.

"Thank you for getting the car out," Loretta said, raising her voice. "Now would you please leave it by the garage doors?"

"Oh, don't be such a fart, lady," Jerry said. "Let's have a little fun here."

"Yeah," Larry said, slamming the wheel right and left.

Loretta could feel the sweat collecting in her armpits. She didn't like the way this was developing.

"Let's go for a ride," Larry said. He'd turned the car around and revved the engine, making it slide toward the street.

"No," she said.

"Goddammit!" Jerry snarled, suddenly turning mean. "I *hate* it when a woman says no."

"Well, I kind of like it myself," Larry said with a crooked grin, looking past Loretta and winking to his brother, "because they never mean it."

"Stop the car right now," Loretta demanded.

"No!" Larry barked with a dumb smirk on his face. "And I'm a man, so I mean no."

Jerry snorted up a wet laugh.

Loretta's heart was beating fast. She wished she could get to her gun, but her purse was on the floor in the backseat.

The engine was screaming as the wheels spun like mad and the car slowly drifted sideways toward the street.

"Trust us," Jerry said. "We're nice guys. We'll have some fun." He laid his clammy hand on Loretta's thigh.

Then Larry laid his grimy hand on Loretta's other thigh. "Yeah, we'll show you fun like you've never had, lady. Right, Jer?"

"Absolutely."

"Stop the car!" she yelled.

But they just laughed at her, digging their fingers into her flesh.

Loretta squirmed and struggled, her heart pounding. If she could only get to her gun.

"Two tons of fun, huh?" Jerry said to Larry as if Loretta weren't even there.

Larry sized her up and nodded. "At least that much."

Loretta could barely move, and their fingers were crawling up her thighs as the car inched closer and closer to the road.

She strained to look over her shoulder, hoping to see Marvelli by the garage, but all she saw was the empty mud field.

"Two tons of fun," Larry repeated, coughing up a laugh.

"Yeah, this is gonna be good," Jerry said, raising his eyebrows. "Real good."

Marvelli was still staring at his muddy boots. "I'm waiting, Tino," he said.

"But I keep telling you," Tino said, gesturing with both hands. "I don't know nothing about nothing about Sammy Teitelbaum. You know more than I do about him."

Marvelli shook his head. "I'll bet you I don't."

Tino kept glancing at the telephone sitting on top of the computer tower. His forehead was getting sweaty. He was probably thinking about all the customers who weren't getting through to lay down their bets. "What do you want from me, Marvelli?" he exploded. "I don't know nothing."

Marvelli sighed. "I know you're not a bad guy, Tino, but you're gonna force me to treat you like one."

"What do you mean?"

"Either I'm gonna get somebody from the police department to come down here and sit on your head, or I'm gonna follow your two nephews around until I catch them doing something wrong, which knowing them, shouldn't take too long."

Tino's mouth drooped like a clown's. "Gimme a break, Marvelli. Jerry and Larry are good kids, basically. If they'd had regular parents when they were growing up, they'd be straight up today. But my friggin' sister ran off with some bum from Alaska and left those boys with my poor mother. They were only in the sixth grade, the poor kids. Then my mother had a stroke, and they ended up with me. No wonder they're confused."

Marvelli was not sympathetic. "There are a lot of confused people in the world, Tino, but they don't all turn into rapists."

"I keep telling you, Marvelli, *they were not convicted.*"

"Doesn't mean they weren't guilty."

"Come on, Marvelli. Get off my friggin' back."

"Not until you tell me what I want to hear."

"Come on, will ya?"

Marvelli pointed his finger in Tino's face. "Those boys aren't careful, Tino. They don't watch what they do like you and your goombahs do. So as soon as I catch 'em doing something wrong, I'll make sure they pay for it big-time. This is a promise, Tino."

"You're just jerking my chain, Marvelli. You're not a cop, you're just a PO. There's nothing you can do to those boys—even if they were as bad as you say, which I know they aren't."

"Last chance, Tino. Speak now or forever—"

BOOM!

A splintering crash shook the whole building. It sounded as if a tank had just broken through the bay door.

Tino jumped out of his chair, instantly pale. "What the hell's going on, Marvelli? *Marvelli!*"

But Marvelli was already running out into the garage space. Daylight was shining in where the big garage door used to be. He ran between the two old tractors and found the door off its tracks and draped over the front of the white Chevy Cavalier, which was halfway inside. The car doors were open on both sides, and Tino's nephews, Larry and Jerry, were scrambling for cover on the gritty cement floor. Loretta emerged from the passenger side, leading with her .38.

"On your bellies, you disgusting maggots," she shouted. "Hands behind your heads." She was holding her gun in both hands, pointing it down at the twins.

"Loretta, what the hell happened?" Marvelli said.

"She tried to kill us," Jerry whimpered from down on the floor.

Larry had his fingers linked behind his neck. He strained to look up at Marvelli. "She stomped on the gas and wouldn't let up. Then she grabbed the wheel. She crashed it on purpose. She's nuts."

Marvelli looked at Loretta. "What the hell're they talking about?"

"Attempted sexual assault," Loretta said. "That's what *I'm* talking about."

"That's a lie," Jerry said.

"We were just helping you get your car out of the mud," Larry whined. "That's all."

"Shut up!" Loretta snapped. "Marvelli, call nine-one-one. Get some uniforms down here. I'm pressing charges."

"Hold it, hold it, hold it." Tino muscled his way past Marvelli. "Let's talk about this first."

Marvelli was trying to suppress a grin because he knew what Tino was thinking. "Okay, Tino, let's talk about it."

"There's nothing *to* talk about," Loretta interrupted. "Call nine-one-one. And stop squirming," she yelled at the twins as she kicked the soles of their shoes.

"Just give me one minute here, Loretta," Marvelli said. He put his arm around Tino's shoulders and led him around to the back of the garage. "The choice is yours, Tino. Either you tell me what I want to know, or I let my partner press charges against your nephews."

Tino was chewing the arm of his glasses. "You can't do this, Marvelli. This is illegal."

"Loretta can press charges. There's nothing illegal about that," Marvelli said. "I might be able to change her mind, though. But you have to make it worth my while. *Capisce?*"

"This is extortion, Marvelli."

Marvelli shrugged. "It's the way of the world, Tino. *Your* world."

Loretta was glaring at them down the length of the trucks. "Make the call, Marvelli," she shouted. "What're you waiting for?"

"Uncle Tino," Larry called out, "do something. I only touched her knee. I swear."

"Please, Uncle Tino," Jerry wailed. "This lady's a nut. She's gonna friggin' shoot us."

Tino whispered to Marvelli. "She wouldn't do that, would she?"

"A woman with a gun is a bad combination. You know that, Tino."

"Marvelli!" Loretta yelled.

"Take it easy, Loretta. I'm working it out here."

"Forget about working it out. Just call nine-one-one."

"One minute, Loretta." He turned to Tino. "So what's it gonna be? Either you tell me about Sammy, or the dum-dum boys go back into the system. And I can guarantee you this: The county prosecutor will definitely want payback for their acquittal on that rape case."

Tino grimaced, clicking the arm of his glasses against his teeth. His eyes roved from Marvelli to Loretta to his nephews on the floor. "You promise to get her to change her mind about pressing charges?"

"I'll talk to her. I think she'll listen."

"No deal. I want a guarantee."

"Then go buy a refrigerator. I said I'll do what I can."

"Marvelli!" Loretta shrieked.

"Okay, okay," Tino said, barely whispering. "Here's what I know. Sammy came by a few days after he got out of prison. He told me he wasn't gonna work for me no more. He said he was working for someone else now."

"Who?"

Tino hesitated. "He told me he got a contract to do some guy. It was gonna be a big hit, he said. 'Mega' was the word he used."

"Who's Sammy working for?" Marvelli pressed.

Tino glanced at Loretta and let out a long sigh before he answered. "I shouldn't be telling you this, Marvelli."

"Yes, you should. Now tell me. Who?"

Tino hesitated again. "Taffy," he finally said. "Taffy Demaggio."

Suddenly Marvelli's gut was burning. His jaw was locked shut, and he could feel the blood pounding behind his eyeballs.

"Marvelli, what's the matter?" Tino asked. "What's wrong? Say something."

Taffy friggin' Demaggio, Marvelli thought.

His hands were cramped into fists.

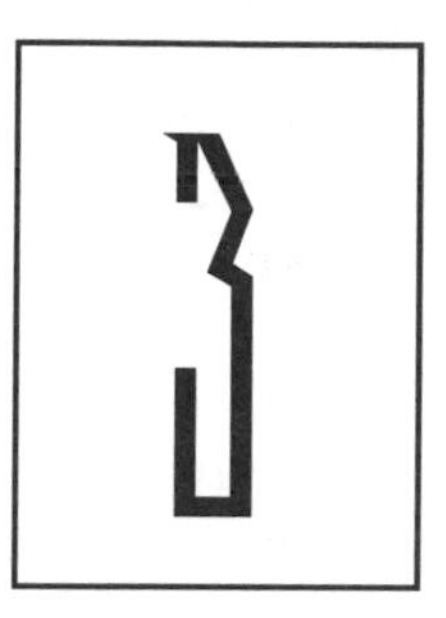

Back at the office Marvelli was pounding his fist on the edge of Julius Monroe's desk. "Taffy friggin' Demaggio," he fumed. "That mother-loving son of a bitch."

Marvelli was still all worked up. He was so mad he was barely coherent, and Loretta hadn't been able to get him to calm down enough to explain what was bothering him. She sat on the couch and watched her partner pacing like a caged tiger, punching his palm and grumbling to himself. She'd decided to just stay out of his way until he simmered down. He was in such a state she didn't dare say anything about his not calling the cops on those two little snot-noses, Larry and Jerry, but she sure was going to chew him out about it later. Where the hell did he get off using an attempted sexual assault against her as a bargaining chip? Those two perverts should be rotting in jail, for crying out loud.

Julius was slumped over his desk, cradling his face in both hands. "Why don't you take it from the top, Marvelli? And slow down the tempo so I can pick up on what you're putting down."

"Okay, okay," Marvelli said, patting the air in front of him with both hands. "This is what I got out of Tino. Sammy is supposedly doing a hit for that bastard Taffy Demaggio. According to Tino, Sammy is up to his eyeballs in debt to Taffy, but Taffy has agreed to settle Sammy's tab in exchange for doing this job."

"So who's the lucky person Sammy's supposed to offer up to the gods?" Julius asked.

"You're not gonna believe this. Gus Rispoli."

Julius clutched his belly and started to laugh, but then just as quickly he stopped and turned serious. "You don't think your crazy brother-in-law could actually pull that off, do you?"

Loretta was confused. "Wait a minute. Hold on. Rewind. Who's Gus Rispoli?"

They both looked at her as if she were from Mars.

"Mizz Kovacs, I am surprised at you," Julius said. "Gus Rispoli is Top Rat, stoolie number one. He is the thorn in the mob's jelly-belly side, and the marinara is leaking out pretty heavy because of him."

She looked at Marvelli. "Translation, please."

"Gus Rispoli is a mob turncoat," Marvelli said. "No, correction: He is *the* mob turncoat. He used to be with the Luccarelli family, same as Taffy Demaggio, but now he's cooperating with federal prosecutors, helping them build cases against the mob. So far the feds have put away eight high-level Mafia guys thanks to Rispoli's testimony—six captains, a consigliere, and an underboss. And they say he's just getting warmed up. The feds are bragging that when Rispoli is through, there won't be a Luccarelli family left."

"No kidding." Loretta was impressed. "But what about Sammy? What if he does whack Rispoli?"

"Well, there's two ways to look at this situation," Julius said, leaning back and linking his fingers on top of his head. "The feds are holding Rispoli at My Blue Heaven. That's the U.S. Marshals' top-secret Xanadu prison for the ratsos in the Witness Protection Program who still have time to serve on their own convictions. Now, nobody but nobody knows where My Blue Heaven is. Just the marshals who work in the program. Rispoli's the prize egg in their basket, so they must be watching him pretty good, keeping him safe and sound, which means there should be nothing to worry about."

"So what's the other way to look at it?" Loretta asked.

Julius dropped his chin and stared at her. "My Blue Heaven is run by the feds. Nobody knows how to screw things up like a fed, my dear. You should know that."

"Oh, I know," she said.

"But," Marvelli said, "there's a third factor in this equation. Sammy. He is crazy, but it's genius crazy. He's very smart, and he doesn't look anything like a wiseguy. I think if anyone could get into My Blue Heaven and pull off a hit, it would be Sammy."

"I don't know about that," Julius said, shaking his head. "Sammy T. may be good, but I think the feds can secure at least one building."

"What about the Zito hit?" Marvelli said. "Word out on the street is that Sammy did that one. Even Tino thinks he did it."

Loretta had heard about this one. Eugene Zito, the underboss of another mob family, had been stabbed through the heart on his own private island in Long Island Sound. The island was tiny, and the only way to get there was by boat. At the time of the murder, there were four bodyguards on the island as well as five other wiseguys from the family. It had been done out in the open on the beach at three o'clock in the afternoon with the two bodyguards on duty just a hundred feet away. Zito had been sunning himself, stretched out on a lounge chair all by himself. The bodyguards thought their boss had fallen asleep, so they didn't disturb him. They didn't realize that he was dead until the sun started to go down. The two bodyguards swore that they hadn't seen or heard anyone else on the beach all day.

"But wait a minute," Loretta objected. "I just read Sammy's file. He was never charged—let alone convicted—on *any* murders. How can he be a hit man?"

"Because he's that good," Marvelli said gravely.

Julius picked up his flute and blew a single pensive note as he stared out into space. The note slowly trailed off into silence. "We better not sit on this," he said. "The guys upstairs will not be jolly if they find out that one of our jumpers pulled off the Academy Award of hits. Throw in a Grammy for being the brother-in-law of one of our parole officers. Mucho embarrassmento for the Bureau of Parole. Mucho crapola for us. Heads will roll, children. Mine, too."

A lightning bolt of panic suddenly shot through Loretta's stomach. She couldn't afford to lose this job. She was already at the end of the line here at the Jump Squad. If she got bounced from this one, her next stop would be behind the drive-in counter at a McDonald's, wearing a paper hat and a wireless headset, shoveling burgers and fries out a window, telling people to have a nice day over and over again all day long. She'd snitch French fries every two minutes, and in no time she'd be as big as a house. And worst of all Marvelli would never come to her window. She'd never see him again. Ever.

Of course, there was always Chicago, she thought.

"Loretta. Loretta!" Julius repeated. He blew a high piercing note to get her attention.

"What?" she said, blinking her eyes as she snapped out of it.

"You were looking a little paler than usual," Julius said. "You still with us?"

"I'm here," she said, but inside she was still dealing with the prospects of doom and gloom. She glanced at Marvelli and felt embarrassed for feeling the way she did about him. In every other apsect of her life, she was direct to the point of being a blunt object. But with Marvelli it was different.

"I called a guy I know at the federal courthouse," Marvelli said. "Taffy Demaggio is scheduled to go on trial at the end of the year. And guess who's gonna be the prime witness against him?"

"Gus Rispoli-oli-olio," Julius sang, capping off his tune with a doleful note on the flute. "This is not good, children. Not good at all. Steps must be taken. Preemptive damage control."

"Why don't we just go out and start looking for Sammy?" Loretta suggested.

A prolonged search, she thought naughtily. Out-of-state overnights. Just the two them.

But Julius was already shaking his head, cutting an arc in the air with his pointy beard. "Where-oh-where do you start looking, Lorett-o? The feds won't tell us where My Blue Heaven is, so we can't scope the target. For now all we can do is let everybody and his sister know what we know, so that when the poop hits the fan, they can't say we didn't tell them it was coming. Got it?"

"Right." Loretta nodded, trying to hide her disappointment.

Marvelli looked doubtful. "I don't know about this, Julius. I think we should do a full-court press. I think Loretta's right. We should be out there actively looking for Sammy."

"We" as in you and me? Loretta thought hopefully.

But Julius just shook his head. "Start with the Marshals Office, Marvelli," he said. "Let them know what's going on and see if they'll give you any help, but don't get your hopes up. Remember: A fed is a fed is a fed. I'll talk to the almighty ones upstairs, see what they have to say about it."

"And what am I supposed to do?" Loretta asked.

Julius just stared at her. "Go to work." He waved his flute like a magic wand at all the piles of case files stacked up around the room. "Take your pick. There's plenty to go round."

Loretta sighed as she got off the couch. "I've got my own pile, thank you."

"Let me know what the marshals say, marvelous one. We'll talk later." Julius picked up his phone and pressed a button for an open line.

Loretta followed Marvelli out of Julius's office and back to the bull pen. "Can I ask you something?" she said.

"What?" Marvelli sat down at his desk.

"What've you got against this Taffy Demaggio guy? I've never seen you like this before. He ever do anything to you? Personally, I mean."

Marvelli's eyes grew large and watery. "Not to me. To Rene."

Loretta furrowed her brows and leaned against her desk. "What did he do to her?"

"It wasn't just Rene," Marvelli said. "It was a lot of people. See, on top of all the usual Mafia scumbag things Taffy has done, he also controlled a medical supply company that sold second-rate equipment to hospitals at inflated prices. Stuff like syringes, catheters, gauze, bandages, IV lines—that kind of stuff. Most of it was crap. He was putting people's lives in danger with that stuff, people who were already sick. There was one case of an old man who got blood poisoning from some chemical used to make cheap plastic IV lines. He ended up dying."

"Did anything like that ever happen to Rene?"

Marvelli shrugged. "Hard to tell, she was so sick. But I know Taffy was selling to the hospital that was taking care of her, so they must've used some of Taffy's junk on her. I mean, how do I know it wasn't a bad blood tube or a faulty syringe that killed Rene? A little piece of plastic that broke off from the syringe and got into her bloodstream, maybe nicked an artery or something. There must be thousands of people who had this cut-rate junk stuck in their bodies. How many of those people died because of this stuff? We'll never know for sure, and Taffy's probably gonna get away with it. If it were up to me, though, he'd get the friggin' death penalty for that scam. And when they gave him the lethal injection, I'd make sure they did it with one of his own crappy syringes."

Marvelli's voice was dripping with revenge. It made Loretta's heart sink. He was never going to get over his wife.

So why am I putting myself through this? she wondered. *I don't stand a chocolate chip's chance in hell with this guy.*

As Marvelli reached for his phone, he looked at his watch. "What're you doing for lunch?" he asked.

"Me?"

"You want to have lunch?" He was flipping through his Rolodex, looking for a phone number.

"Yeah . . . sure." She was wary, though. She didn't want to read anything into this. Sometimes lunch is just lunch.

"I gotta make a few calls," he said as he punched out a number, the receiver cradled between his ear and shoulder. "We'll go about twelve-thirty. Is that okay?"

He raised his eyebrows, waiting for her response, but his expression turned serious as soon as someone answered his call.

She glanced at him sideways as she picked up a file at random from her desk, trying to look busy. Her heart was thumping, wanting to be hopeful, but her head was cautious. He didn't really mean anything by this, she told herself. It wasn't like a date or anything. It was just two co-workers going to lunch. That's all.

But when she looked up, he was looking at her, eyebrows up, still waiting for an answer, and instantly her head switched sides. Maybe it wasn't just lunch, she thought. Maybe it could lead to something else.

She nodded and flashed the okay sign. "Twelve-thirty," she mouthed, confirming the time.

She sat down at her desk and started going through case files, intending to catch up on her paperwork, but she had a hard time paying attention to anything that wasn't Marvelli.

The mud-spattered white Chevy pulled into an empty space in front of the Five Roses Dinner, a chrome-sided shoe box of a building that would have been stylishly retro if it weren't absolutely authentic. The diner had opened for business in 1961, and the five loud, leggy, gum-chewing, teased-hair-out-to-there sisters who had started this place back then were still waiting tables. None of them was actually named Rose, but they all answered to that name and any variation on it: Rose, Rosie, Rosa, Rosemary, Roseanne, Rosalie. . . . They were in their sixties now, and they didn't show as much leg as they used to, but they were just as loud, and their meat-loaf special was to die for.

Marvelli always came here for the meat loaf, and now that his appetite seemed to be coming back, Loretta had high hopes for a complete meat-loaf cure. He needed a shot of something to get him back on track, and an extra-thick slab of chopped meat, a generous scoop of mashed potatoes, and the veg of the day, all swimming in brown onion gravy with a Parker House roll on the side and a hot cup of coffee just might do the trick.

But when Loretta went to open her car door, she realized that

Marvelli wasn't opening his. He was just sitting there, staring into space, rapping his knuckles on the dashboard.

"What's the matter?" she asked, nervous that he was slipping back into his funk.

"Goddamn feds," he grumbled.

"What about them?" Loretta asked.

"I called the marshals before we went to lunch and tried to let them know what was going on with Sammy, but they didn't even want to hear me out. The guy I talked to wouldn't even admit that My Blue Heaven exists. But then in the next breath he told me that *if* such a place did exist, no one would ever be able to find it. I tried to tell him that Sammy is an unusual case, he might pull it off, but the guy wouldn't even listen to me. After that conversation, I tracked down this woman at the FBI, some witch named Springer. She's the one who handles Rispoli whenever they bring him east to testify. What a pain in the ass she was. She practically told me to go drop dead."

"What can I tell you, Marvelli? They're feds," Loretta said. "Come on, let's eat."

Marvelli muttered something she didn't hear as he opened the door and got out of the car. They headed up the brick steps to the front door, and Marvelli's cell phone suddenly started to ring.

"Hang on a minute," he said to her as he pulled it out of his pocket, pressed the answer button, and held it to his face. "Hello?"

"Hello. Officer Marvelli? This is Special Agent Veronica Springer." The FBI agent was sitting behind the wheel of a dark blue Oldsmobile Cutlass parked across the street from the Five Roses Diner. She was holding a cell phone to her ear, staring at the two figures standing in front of the diner. The man with the cell phone was obviously Marvelli, but she wondered who the fat woman was.

"What can I do for you, Agent Springer?" Marvelli said. She detected a touch of frost in his voice.

"I apologize if I gave you short shrift earlier today," she said, "but I didn't know who you were then. I've made a few calls in the meantime, and yes, I would like to talk to you."

"You checked up on *me*?"

"No, no," she lied. "On Sammy Teitelbaum. I think we should get together to discuss this situation."

"When?" Marvelli said.

"How about right now? Where are you?"

"I'm just about to have lunch," he said. "You know a place called the Five Roses Dinner on—?"

"I know it," she interrupted. "I can be there in fifteen minutes."

"Okay."

"Fine. How will I know you when I get there?" she asked.

"How will I know *you*?" he countered.

Agent Springer narrowed her eyes. *Belligerent,* she thought. *Typical Italian, but cute.* She was staring at his butt.

"I'm five foot three," she said. "I've got short, straight, light blond hair. I'm wearing a navy blazer, a cream-colored blouse with a banded collar, and gray slacks. Is that enough for you?"

"I'll spot you. See you in fifteen." He hung up. Rather abruptly, she thought.

She blipped her phone off and put it back in her pocket as she watched Marvelli and the fat woman go into the diner. *He could do better than her,* she thought. *A lot better.*

Springer started the engine, pulled out into the street, and drove down to the end of the block to a gas station on the corner. She drove past the pumps and pulled up to a pay phone. It was set low enough on the pole so that she didn't have to get out of the car to use it. She lowered her window and reached for the receiver, then reached out again to dial.

After two rings a recorded voice came on the line. "Please deposit fifty-five cents for the next three minutes."

Springer had the change ready. She dropped two quarters and a nickel into the slot. It started to ring again.

"Hello?" a man answered.

"Let me speak to Taffy, please," Springer said.

"Who's this?"

"Tell him it's the First Lady."

"What is this, some kind of joke?"

"Just tell him," she said. "He'll know who it is."

The man dropped the phone. She could hear the man yelling. "Hey, Taf, some broad wants to talk to you. She says she's the First Lady."

It was thirty seconds before someone came back on. "Sweetheart," a new voice said, "how the hell are you?" She recognized the voice right away. Smooth as silk. Taffy Demaggio.

"I have to ask you something," she said.

"Is this something of a social nature?" he asked with a snicker.

"No."

"You're on a pay phone, I hope."

"Of course."

"So what can I do for you, Veronica, my love?"

"Save the Casanova routine for your bimbos. I need you to give me a straight answer about something."

"With you I am nothing but straight, my dear. You can ask me anything."

"Did you hire a guy named Sammy Teitelbaum to kill Gus Rispoli?" Her voice was cool, but she was sitting on her temper, digging her fingernails into the Oldsmobile's crushed velveteen upholstery.

"Sweetheart, I don't know what you're talking about."

"That's not an answer, Taffy."

"Is that anger I hear in your voice, Veronica?"

"Cut the crap, Taffy. Putting a contract out on Rispoli isn't going to help your case any."

"Oh, no? Why not?"

"Because."

Taffy lowered his voice. "Look, Veronica, I told you before. I want some guarantees. I don't want to have to go back to court on any other charges, not even a parking ticket. Otherwise just forget about it."

Springer's stomach was churning, but she was determined to

stay calm. She wasn't going to blow this. "Don't you have any faith in me, Taffy? Didn't I bury that murder investigation for you?"

"Yeah, but—"

"Yeah, but nothing, Taffy. That would have been a second-degree murder charge at the very least. It wasn't easy, but I managed to derail the entire investigation. For you."

"That whole thing was an accident, pure and simple. Believe me, I would never have been charged with anything."

Springer kept her mouth shut, but she begged to differ. Cathy Dunne was the victim's name. Twenty-eight years old. Official cause of death: asphyxiation. Real reason: rough sex with Taffy. He was into that. She was strangled with her own bra. He'd wrapped it around her neck and used it as a bridle as he mounted her from behind. The ligature marks combined with the bruises and contusions on her face and limbs would have put Taffy away for thirty years minimum. It wasn't easy convincing the local police that a nice Irish girl from Palisades Park was really an IRA terrorist and that for diplomatic reasons, the Bureau should handle the case. Thank God Taffy had taken Ms. Dunne to a summer house on a lake in some one-horse town in Upstate New York. If he had done it anywhere else, Springer would never have been able to bury it.

"So what about our deal, Veronica?" Taffy said. "You gonna come through for me or what?"

"I cannot get those other charges dropped, Taffy. I told you that."

"Not even the hospital thing?"

"Rispoli had intimate knowledge of that scam. He's set to testify. There's nothing I can do about it. I'm sorry."

"But hypothetically speaking, if there were no Rispoli, there'd be no case against me."

"Hypothetically, yes."

She clawed the upholstery. He did put out a hit on Rispoli, she thought. Stupid bastard.

"Well, sweetheart, you know where I stand on this thing. Either you get me off completely or we don't have a deal. I do not want to be tried ever again, and if you can't get the medical-supply thing dropped in exchange for my cooperation, then . . . Well, I'm just going to have to explore other avenues, as they say."

Springer chewed on the insides of her cheeks. She didn't want to lose him, but she didn't know how to give him what he wanted.

"Are you still there, sweetness? I don't hear you breathing."

Her head was spinning. She was going to lose him. But Taffy was too big a fish to lose. She couldn't let him get away, not when she was this close. If she got him to flip and turn state's evidence, she could write her own ticket in the Bureau. It would mean a promotion, a raise, status, prestige. She would be the first female agent in the history of the FBI to earn a position of real power. All those good ol' boys at the Bureau could kiss her sweet little ass. She was sick and tired of banging her head against the glass ceiling. She closed her eyes and rubbed her temples. It made her nauseous just thinking about how close she was to realizing this. But close wasn't good enough.

"Sweetness, are you there?" Taffy said. "Talk to me."

"How about if I helped you?" she suddenly blurted out.

"Helped me what?"

"Helped you eliminate . . . your problem."

"What? *You* want the contract?"

"That's not what I'm saying. You've already got someone to do the deed. What if I were to provide the opportunity? Provide you with information." Her heart was pounding.

"In theory that sounds very nice, but you've got to put something on the table, darling."

"I'll put something on the table, Taffy. Don't you worry about that."

"But when?"

"Soon."

"Soon? What does that mean?"

"Let me think this through. I'll get back to you."

"You can call me anytime, beautiful. You know how much I love to talk to you. Maybe we can get together sometime, have dinner."

Springer touched her throat, imagining a lacy bra tightening around her neck. "I'll be in touch," she said quickly, then hung up the phone and rolled up the window.

She had stomach cramps as Taffy's face materialized behind her closed lids. The man was undeservedly handsome and utterly ruthless. A mature hunk with a very nasty bite. But he was the key to her future, the key to a corner office at the Hoover Building in Washington. Without Taffy, she would stay where she was, treading water as an FBI liaison with the Marshals Service. It was a dead-end job; she had to move on. Taffy unfortunately was the only egg in her basket. She needed Taffy.

But the only way to hang on to him was to make him happy by eliminating Gus Rispoli. She bit her bottom lip and tapped her foot impatiently on the floorboard. It wasn't right, she thought with a sigh, but what has to be, has to be. Anyway, it wasn't as if Rispoli were Mother Teresa.

She rolled down the window again and reached out for the receiver, dialing Marvelli's cell phone number.

"Hello?" Marvelli said.

"Officer Marvelli? Veronica Springer."

"Yeah, what's up?"

She was digging into the upholstery again. "Listen, would you do me a favor? I'm on my way, but would you order lunch for me? I'm on a tight schedule."

"Sure. What do you want?"

"A turkey burger, no bun, some cottage cheese, and whatever fruit they have."

"Anything to drink?"

"Just water."

"You got it."

"Thanks."

She put the receiver back on the hook, then looked down at her other hand on the seat. There was blue fuzz under her fingernails and deep gouges in the velveteen next to her thigh.

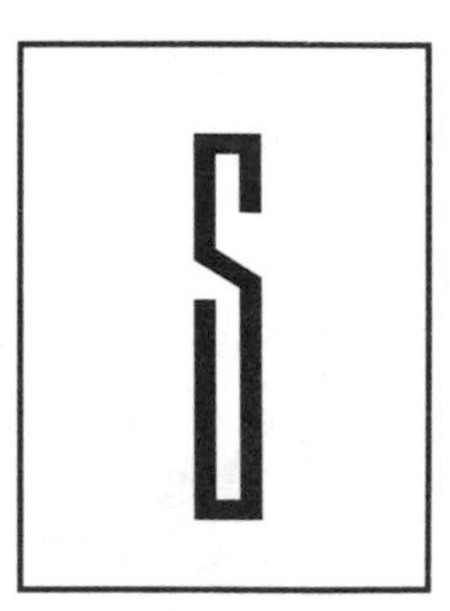

"Who was that?" Loretta asked as Marvelli put the cell phone back in his pocket. She was sitting opposite him in a booth.

Marvelli started sprinkling salt on the meat-loaf special. "That was Agent Springer," he said. "She wants me to order lunch for her. She says she's on a tight schedule."

Marvelli raised a finger to catch the eye of a passing waitress, one of the five Roses. "Rosie," he said, "you don't do turkey burgers, do you?"

The woman tilted her head up and down until she had Marvelli focused in the right part of her trifocals. She had pencils stuck in her puffy hair on both sides of her head. "Turkey burgers? Are you kidding me?"

"I didn't think so," Marvelli said. "Just give me a regular burger on a plate—well-done, no bun—a scoop of cottage cheese, and whatever fruit you've got."

The waitress shook her head. "All's I got is cling peaches in the can and fruit cocktail in cherry Jell-O."

Marvelli shrugged. "I dunno. The Jell-O, I guess. If she doesn't eat it, I will."

"Okay. You got it." The waitress hurried back toward the kitchen.

"And put that on a separate check," Loretta called after her. She wasn't about to start treating feds to lunch.

Marvelli was digging into his meat-loaf special, cutting into the slab of meat with the side of his fork. She was happy to see him eating and even happier that he was planning to eat Agent Springer's Jell-O if she left it. The bottomless pit was open for business again. Marvelli was coming out of it.

"You know, I've been thinking," he said with his mouth full. "Julius is all wrong. We gotta get out there and start looking for Sammy ourselves. Sammy's nuts. I know him. He'll figure out a way to get to Rispoli. We can't just sit on our hands with this."

"We?" Loretta was trying to be nonchalant as she tore open a Parker House roll.

"Yeah, we should both be out there," he said. "I know what he's like, but he knows my face. I need someone else to be the point man."

She stared at him from under her arched brows.

"Or point woman," he corrected himself. "Whatever."

"But where do we start? If we can't find out where Rispoli is, how do we find Sammy?"

"I've got a few ideas," he said as he scooped up a drippy forkful of creamed spinach. "With a little luck I think we can find him. I really do. I'm gonna tell Julius that I think he should approve a few overnights for us. Let us at least try."

Loretta nodded as she ate, trying to be noncommittal, but inside she was a Rockette doing high kicks to the ceiling. Overnights, she thought. That's all they needed. A couple of overnights. It would be good for both of them. He needed to realize that his wife wasn't the only woman in the world, and she had to break her celibacy streak. Being horny for year-long periods was not good for your health, she'd decided. If she and Marvelli got together for a little romance, it would be therapeutic. It didn't have to be hot and heavy. She wasn't looking for commitment. Just a little dose of hugging and kissing and . . . whatever. It would be good for them.

"There she is," Marvelli suddenly said, nodding toward the cash register. "Agent Springer."

Loretta turned around and saw a petite blonde in a navy blazer standing by the cash register, eyeing the crowd. She had extremely light blue eyes.

Soccer mom, Loretta thought. She imagined Springer living in some tidy little suburb, driving a minivan, and wearing holiday theme sweaters that went with the seasons—rows of pumpkins across her chest in October, Pilgrims in November, reindeer in December, hearts and flowers in February.

Marvelli waved to the woman. She nodded and flashed what probably passed for a smile at the Bureau as she came over to their booth.

"Officer Marvelli," she said, extending her hand. "Good to meet you."

"Hi, how you doing?" Marvelli put down his fork and shook her hand. "This is Loretta Kovacs. We work together at the Jump Squad."

"Pleased to meet you," Agent Springer said.

"You, too." Loretta shook her hand. It was ice cold and bony.

Marvelli shoved over and made room for Springer in the booth. "Have a seat. I put in your order. It should be coming right out."

Loretta didn't like the way Marvelli was looking at her. He was trying too hard to be cordial. Why? Did he forget that she was a fed?

Springer glanced down at their plates. Her expression was neutral, but Loretta could just guess what a cottage-cheese eater thought of mashed potatoes and gravy.

One of the other Roses—this one was a little older and more lined than the Rose who'd taken the order from Marvelli—arrived with Springer's lunch, setting the plate down in front of her. Springer examined the contents with clinical detachment, as if it were an autopsy specimen.

"Anything to drink, hon?" the new Rose asked.

"Just water, please," Springer said curtly.

When the waitress left, Springer scrutinized the block of Jell-O wiggling between the burger and the cottage cheese.

"It was either Jell-O or cling peaches," Marvelli explained. "Sorry."

"That's okay," Springer said as she looked around for the waitress. "I'm not that hungry. But I could use some water."

Marvelli speared another piece of meat loaf. "So you've changed your mind about my brother-in-law?"

"I made some inquiries about Teitelbaum," she said. "Apparently he is known in the Luccarelli family, and he had been associating with members of Taffy Demaggio's crew before he went to prison. It's possible that Demaggio could have hired him to kill Rispoli."

Marvelli sucked on the straw in his root beer. "Yeah, but could he really find My Blue Heaven?"

Springer didn't say anything for a second. She was looking around for the waitress again. Loretta noticed that she had her hand in the side pocket of her blazer.

"Who told you about My Blue Heaven?" There was a note of skeptical amusement in Springer's voice as if she were prepared to deny its existence, the way the marshals had.

"Everybody knows about My Blue Heaven," Loretta said. She had put down her fork and was leaning on her elbows, waiting for Springer to start eating before she continued with her own meal.

"Look, let's not focus on My Blue Heaven," Springer said. "That facility is very secure and very well hidden. Instead, let's focus on Mr. Teitelbaum. How good is he? Is he that extraordinary at his trade that he could realistically get to Mr. Rispoli?"

"I don't know how skilled he is," Marvelli said, "but he is reckless, and he doesn't give a damn about his own safety. He's a kamikaze."

Loretta noticed that the hand Springer had had in her pocket was now a closed fist on the table.

Springer was frowning. "This concerns me. Rispoli doesn't spend all his time at My Blue Heaven. We take him out fairly frequently for court appearances. That's when he'd be vulnerable."

Yet another one of the Roses came by with a glass of water. "Who gets the water?" she asked.

"Here," Springer said. She reached for the glass and took a sip. The closed hand went to her mouth, and she took a second sip. She set down the glass but didn't make any moves toward her lunch.

Diet pills, Loretta thought. Agent Springer's on diet pills. She's waiting for them to kick in, so she won't eat so much. Loretta knew that trick all too well. It never seemed to work for her, though.

Agent Springer started playing with her spoon, rocking it back and forth on the tabletop between her thumb and pinkie. "Rispoli's security is my responsibility whenever he's in this area. Naturally, I'd want to know if there were a bona fide contract out on his head. That's why I think it would be in both our interests if we shared information in this matter." She was looking at Marvelli, addressing all her comments to him.

Loretta dug a trough in her mashed potatoes and watched the pool of gravy on top flow out. She wanted to eat, but now she felt self-conscious.

Marvelli was grinning. "Share information, huh? Correct me if I'm wrong, Agent Springer, but according to Bureau rules, 'share' means we tell you what we know, but you only tell us what you want us to know."

Springer shook her head. "Absolutely not. I'm sure you've heard all kinds of stories about feds who have screwed local law-enforcement personnel—and I admit, it has happened—but I don't work that way. The way I see it, it's a simple equation. You want to find Mr. Teitelbaum; I want to keep Mr. Rispoli alive. In the process of pursuing those goals, I may discover things that would be helpful to you, and you may discover things that would be helpful to me. All I'm suggesting is that we keep each other informed."

Marvelli sucked on his straw again and nodded. "Sounds fair."

Dummy, Loretta thought. She finally speared a piece of meat loaf and started chewing with a scowl on her face. *Why was Mar-*

velli being so patient with Springer? He's knows better than to trust a feebie. Or was it her big blue eyes and her cute little figure? God, men are dopes.

Suddenly Agent Springer dabbed her mouth with a napkin and slid out of the booth even though she'd hardly eaten a thing. "I have to get going," she said, pulling a pair of sunglasses out of her breast pocket. She flashed a tight smile and nodded to Loretta. "Nice meeting you." Her smile was wider for Marvelli. "Let's stay in touch, okay?" She went into her pocket and laid a twenty-dollar bill on the table. "My treat," she said. "I'll be talking to you."

Loretta watched her walking toward the front door. She wanted Springer to have a big butt or thick ankles, but she didn't.

Marvelli was sopping up gravy with his Parker House roll. "She seemed okay," he said.

"You think so, huh?"

"You don't like her?"

"I didn't say that."

"You don't have to."

"Did you see her popping those pills?"

"She was popping pills?"

"Yup."

"Maybe they were aspirin." Marvelli was craning his neck to peruse what was left on Springer's plate. "You want to split her Jell-O? She didn't touch it."

"No thanks."

"You sure?"

"I'm sure. You go right ahead."

"Okay." He balanced the block of red Jell-O on his fork and plopped it onto his bread plate. He cut it into quarters and shoveled a piece into his mouth. "Not bad," he said with his mouth full.

Loretta just glared at him. *Springer seems okay,* she thought sarcastically, remembering his words. *What a dope.*

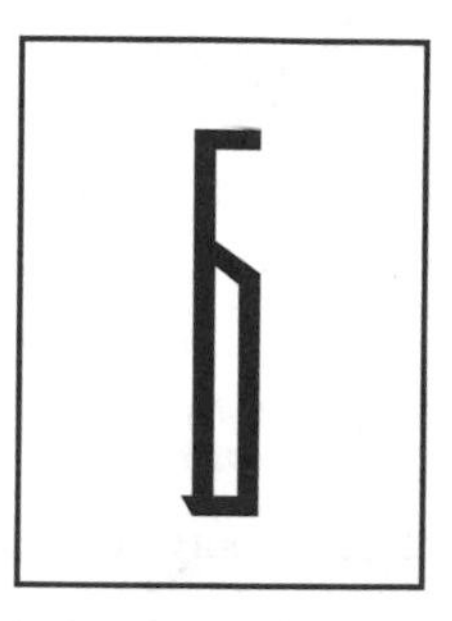

Sitting behind the wheel of her old cranberry-red Saturn, Loretta squinted and tilted her watch toward the light coming from the fluorescent overheads that barely illuminated the parking garage. Outside her window most of the other spaces were empty. Just nine parked cars were scattered around the floor. She'd been here twenty minutes, and she hadn't seen a soul. Even the attendant's booth had been empty when she'd come in and taken a ticket from the automatic dispenser. Loretta had followed Marvelli's directions and parked in a dim corner to stay out of sight, but where the hell was he? she wanted to know. It was almost one A.M., and she was getting cold sitting here.

Marvelli had called her earlier that evening. She had been looking through a new law-school brochure that had come in the mail that day, one of the ones her sister Bonnie had ordered, when the phone rang. "Loretta, it's me," he'd said. "What're you doing?"

Instantly she got her hopes up, but she realized just as quickly that she was jumping to conclusions. "Not much," she said. "Just reading."

"Listen. There's a parking garage on Bergen Avenue in Jersey City called Park and Go. It's just south of Journal Square. Meet me on the fourth floor between twelve-thirty and one."

"Tonight?"

"Yeah. I'm meeting someone who may help us find Sammy."

She'd stared down at the holes in her Acorn sox. "Why do you want *me* to go? Officially I'm not on this case."

"Well, yeah, but I thought you were interested in doing this one with me."

"What about Julius? Did he say he wants both of us on it?"

"Just meet me there. I'll fix it with Julius."

She was thrilled that he wanted to include her, but she had some misgivings about this mysterious late-night rendezvous in a parking garage. "So who are we meeting?" she asked

"Not on the phone," he said, lowering his voice. "Just meet me there. And park in a dark corner." He hung up, leaving her with a dial tone in her ear.

So where the hell is he now? she thought, clamping her armpits over her cold fingers as she stared out the windshield.

She wished she had a hot cup of coffee and not just for the warmth. Life without caffeine was getting to be a drag. She'd graduated from the fuzzy-headed stage to the cranky jitters. Not that she needed any help being cranky.

Her mind started to wander, and her lust for a cup of coffee reminded her of restaurants and diners, and that reminded her of the Five Roses Diner, which in turn reminded her of Special Agent Veronica Springer and the way Marvelli had been with her. She wondered if Marvelli found her attractive. Springer wasn't a dog, but she wasn't exactly someone you'd want to cuddle with. And she was a pill popper. How could he find her attractive? If he did find her attractive.

Loretta was blowing on her fingers when she suddenly heard a soft thunk coming from the other side of the garage. She froze and listened. After a few seconds she heard a distant ding. The elevator, she thought. Marvelli took the elevator? Why would he do that?

She watched for him to come down the slope of the concrete floor, listened for his footsteps, but there was nothing. A chill traveled down her arms and through her stomach. She couldn't see the elevators from where she was parked. Thick concrete supports in the middle of the floor blocked her view. Someone was hiding behind those supports, she kept thinking. Someone who'd seen her come in by herself. Someone who wasn't Marvelli.

She reached for her purse and pulled out her .38, quickly flipping open the cylinder to check her load even though she knew it was full. Then she reached into the backseat and pulled her "inflatable friend" up front. The blow-up dummy had a placid but masculine face, a weird orangy complexion, and he wore a gray business suit that fit him like a paint job. Her mother had given it to her for protection, so that it would look like someone was always driving with her. Loretta sometimes left him behind the wheel when she had to park in an unfamiliar neighborhood after dark.

He was looking a little saggy, so she quickly opened the plug at the small of his back and blew him up a little. *Plastic oral sex,* she thought as she exhaled. *About as close as I come to the real thing these days.*

She closed the plug with her tongue and quietly opened her door, staying low as she stepped out, and pulled her "friend" behind the wheel. She closed the door softly, nudging it shut with her hip. Again she stopped and listened. The garage was silent, but she sensed that someone was out there.

She moved around to the back of the car where the shadows were darker and strained to get a better view of the massive support columns, but they were at least three feet wide. Someone could easily be hiding behind one of them.

Ten parking spaces away, three cars were parked in a row—two dark-colored sedans and an old cream-colored station wagon. If she could get behind those cars, she could see what was behind the support columns. But to get there, she'd have to move out into the open.

She pressed her lips together, trying to think of another way to get there. A knee-high metal pipe barricade ran the length of the garage along the outside wall. Beyond the barricade were open windows, two feet wide and ten feet tall. A high cyclone fence kept the curious and the stupid from having an accidental fall, but in the corner the fence had been pulled away from its post, leaving enough room for someone to squeeze through.

Loretta got down on her knees, crawled to the corner, and carefully pried the fence up, poking her head through. A six-inch ledge ran under all the windows on the outside of the building. She could hold on to the fence and step sideways along the ledge until she got to a window that gave her a better view. There was just one problem—the distance *between* the windows. She'd only have sheer wall to hang on to for the five or six feet between the windows. Not good, she thought.

Suddenly the scrape of shoe leather on concrete echoed through the garage, and Loretta froze, not daring to even breathe. Someone was definitely out there. Maybe more than one someone. She couldn't stay where she was.

She slowly pulled back the cyclone fence and crawled through the opening on her hands and knees, frowning at the encrusted pigeon droppings and gooey grime that was getting on her palms. The air was chilly, but there was no wind, thank God. Still, it was four stories down to a pitch-black alley below, and even though Loretta wasn't afraid of heights, her balance was only so-so, and she had never been terribly surefooted.

The sound of quick footsteps reverberated off the concrete walls. Loretta imagined whoever-it-was moving his position, ducking behind another support, and coming closer. She could not stay there, she thought. She had to get a better vantage point, so she could use her gun to hold the intruder at bay. But she had to go out on the ledge to do that, and she was going to need both hands to hold on to the fence. She tried to stick the .38 into the waistband of her jeans, but it was too uncomfortable against her skin. Her fleece pullover didn't have any pockets, and she didn't want to try sticking the gun in her jeans at the small of her back for fear that it would pop out and fall into the alley. In desperation she uncocked the hammer and put it in her mouth, clamping the wood-grain butt between her teeth. It tasted horrible, and the smell of gun oil was enough to make her gag, but she had no choice.

Holding on to the fence, she slowly got to her feet. When she turned her head to look down, the gun shifted in her mouth, pivoting on her eye teeth, and she quickly had to close her lips around it to keep from losing it. She winced, wishing she could spit.

Carefully she sidestepped along the ledge. It was wider than her foot, and walking it wasn't as scary as she'd feared. But then she came to the wall. There was no cyclone fence to hold on to, and the ledge wasn't as wide here. She stopped and took measured breaths, trying to psyche herself. The distance was a little more than two full arm lengths, she estimated. If she hugged the wall and stayed as flat as she could, it shouldn't be a problem. But when she took her first step and realized that there was only enough room for the ball of her foot, she changed her mind about that. There *was* a problem. A big problem. She could fall.

But the click of rapid footsteps inside the garage was like a straight pin to the butt. Loretta held her breath and stuck her foot out, testing her footing before she let go of the fence. She heard the footsteps again, and her thumping heartbeat threatened to knock her off the ledge. Reluctantly she let go of the fence and moved farther out, her face so close to the wall her gun was scraping against the concrete, forcing her to tip her head back.

A sudden stiff breeze blew through her ears, and she imagined herself being blown right off. It died down as quickly as it came, and Loretta took another step, anxious to get this over with. Crusty guano crunched under her sneakers as she reached out and wiggled her fingers, desperate to find the edge. She wasn't quite there yet, but she figured another small slide step would do it. She moved slowly, inch by inch. When her fingertips finally touched the cyclone fence, she started to breathe again. She got a good grip on the fence and moved a little faster. When she finally cleared the wall and was able to put her whole foot down on something solid, it felt as if she were standing on a football field compared to where she'd been.

Unfortunately this stretch of the ledge was better lit than the last part, and whoever was inside could probably see her. She took the gun out of her mouth just in case she'd need it fast and sidestepped quickly across the ledge until she got to the next wall. But her hands started to shake at the prospect of having to cross another wall. Her heart fluttered. She suddenly had a headache like a steel rod going through her skull. She needed a coffee badly.

Putting the gun back in her teeth, she hugged the wall and started across the narrow part of the ledge. She listened for footsteps, but she could only hear the breeze in her ears, and suddenly she panicked. She was convinced that whoever was out there knew she was here and was staring at her right now. She turned her head abruptly to look back, thinking he could be on the ledge, but the gun got in the way, scraping against the wall and unsettling her balance. Her heart leaped as she started to tip backward. She dug her fingers into the hard concrete, but there was no purchase, so she quickly dropped her chin and for the moment that seemed to help. She stood there with her forehead against the bricks, breathing hard. Her heart was doing a drum solo, and her legs were shaking like dogs on their way to the vet. She was petrified, afraid to move an inch.

Come on, Loretta, she told herself. *Go. You made it across the last one. You can do it again.*

She took as deep a breath as she dared, then forced herself to go on. Her foot was shaking as she slid it forward, dislodging more crusty gunk from the ledge, but she kept going, telling herself that there was no alternative. Either she kept going or she stayed put, and if she stayed put, she'd either get caught or she'd fall. Stretching her arm across the rough surface of the wall, she prayed for the edge, forcing her legs to obey until finally she felt it with the tip of her middle finger. *Thank God,* she thought.

Her fingers found the cyclone fence. She grabbed hold and moved a little faster. When she was able to take the gun out of her mouth, she let out a long breath. She felt safer here. Not only was she shielded by a parked car, but there was another hole in the fence a few feet away. In the dim light, she could see a corner that was pushed out. She wouldn't have to go back across the ledge to get back in. *Thank you, God.*

Forgetting about the stalker for a moment, she gripped the fence and sidestepped quickly toward the hole. She glanced over her shoulder at the dark alley down below. All she wanted was to get off that ledge. She'd worry about the damn stalker when she got back inside.

But then she looked down the length of the parked car, and she noticed something that made her freeze. Crouched down in the car's shadow was a man. He had his back to her, and apparently he hadn't noticed her. In the dim light she couldn't make out what he was wearing or what he looked like. She hung on to the fence, not daring to move for fear of making a noise. She glanced down at the hole in the fence and thought about diving through, but he'd surely hear her before she could make it. But what she did have was the element of surprise. She decided she had to take advantage of that and do something before he did.

She quietly stuck the barrel of her gun through the fence, peering down the sights and drawing a bead on his back. The first aggressive move he made, she'd shoot him. In the position she was in, she had no choice. If he had a gun and shot first, she'd be dead. Even if the wound weren't fatal, the fall would be. It was either him or her.

She sucked in a deep breath. "Freeze!" she shouted, her finger already pressing on the trigger, ready to get off the first shot. "Don't move or you're dead."

The dark figure flinched but didn't turn around. Then his head turned slowly and half of his face went into the light. "Loretta!" he said. "Don't shoot! It's me."

Marvelli! she thought, and suddenly her heart really went wild. She'd almost shot Marvelli.

"Loretta, what the hell're you doing out there?" he said, sounding annoyed. "I told you to just wait for me."

"I thought you were a—never mind," she said. It was too hard to explain.

She made her way to the hole in the fence as Marvelli came

over to help her. He held the broken flap of the fence open as she carefully got down on her knees and crawled through. Her nerves were jangling, and her hands were trembling as she stood up and brushed herself off. She wanted to throw her arms around him. She needed a hug. But the ticked-off look on his face stopped her.

"Are you nuts, Loretta? You could've gotten killed out there."

"You could get killed in here, too," she snapped back. She was stung by his attitude. "Where the hell were you? You said you'd be here."

"What're you barking at me for?" he said. "I've been here for fifteen minutes. Looking for you."

"Then *you're* the one I heard?"

"Well, who did you think it was? You expecting someone else?"

"Only your friend," she said, glowering at him. She was embarrassed that she'd overreacted. "I thought we were supposed to meet him here," she said.

"He's late. He told me he might be. Is that a problem?"

"No," she muttered, and turned her back on him.

Silence came between them like an air bag full of resentment.

"I'm sorry," he said after a moment, softening his tone. "Maybe I shouldn't have called you. This isn't your case. I just thought . . ." He let his words trail off.

She turned around to face him, and the pathetic back slant of his puppy-dog eyes melted her like a scoop of ice cream sliding down the hood of a car in the sun.

"Marvelli?" she said. She coughed to clear her throat. "Marvelli, we have to talk."

"About what?"

Her heart was pounding. "Let's go to my car," she said. She was stalling, wondering if this was the right time, the right place, wondering if bringing up her feelings was a good idea at all.

She walked toward her car in silence, thoughts racing through her head. What was she going to say to him? How would she start? She was going to sound like an ass. He'd think she was a nut. He'd never speak to her again.

Maybe just change the subject, she thought. Talk about something else.

But she couldn't avoid her feelings any longer. She was very attracted to him, and it was driving her crazy.

"Marvelli," she said as they came up to her car, "I don't know how to say this, but—"

"Wait!" He suddenly stepped in front of her. "Get down!" He dropped to a crouch and tried to pull her down with him.

At first she was confused, but then she realized that he must have seen her inflatable friend in the driver's seat. She was surprised that it had fooled him.

"It's okay," she said, standing up. "It's only a dummy."

But when she peered through the windshield, the placid orangy plastic face she'd expected wasn't staring back at her. This dummy was flesh and blood, and he didn't look like anyone's idea of a friendly businessman because he was holding a big black automatic, pointing it right at Loretta.

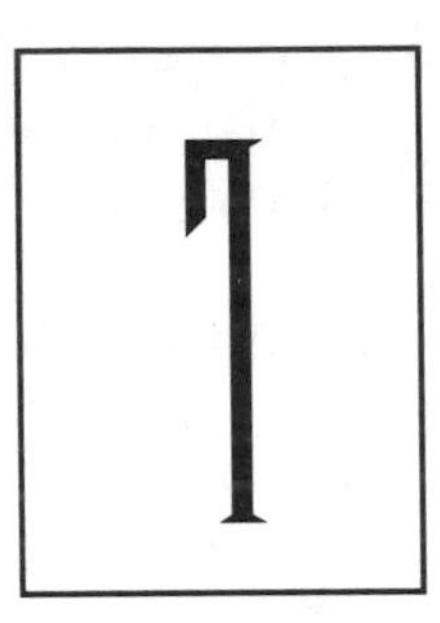

Loretta slowly raised her hands above her shoulders, shifting her gaze back and forth between the heavy-browed man sitting behind the wheel of her car and the big black 9-mm in his hand. He had thin dark hair combed straight back over a piston-shaped head. His lips were meaty, and his eyes slanted up as if his scalp was too tight. The gun was in his left hand, propped on the side mirror, staring at her like a big black one-eyed crow.

"Easy," she said to the man. "Just tell us what you want."

"Why don't you tell me what *you* want?" he said. He sounded grumpy.

Loretta was confused, but at least he wasn't shooting.

"What's with the gun?" Marvelli said as he approached the driver's side.

"What're you doing?" Loretta blurted, afraid that he was going to get himself shot.

"Don't worry," Marvelli said. "This guy can't shoot his way out of a paper bag. He's a fed." Marvelli extended his hand toward the man and grinned. "I didn't recognize you there for a minute, pardner."

"You either," the man said, retracting the gun and shaking Marvelli's hand.

Loretta was scowling at the two of them. "Do I get an introduction?"

"Get in first," the man said. He nodded toward the passenger door.

Loretta resented being invited into her own car, but she got in anyway.

Marvelli climbed into the backseat. "Loretta, this is Mike Tarantella. He's a feebie."

Loretta raised her eyebrows in surprise. "You never told me you had any friends at the FBI."

"No one has 'friends' at the Bureau," Marvelli said as he watched Tarantella's eyes in the rearview mirror. "Mike just happens to owe me a few favors."

"You're hurting my feelings, Marvelli," the agent said. "I thought we were *paesans.*" There was a pungent note of insincerity in almost everything Tarantella said.

"Sure, we're *paesans,*" Marvelli said. "That's why I called you."

"So what can I do for you? Ask me anything."

"Okay. Where's My Blue Heaven?"

Tarantella started to laugh. It sounded like gravel in a coffee can. He squeezed his eyes shut and pinched his nose, hissing like a radiator.

"What's so funny?" Loretta asked. She wanted him out of her seat.

"Are you two kidding or what? I don't know where My Blue Heaven is. Nobody knows except for the marshals who work in Witness Protection."

"I'll bet Veronica Springer knows," Marvelli said.

Tarantella abruptly stopped laughing. "How do you know her?"

"We just met. I got in touch to let her know that we've got a jumper who's been hired to whack Gus Rispoli."

Tarantella nodded, mulling this over. "And let me guess. Agent Springer was *very* cooperative."

"Well, she wasn't *un*cooperative," Marvelli said.

"What the hell're you talking about?" Loretta said, frowning at Marvelli over the seat back. "She blew us off. In a nice way maybe, but she didn't give us the time of day."

Marvelli frowned back at her. "We agreed to keep each other informed."

"I'll bet you believe in the Tooth Fairy, too, Marvelli," Tarantella said.

"What do you mean?"

"Well, let's just say I've heard some stories about her, and the words 'ruthless' and 'ambitious' do tend to come up a lot when people describe her. So do the words 'sneaky' and 'underhanded.' But I don't really know the woman, so I couldn't say for sure."

"Sounds like you know plenty," Loretta said.

Tarantella shrugged and flashed a sly grin. "You know how we feds are. We got hidden agendas up the wazoo. Can't depend on anything we say."

She grinned back at him. She was beginning to like this guy.

"I did some work with her on a few cases, but that was years ago," Tarantella said, "before she lost all the weight. She was actually sort of nice back then."

"She used to have a weight problem?" Marvelli asked.

"Oh, yeah," Tarantella said. "She almost lost her job she was so big. Field agents have to stay within certain weight requirements. But she managed to take it off. And she did it pretty fast."

"Really," Marvelli said. "How big was she?"

Tarantella shrugged. "I don't know. I'm not a doctor."

"Hard to believe Springer used to be heavy," Marvelli said. "She doesn't look it."

Loretta wanted to smack him. He was acting as if Tarantella had just told him Springer used to be a man. So what if she used to be fat? Was she tainted because she wasn't always a perfect size 6? Or was he afraid that if he got involved with her, she might suddenly blow up one night and turn into a blimp?

"So getting back to the original question," Loretta said to Tarantella, ignoring Marvelli, "do you have any idea where My Blue Heaven is?"

The agent shrugged and shook his head. "All I've heard are rumors. I've talked to people who've been there, and *they* don't even have a clue. To get there, you have to fly to Chicago, then the Marshals Service puts you on a plane with the windows blacked out. You land on some tiny airstrip in the middle of nowhere, and they put you on a bus, also with windows blacked out. You never get to see anything until you're actually inside the compound."

Loretta shook her head and sighed. "Great. This is very helpful. I'm so glad I'm losing sleep for this."

"Come on, Mike," Marvelli said. "You must know more than that. You're just not saying."

"I swear to God, Marvelli. That's all I know."

"Mikey, please. I've known you a long time. I know you know more. You must."

"I'm telling you, Marvelli. *Paesan* to *paesan*. That's all I know."

"Okay, fine. If you want to be that way about it . . . But next time you need a favor from me, don't even bother making the call."

Tarantella smiled sweetly in the rearview mirror. "Come on, Marvelli. I'm being straight with you. Why won't you believe me?"

Marvelli shook his finger at Tarantella's reflection. "Next time you want some mook picked up on a parole violation so you can smoke him, don't ask me to put the guy's file on top of my pile. I'm gonna be too busy."

"Marvelli, please. We go back a long way—"

"I'm gonna be busy, Mike. I'm telling you right now."

Tarantella's face compressed. He sneered and bared his teeth. "All right, all right," he said. "This is all I know. I swear. And this is only what I've heard, so I can't confirm any of it. My Blue Heaven is supposedly somewhere in the Pacific Northwest. That's all I know."

"What else?" Marvelli insisted.

"What do you mean, 'what else'? I told you. That's all I know."

"You know more, Mike. I know you do. Spill it or take my name out of your Rolodex. I'm serious."

Tarantella turned around and glared at Marvelli face-to-face. "The place is on the water. Now, that's all I know."

"Salt water or fresh?"

"The ocean," Tarantella snarled. "Now, don't ask me another friggin' thing because I don't know anything else. Okay?"

"Right," Marvelli said sarcastically. "But this'll do for now . . . *paesan.*"

"This isn't gonna do you any good," Tarantella said. "You're never gonna find the place, and neither is your jumper. If I were you, I'd start working another angle."

"We'll see," Marvelli said. He was wearing a funny little grin, like a cat hiding a canary in its mouth. Loretta noticed and so did Tarantella because they were both staring at him, waiting for him to share his thoughts. But he didn't say a word.

"Anything else I can do for you, Marvelli?" Tarantella asked.

"Nope."

"You sure?"

"Yup."

"Well, I'm gonna get going then." But he didn't make any moves to go. "If you need anything else, you know where to find me, right?"

"Yup."

"Okay then."

"See ya around," Marvelli said.

"Nice meeting you, Loretta," Tarantella said.

"Yeah, you too," Loretta said.

Tarantella paused with his hand on the door handle. Finally he opened the door and let himself out, staring poker-faced at Marvelli through the window as he closed the door. He walked across the empty garage, his heels clicking on the concrete all the way to the elevators. Loretta didn't say anything until he was out of sight.

She turned around and looked at Marvelli between the seats. "So what're you thinking? I know you're cooking something up."

Marvelli opened his door and started to step out. "Meet me at the White Castle up on Kennedy Boulevard."

"What?"

"The burger place. You know. It's just over the border in Union City."

"I know where it is," she said, about to be exasperated with him. "Who're we meeting now?"

"No one," he said. "I'm just hungry."

"It's almost two o'clock in the morning. How can you eat now?"

He shrugged. "Just meet me there. You don't have to eat. You can just have a coffee."

"I wish," she muttered.

"Oh, I forgot you gave it up. You can have a soda or something." He started to close the door.

"Hang on," she said. "What about Sammy Teitelbaum? What're we gonna do about him?"

"I'll tell you when we get there." He shut the door and walked away.

Loretta glared at his back, but her eyes were drooping, and her head was fuzzy. She wanted to get to bed.

"Have a coffee," she grumbled sarcastically. "Sure. Why not? Maybe I should have two."

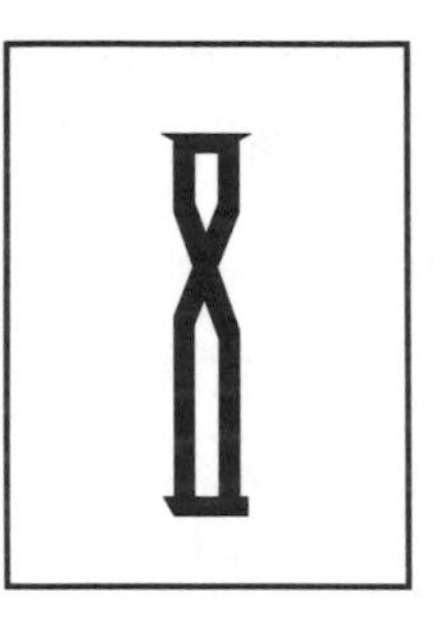

When Loretta arrived at the White Castle, Marvelli was already sitting at the stainless-steel counter along the front windows, eating. He waved to her through the plate-glass window as soon as she got out of her car, his mouth full of something, chewing away like a cow in cud heaven. She dragged herself across the blacktop lot, yawning all the way, and pushed through the steamy glass door.

Two Hispanic women—one in her teens, the other in her fifties—stared at her with bored expectation from behind the counter. Their dark hair was imprisoned in nets, and the teenager's eyeliner was melting in the heat rising from the grill. Two neat lines of little square hamburgers sat heating on the grill next to a mound of chopped fried onions. Some of the burgers already had buns balanced on their backs like turtle shells, ready to be scooped up and put together at a moment's notice.

But the smell of the burgers did nothing for Loretta. It was the smell of the coffee dripping into a clear Pyrex pot that caught her attention. The aroma tantalized, teased, and mocked her all at the same time. She felt like a junkie in a drugstore.

Other than Marvelli, there was only one other customer, a bus driver engrossed in a newspaper laid out on the counter. Swirls of steam quietly rose from a jumbo cup of coffee poised in his hand. He was a big man with a big gut and a big butt. The wages of sitting behind the wheel of a bus all day, Loretta thought.

Marvelli was hovering over a cardboard tray full of those little square hamburgers, each one in a little white open-sided box. Loretta counted the boxes, both full and empty. An even dozen. Plus two orders of fries and a humongous paper cup full of soda that she could have stuck her fist in halfway to her elbow. He was still wearing that funny little smile that he'd had back at the parking garage.

"Are you pregnant?" she asked as she took the stool next to him. "Looks like you're eating for two. Or three. Or four."

"What're you talking about?" he said, taking another bite. "It's not that much."

"Twelve hamburgers isn't much?"

"Nah. They're small." He picked out a fresh one and held it out to her. "Here. You want one?"

She shook her head. "No thanks." It had taken her years to stop midnight snacking, and she still broke the rules now and then, but not for greasy burgers in the wee hours. Ice cream, of course, was a different story.

"You want anything?" he asked. "A coffee."

She shook her head.

"A soda?"

Cola had caffeine, she thought, and she shook her head again. "I don't want anything. I'm fine," she said. "So tell me. Why do you look so happy?"

"I've got an idea on how we can catch Sammy." He shoved the remainder of the burger he was holding into his mouth and held up one finger to say that he needed a minute to swallow. He was eating like an anaconda. At this rate his descendants would eventually develop the ability to unhinge their jaws so they could eat an entire roast pig in one bite.

"So what's your idea?" she said, propping her chin on her fist.

Marvelli picked up another burger. "If Sammy's going to the Northwest, I know one place where he'll definitely put in a stop: Seattle."

"Why Seattle?"

"Because my sister-in-law Jennifer lives there. Rene's kid sister. She and Sammy are married, but they separated when he went to prison. He's still crazy about her, though. Obsessive crazy. If he's anywhere in the area, he'll definitely look her up."

"So what're you gonna do? Overnight your sister-in-law a pair of cuffs and tell her to hold Sammy if he shows up?"

"No," Marvelli said, pausing to suck the straw in his bucket of soda. His eyeballs nearly touched, he sucked so hard. "I think we should go out there and wait for him, use Jennifer as bait."

"What do you mean 'we'?" Loretta didn't want to get her hopes up.

"I can't do this one alone, Loretta. Sammy knows me. Once he spots me, he'll head for the hills. But he doesn't know you, and he probably won't suspect a woman."

"Julius will never go for it," she said.

"Yeah, he will," Marvelli said. "You heard him yourself. If Sammy pulls off this hit, the Bureau of Parole will get crucified, especially by the feds. Julius will find the money to send us out there when I tell him about my sister-in-law. Don't worry." Marvelli chomped into another burger.

Loretta was skeptical. "How do you know Sammy hasn't already been to see . . . what's her name?"

"Jennifer."

"Maybe he's already been there and gone."

"I sincerely doubt it. Annette, my mother-in-law, talks to Jennifer every other day. They talked last night. If Jennifer had seen Sammy, I would've heard about it." He rolled his eyes. "Believe me."

"I take it your mother-in-law doesn't like Sammy?"

"She despises him. Hated him from the moment she met him. She's afraid he and Jennifer will get back together. Those two have that kind of relationship. One minute she loves him, the next minute she wants to kill him."

"I had one of those once," Loretta muttered.

"What happened?"

"When I realized I was spending more time wanting to kill him, I decided I'd better leave him before I actually did it."

"Good move." Marvelli slid another burger out of its box.

Loretta looked over her shoulder at the globe-shaped coffeepots sitting on the big double-decker coffeemaker. She could have a decaf, she thought, but that wouldn't help her kick the habit. It would just make her want a real coffee. Better to just go cold turkey, she decided.

"So how long has Jennifer lived in Seattle?" Loretta asked.

Marvelli shrugged. "Only a couple of months. She said she wanted to be on her own. I guess she needed some space."

"How come?"

"Well, she got married right out of high school. She and her bum of a husband were only together about a year when he went to jail. In the meantime Rene started getting real sick, and Jennifer moved in with us to help take care of her. It was like one thing right after another for her. After Rene died, the kid needed a break. I hated to see her go, but . . ." He shrugged. "Hey, what can you do?"

Loretta noticed that Marvelli had stopped eating. He was staring down at the clutter of empty burger boxes, his face suddenly sad and vague. Loretta knew what he was thinking. He was thinking about Rene.

Loretta's brow wrinkled. She felt sorry for him. He wasn't over his wife yet, and she wouldn't be surprised if he never got over her. In his mind he was still married to Rene. No woman was going to get anywhere with him. She sighed and glanced back at those coffeepots again, four of them, two on the top shelf, two on the bottom. Her new forbidden fruit. She closed her eyes and rubbed her face. God, she needed something.

"Can I have one of these?" she suddenly said, reaching over and taking one of the burgers.

"Sure, go ahead," he said. "Take what you want. There's plenty." He emerged from his fog for only a moment, then went right back in, staring out the window at the starless night.

She looked at him sideways as she bit into the burger. She was eating, and he wasn't. Great, she thought. He was going to mourn for the rest of his life, and she was going to keep eating. Wonderful.

"Guess we'll have to leave for Seattle pretty quick," she said.

"Ummm . . ." He was a million miles away.

"I don't supposed the feds out there will be any more helpful than they are here."

"Ummm . . ."

She stared at him glumly as she chewed, then reached for his gigantic cup and helped herself to a sip. He didn't seem to notice. She finished the tiny burger and picked up another one. "So tell me," she said. "What's your sister-in-law like?"

"Hmmm?"

Loretta sighed. "Never mind."

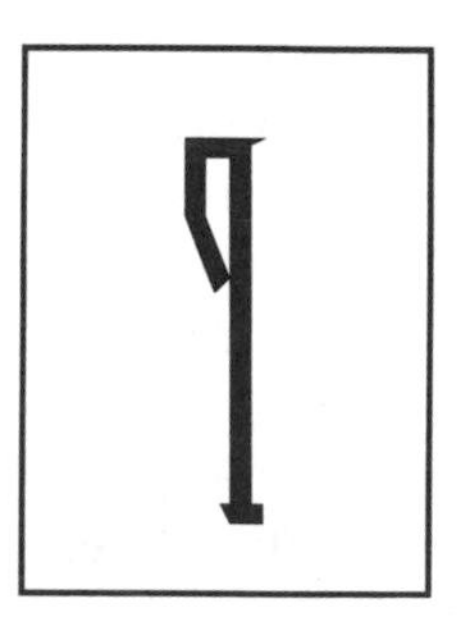

The sky had been a bit overcast when their plane touched down at Seattle-Tacoma International, but now it had darkened to the color of pewter. Loretta and Marvelli were in the back of a cab, heading up Fifteenth Avenue. Loretta scanned the sidewalks as they whizzed by, taking in the locals—men in business suits, old Japanese ladies in long skirts, scruffy street people wearing newspapers tied around their legs, teenagers with nose rings and brow rings and belly-button rings and hair the colors of Fruit Loops. She tilted her head back and stared up at the gloomy sky through the rear window. How the hell did a place with this much crappy weather get so hip? she wondered.

Marvelli was staring intently out his window, his brow deeply furrowed. He'd been pretty quiet since they'd left New Jersey. Loretta was beginning to worry about him.

"Did you tell your sister-in-law we'd be coming straight from the airport?" she asked.

Marvelli shook his head. "I didn't tell her anything."

Loretta sat up. "She doesn't know we're coming?"

He shook his head again. "I didn't want to tell her, just in case she told Sammy."

"Sure. Of course."

Loretta stared at his grim profile. Maybe he was concerned that they'd walk right in on Sammy, that they'd have to take him there and then, bim-bam-boom. Loretta hoped it wouldn't be that easy. She wanted to see a little of Seattle before they had to go back.

The cab pulled to a stop at a red light. "It's up on the next block," the cabbie said, turning around in his seat and flashing a gold-toothed grin. His skin was golden, and his features were Asian, but he was wearing a multicolored Rastafarian knit cap so stuffed with dreadlocks it puffed out from his head like a tin of Jiffy-Pop popcorn hot from the stove. His photo ID on the dashboard identified him as Cedric B. Ong.

The traffic light turned green, and Cedric stomped on the accelerator. At the middle of the block he pulled into the right lane, looked over his shoulder for oncoming traffic, then made an abrupt U-turn, screeching to a stop on the other side of the street. He flipped the lever on the meter and looked back at them over his blue-tinted granny glasses, flashing his gold teeth. "Here you go, mon."

Cedric was obviously proud of his daredevil driving skills, but neither Loretta nor Marvelli were impressed. They both lived across the river from Manhattan, and by New York standards Cedric was still in the minors.

Marvelli handed him a few folded bills. "Keep the change," he said.

"I and I thank you, mon," Cedric said with a grateful nod, but Loretta could tell that he was a little disappointed that he hadn't gotten a rise out of them.

"Next time try driving on the sidewalk," Loretta said as she slid across the seat, dragging her garment bag with her.

Cedric B. Ong scratched whatever he had living under that hat, looking a bit confused as he pulled away.

"This way," Marvelli said. He hoisted his oversized gym bag over his shoulder and started walking toward a storefront. He was wearing a pair of pressed, dry-cleaned jeans and a white-on-white pinstriped dress shirt with a huge high-roll collar under a double-breasted salt-and-pepper sports coat. He just might fit in here, Loretta thought. He was so out of date he was practically retro.

A mechanized sign in the storefront window showed an old-fashioned percolator tipping back and forth, pouring invisible coffee into a huge French coffee cup. "The Grind" was spelled out in jagged lettering that was supposed to indicate a caffeine jolt. As they approached the front door, a young man dressed in black jeans and a black T-shirt came out, and immediately Loretta was overtaken by the pungent aroma of espresso beans. It went right to her head and gripped her frontal lobes. She loved espresso. She wanted some badly.

"This is not gonna be easy," she muttered as Marvelli pushed through the door.

"What'd you say?" he asked.

"Nothing."

The Grind was a homey place with exposed brick walls, a scarred but well-varnished hardwood floor, and ten mismatched tin-topped kitchen tables with vinyl-seat chairs. It was early afternoon so there were only a few patrons, most of them reading. Two young guys were surfing the Internet on the two computers over in the corner.

"Frank! What the hell're you doing here?" The accent and volume level were unmistakably New Jersey. Loretta glanced up to see who belonged to the voice.

Standing behind the glass pastry case was a woman in her midtwenties who was drop-dead gorgeous. Long heavy blond hair covered her shoulders and curved around a set of breasts that stood up at attention and defied gravity. She was tall and slender, and her waist was so small it was hard to believe her frame could support those breasts. She came clumping around the counter in clunky black heels and a denim micro-mini that hardly seemed worth the effort.

"Jennifer!" Marvelli shouted, dropping his bag and throwing his arms around her.

As they embraced, Jennifer bent her knee and lifted one leg behind herself the way sexy babes do in the movies. Loretta sniffed the overpowering smell of coffee as she stared at Marvelli hugging a great pair of legs, a great head of hair, a great ass, and a great set of boobs.

So this is Rene's sister, she thought.

"So how you doing, kid?" Marvelli said. Jennifer's hair was tickling his nose. He wished she'd let go already, but she was squeezing him tight, and it was starting to make him a little uncomfortable.

Marvelli gently tried to pry his sister-in-law loose. "Jennifer, Jennifer, I want you to meet my partner." He managed to disengage from her hug, but she still clung to him, standing side by side with her shoulder in his armpit, her head nuzzled against his chest. He knew she didn't mean anything by it—she'd always been affectionate like this—but she was the same size as Rene, and she sort of resembled Rene, and she reminded him of Rene, and Rene was gone now, and he was feeling something, he didn't know what, and it was all very weird.

"Jennifer, this is Loretta Kovacs," he said, "my partner."

"Hi," Jennifer said, pushing the hair out of her eyes and hooking it around her ear. Rene used to do the exact same thing with her hair, he thought.

"Nice to meet you," Loretta said. For some reason she looked a little irritated, but it didn't take much to irritate Loretta. In most situations she sort of came preirritated.

Jennifer squeezed Marvelli sideways. "I'm so happy to see you. I really miss you, Frankie."

Marvelli smiled nervously. No one called him Frankie outside of his family, and he was supposedly here on business.

"Frankie's the big brother I never had," Jennifer said to Loretta. "I mean, how could you *not* love this guy?"

Loretta shrugged. "I don't know. How?" A tight smile was plastered to her face.

Jennifer pulled him down by the neck and gave him a big smooch on the cheek. "You're the only thing about Jersey I miss, Frankie. You and Nina."

"Nina says hi, by the way," Marvelli said.

"Nina's his daughter," Jennifer explained to Loretta.

"I know. We've met," she said.

Jennifer beamed. "Isn't she a doll?"

Loretta nodded. "She certainly is."

"Nina's lucky she's got you for a father, Frankie."

"Enough, Jennifer. You're gonna give me a big head."

"No, it's true," she said to Loretta. "This man is a prize. You know, when I first found out he was going to marry my sister, I was really jealous. I mean, I was just a kid at the time—about twelve or thirteen, Nina's age—but I had such a crush on him you wouldn't believe."

"Looks like you're crushing him now," Loretta said. Her smile got tighter.

"No, seriously." Jennifer's eyes widened. "I really wanted to marry him. I was so upset I crashed their honeymoon."

Loretta looked at Marvelli. "Really?"

"Yeah, she did," he admitted. "Hitchhiked all the way up to Cape Cod. We'd rented this cottage on the bay. God, you should've heard Rene when she answered the door and there was her little sister standing there." He shook his head and looked at Jennifer. "I thought you two were gonna duke it out right then and there."

Jennifer shrugged it off. "What can I say? I was just a kid. Anyway, it's your fault for being so cute, Frankie." She pinched his cheek. He didn't like her doing that, but he didn't say anything.

Memories of that cottage on Cape Cod suddenly cluttered his thoughts. He remembered how the light slanted across the white-painted wood floors, how at midday you almost had to wear sunglasses inside. He also remembered Jennifer sleeping in the breezeway on a white wicker couch, pouting the whole time because he and Rene were in the bedroom, doing what people do on their honeymoons. They weren't terribly sensitive to Jennifer's feelings, as he recalled. They were pissed that she'd come, and they weren't going to change their plans on account of her.

But Marvelli's memories were getting confused. Jennifer now was about the same age that Rene was then, and holding Jennifer reminded him of holding his wife on their honeymoon.

He didn't like what he was feeling because he didn't understand it, and it scared him. He moved away from Jennifer to give himself some space, but she hung on to his hand. He nodded toward the counter. "So how do we get some of this famous Seattle coffee I've been hearing about?"

"Hey, whatever you want," Jennifer said. "You name it."

"How about an espresso?" he said. "Make it a double."

"You want anything to eat with that? As if I have to ask."

"Sure, anything," he said, but in truth he wasn't hungry at all. He was too confused to be hungry.

Jennifer turned to Loretta. "How about you? What can I get you? Don't worry, it's on me."

"Do you have any herb tea?"

"Twenty-three different kinds. But I do make a mean mochaccino. Can I tempt you?"

"No," Loretta said flatly. "Just tea. Mint if you have it."

"Sure." As Jennifer turned to go back behind the counter, she gave Marvelli a look as if to say, What's with her?

Actually Marvelli was a little baffled himself. Loretta was definitely putting out some pretty hostile vibes, but he couldn't imagine why.

As Jennifer got busy behind the counter, Loretta sidled up to him. "In case you forgot, we're here to find Sammy Teitelbaum."

"I know," he said. "Is there a problem?"

"No. Why do you think there's a problem?"

"I don't know. You seem ticked off about something."

"I don't have a problem."

"Oh . . . I thought something might be bothering you."

"Nothing's bothering me."

"Okay. No problem." Something was definitely bothering her. He could tell.

"You want me to ask her about Sammy?" Loretta said.

"No, I'll do it."

"Okay. Fine."

But Loretta just stared at him as if she expected him to do it immediately. He would have preferred to have his espresso and visit a little longer before he got down to business.

"You want me to ask her?" Loretta repeated.

"I said I'll do it." She was getting on his nerves now.

He walked over to the counter where Jennifer was working the espresso machine. "Say, Jen, did you know that Sammy got out of prison?"

"Yeah," she said, squinting against the steam rising from the machine. "As a matter of fact he came by to see me the other day. Right out of the blue."

Marvelli caught Loretta's eye. "Oh, yeah? He was out here in Seattle?"

"You know Sammy. He's like a bad penny. He's liable to show up anywhere."

"As long as you're there." Marvelli grinned at her.

She looked a little embarrassed. "It's not what you think. I'm through with him. Really. We're not getting back together. I told him I want to go through with the divorce."

Marvelli nodded, sympathetic but noncommittal. "Sammy's a difficult guy."

"That's one way to put it." She shut off the espresso machine and slid a brimming cup across the glass counter toward Marvelli. "Now, how about a piece of German chocolate cake? I know that's one of your favorites."

"Sure. Fine," he said. He wanted to know where Sammy was, but he didn't want her to know that he and Loretta were here to arrest the little schmuck. In the past Jennifer had always forgiven Sammy, no matter what he'd done. They'd broken up a hundred times, and each time she'd taken him back. He didn't want her tipping Sammy off.

Jennifer was pouring hot water into a clear glass teapot. Loretta was looming over his shoulder, waiting for him to get on with it.

"So what's Sammy doing out here in Seattle?" Marvelli asked.

Jennifer set the teapot and a blue mug down on the counter. "I don't know. He probably just came to annoy me." She pulled out a brown plastic tray and started moving everything onto it. "He mentioned something about having a little job to do out here, but you know Sammy. You can't believe anything he says."

Marvelli exchanged glances with Loretta. Her face was stone. "Sammy didn't happen to mention what this little job was, did he, Jen?"

Loretta threw her garment bag down on the bed. "I think your sister-in-law is lying," she said. "I think she *does* know where Sammy is."

Marvelli dropped his gym bag and went directly to the little refrigerator in the corner of the hotel room. He turned the key to open it and scanned the shelves—beer, wine, premade daiquiris, margaritas, and Bloody Marys, Coke, Sprite, ginger ale, Dr. Pepper, fizzy water, pretzels, nuts, candy, Slim Jims, Twinkies. "I hope I have one of these in my room," he said.

"Will you get serious?" Loretta snapped as she emptied her pockets onto the dresser. "We have to find this guy."

Marvelli slammed the refrigerator shut and glared at her. "Look, don't tell me what I already know. Just because you don't like my sister-in-law, don't bite *my* head off."

Loretta just stared at him, her face growing hotter. How did he know she didn't particularly care for Jennifer? She hadn't said anything. And why was Marvelli getting so angry? He never got angry. Was this because of Jennifer? Did he feel he had to protect her?

"Look, I'm sorry I yelled at you," Marvelli said. "I'm just tired from the flight."

"Yeah. Me, too," she said, but she knew that wasn't the reason.

Marvelli picked up his gym bag. "I'm gonna go find my room and call the local Marshals Office. Maybe these guys will be more cooperative than the ones in Jersey." He reached for the doorknob.

"You want to have dinner?" she asked quickly.

He looked over his shoulder and laughed. "I always want to have dinner."

"With me, I mean."

"Well, who else? I just assumed . . ."

"I thought you might be doing something with Jennifer tonight."

He shook his head. "She's working till eleven."

"Oh." But did that mean he would have had dinner with her if she were free? Loretta wondered. Or had he planned on having dinner with his partner all along?

"I'll call you later. I'm gonna try to take a nap." He opened the door and let himself out.

She stared at the back of the door and let out a long, slow breath. "What the hell am I doing here?" she muttered. "What the hell am I doing here *with him*?"

She unzipped her garment bag and hung up her clothes in the closet, then put her socks and underwear in the top dresser drawer. All the while she mulled over her situation—not just with Marvelli, her whole life situation. She felt as if she were just barely treading water and that it wouldn't take much of a swell to put her under. Working on the Jump Squad was the end of the line for her. At one time she had been an assistant warden at a women's correctional facility, but that seemed like a hundred years ago. She was still in her twenties back then, and her star was rising. But then fate stepped in. The first riot ever to take place in a women's prison in the state of New Jersey happened under her watch, and instead of cracking down fast, she'd tried to negotiate with the rioters and ended up being taken hostage. That had been the beginning of her downslide. She lost that job, and from then on her career path just kept going down, down, down, like a Slinky going down a long flight of stairs.

Loretta unbuttoned her blouse and stepped out of her slacks. She felt gritty and annoyed; she needed a long, hot shower. She pulled off her socks, unhooked her bra, and pulled down her panties. As she turned toward the bathroom, she noticed herself in the mirror over the dresser, and she glared at what she saw. Thrusting out her arms to the side, she gave herself the full frontal nudity shot. She jiggled her boobs, pinched her love handles, and slapped her rump.

"Like it or lump it, Marvelli," she growled as she headed for the bathroom. "I am what I am."

As she turned on the shower, she felt like a fool for feeling the way she did. She was still pining away for Marvelli, and that wasn't good. Yeah, she was grouchy and a little woozy from caffeine depravation, but her big problem was really Marvelli. She'd thought that she'd gotten over him, but that was just denial. She'd been trying to convince herself that she really wasn't interested in him because she knew he wasn't interested in her. It was rejection protection.

She felt the water spraying from the shower head and adjusted the temperature, making it hotter. She had to get with it, she told herself. She had to stick to her original plan. The Jump Squad was just a stepping-stone. She was going to get into law school and take classes at night. The way she had it figured, it would take four, four and a half years to finish up. In the meantime she would try to get herself transferred out of the Jump Squad so she could be just a regular parole officer with a regular caseload, none of this chasing-down-jumpers crap. But even if she had to stay with the Jump Squad, she'd make do. Because in her mind the Jump Squad was only temporary. It was not going to be her life.

And neither was Marvelli.

She glanced into the mirror over the sink to see how convincing she looked, but the mirror was all steamed up. She wiped away a patch with her hand so she could see her face. *Men are not necessary,* she told herself. *Marvelli is not necessary. My heart will keep on beating; the blood will keep on pumping. A man is not necessary to sustain the life of a woman.*

She stared at herself for a moment, then drew an *X* across her face. "Yeah, right."

She parted the shower curtain and stepped into the pulsating stream. The water was just a little too hot, but she endured it until it was tolerable. She let the spray douse her hair and drip down her breasts, then turned around so that it pounded into her shoulders and melted the tension. She wanted to melt herself down to a puddle of goo and remold herself, come out of the shower a new person. Not someone else, she thought, just an improved version of herself.

But as the hot water drilled into her shoulder blades and flushed the skin on her back, the pinprick sting triggered a sudden memory. The heat, the bumps, and the burns she'd endured. The spinning, the nausea. When the rioting prisoners had taken over the Pinebrook Women's Correctional Facility, Loretta had tried to negotiate with one of the leaders of the riot, a lifer named Brenda Hemingway. Brenda was a gorilla of a woman who had a lot of anger pent up inside of her and nothing to lose. Brenda also had four inches and sixty pounds on Loretta. She had roughed Loretta up and humiliated her, stripped her, tied her up with electrical cord, and tried on her clothes. But that wasn't the worst of it.

Brenda Hemingway had forced Loretta into an oversized industrial clothes drier in the prison laundry and turned it on, then laughed like a jackal, peering through the small round window as Loretta spun round and round, the perforated metal heating up and scorching her bare skin, the metal fins banging into her elbows, knees, and head. Loretta remembered being terrified that she'd throw up and make the ordeal even worse. She felt sick to her stomach just thinking about it.

She clenched her jaw and swallowed to keep from upchucking, gritting her teeth as those old feelings of anger and humiliation reemerged, like a sickening odor that just wouldn't go away.

She squeezed her eyes shut, wishing there were some kind of operation that could suck Brenda out of her head. A Brenda-ectomy or Brenda-suction. Brenda's boulder head, her fat pink tongue, and her rows of yellow teeth spun through Loretta's memories, boring into her and coring out her insides. Her eyes snapped open. This had to stop, she thought. She was not weak, she was not afraid, and she refused to let her life be ruined by something that had happened a long time ago. She was better than that.

She picked up a small plastic bottle of hotel shampoo and poured some into her hand. *Gonna wash that woman right outta my head,* she thought. *Let her go down the drain.*

One of these days.

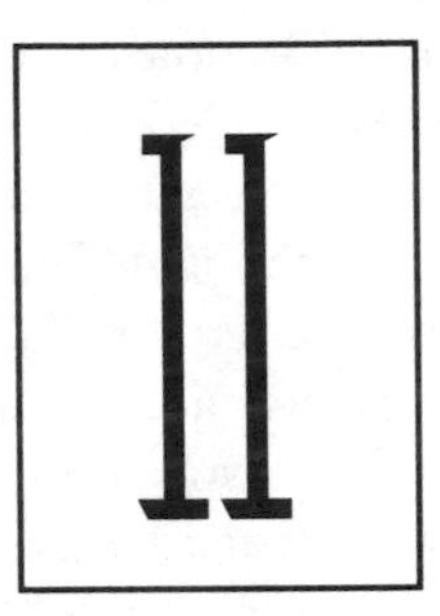

"This is a wild-goose chase, Marvelli." Loretta was behind the wheel of a rented forest-green Ford Taurus, heading south on Route 5. She felt slightly woozy and a little disoriented, and she was on the verge of losing her patience with him. It was caffeine withdrawal, she told herself. At least most of it was. Marvelli was being a real pill.

"I don't think this is a wild-goose chase at all," Marvelli said. He had his nose in a crumpled map of Seattle spread out on his lap. "Take this exit right here."

Loretta flipped the directional stick, checked the rearview mirror, and pulled into the right lane. "We've been to five bookstores already. What do we do next? Hit the libraries? This is insane."

"No, it's not," Marvelli said. "Sammy called Jennifer this morning, and he told her that he was gonna check out the bookstores in town. Sammy loves bookstores. Remember, he's got a Ph.D. in English lit."

"I know. You told me," Loretta said, doing nothing to hide how annoyed she was. She steered the car down the exit ramp. "Now where do I go?"

"Hang on one second." Marvelli studied the map.

The ramp merged with a busy access road lined with old red-brick factory buildings, some with ornate turn-of-the-century carved stone facades. "Which way, Marvelli?" she said impatiently.

"Take it easy," he said, still studying the map. "If you can take a right at the next light, do it."

"And if I can't?"

"Then take the next right."

"We're gonna get lost," she muttered. "I know it."

Marvelli looked at her. "I tried calling Agent Springer again, but she hasn't returned any of my calls."

"Why do you bother with her? She obviously doesn't want to help us. She thinks we're dirt."

"I don't know about that," Marvelli said. "She may come around."

Loretta rolled her eyes. "Don't tell me you're sweet on her, too."

Marvelli frowned. "What do you mean, 'her, too'?"

Instantly Loretta's face flushed. "Nothing."

"No, say it. I can tell something's bothering you. Spill it."

Loretta gripped the wheel with both hands and kept her eyes on the road. She was tempted to tell him what was really on her mind.

"Come on, Loretta," Marvelli said. "Don't clam up on me. You're not shy."

She glanced at him sideways, wanting to say something but not wanting to get into it with him. "You really want to know what's bothering me?"

"Yeah, I do. Is it Springer?"

Loretta shook her head. "It's your sister-in-law. In case you haven't figured it out, she's after you."

Marvelli made a face. "What're you talking about?"

"Jennifer. She wants you."

"You're crazy."

"It's as plain as day."

"Get out."

"All right, don't believe me."

"You're dreaming."

"Fine."

Silence filled the inside of the car like fog as they cruised down the busy avenue, which quickly switched from industrial to commercial with fast-food restaurants and strip malls on either side.

"Well, why should you care?" Marvelli suddenly blurted out.

Loretta was suddenly embarrassed. She should have kept her mouth shut. "I *don't* care," she said, trying to cover her tracks. "It's just that I don't think it's right, that's all."

"What isn't right?"

"So soon after your wife's death. You're still in mourning, and Jennifer's putting the moves on you. She ought to have a little more respect for her own sister's memory."

"What the hell are you talking about?" Marvelli was getting mad. "Jennifer is not like that."

"Well, that's the way it looked to me," Loretta said, concentrating on the road so she wouldn't have to look at him. She wished she had never brought it up.

"Well, you're wrong." Marvelli was glaring at her. He'd never glared at her before. If fact, he very rarely got angry. Was he angry now because he did have some real feelings for Jennifer? Why else would he be defending her so hotly?

"There's the bookstore," Marvelli grumbled. "Up ahead on the left."

Loretta spotted a big blue-and-white sign perched on a pole at the side of the road—D&M Booksellers. She pulled the car into the left lane and turned into the parking lot. The store looked just like every other D&M bookstore she'd ever seen.

"Don't park by the front door and don't slow down," Marvelli ordered. "Take that space over there. That one." He pointed to a space in the far corner of the lot in front of the store. "And back in so we can see who goes in and out."

She didn't care for his brusque tone, but she did what he wanted. She turned off the engine, unbuckled her seat belt, and started to open the door. "I have to go pee."

"No. Wait," Marvelli said, grabbing her forearm.

She glared at him. Her skin tingled under his touch, but it wasn't a good tingle. It was a resentful tingle.

"See that guy walking toward the front door? He just threw away his cigarette."

"The skinny guy with the buzz cut and the horn-rimmed glasses?"

Marvelli nodded. "That's Sammy."

Loretta stared at him. Sammy wasn't at all what she had expected. He was wearing a brown jean jacket, baggy khakis, and black Chuck Taylors. He looked like a slacker, a dweeb, a perpetual grad student, a loser. What he definitely didn't look like was a hit man for the mob. Of course, the good ones never did.

"Let's grab him," Loretta said, opening her door.

Marvelli grabbed her arm again. "Hang on. He knows me, so you're going to have be the one to approach him."

"No problem," she said. Her purse was in her lap. Her .38 was in the inside pocket. The cuffs were somewhere on the bottom.

"Crap," Marvelli muttered. Sammy was going into the bookstore. "I was afraid of this."

"Don't worry. I'll get him," Loretta said, swinging her door open. "What section do you think he'll go to?"

"The weird section."

"No, seriously."

"Lit crit, philosophy, fiction, maybe true crime for a little professional reading."

"Okay, give me ten minutes. If I don't find him, I'll come out and get you." She started to close the door, then stopped herself. "By the way, do you think he'll put up a fight?"

Marvelli shrugged. "My guess is he'll run first. I don't think he'd hurt a woman."

"What makes you say that?"

"I dunno. Just a guess."

She frowned. "That's very reassuring, Marvelli. Are you telling me he's a sexist killer?"

"Look, just don't make a scene in the store. If he runs, let him run. I'll catch him coming out the door."

"What if he goes out the back way?"

"He must've come in a car, right? I can see every space in the parking lot from here. When he goes to his car, I'll get him."

"Okay." Loretta shut the door and walked across the parking lot to the bookstore. She pushed through the front doors, then through a second set of doors in the vestibule. But as soon as she stepped inside, she wrinkled her nose, assaulted by a smell.

It was coffee. The aroma was strong, pungent, and enticing. She glanced around the store and immediately spotted the café. It was on a raised platform right in the middle of the floor. She resisted the temptation to have a cup and marched directly to the store directory. The literary criticism section was on the second floor. She decided to start there.

She got on the escalator, holding her breath as she glided up over the café. When she got off on the second floor, she scanned the signs on the outside walls, looking for the Lit Crit section. Line drawings of supposedly great contemporary authors decorated the walls above the high bookshelves. Some were pleasant faces, some were very intense, but Loretta was totally unimpressed. She'd tried reading most of this bunch, and they had all bored her to tears.

The Literary Criticism section was toward the back, just beyond the Travel section. She slipped into an aisle, pretending to be browsing, and wove her way through the shelves of books, passing through the Pet Care section, Movies and Television, and Antiques and Collecting. The shelves were tall, so it was hard for her to see over the tops. It was sort of like walking through a maze.

She unzipped her purse and felt around for her gun, making sure it was there. The cuffs were down at the bottom under her wallet and all the crumpled Kleenex that always seemed to accumulate in there. She slowed down as she came up to the Travel section, cutting into that aisle. She didn't want to approach Sammy from the main aisle, hoping she could take him by surprise.

She strolled down the aisle, pretending to be looking for something, scanning the shelves of travel books that were arranged alphabetically by country—Argentina, Belize . . . Germany, Kenya . . . Paraguay, Puerto Rico . . . Switzerland, Thailand . . . Uruguay,

Venezuala . . . Zanzibar. When she got to the end of the aisle, she paused and put her hand inside her purse, gripping the butt of her gun. She turned the corner slowly, hoping she wouldn't have to use her weapon. But when she rounded the corner, there was no one there. She wandered farther into Lit Crit, but the whole section was empty.

She let go of her gun and adjusted the purse strap on her shoulder. She started to walk back toward the main aisle when suddenly she felt a tug on the strap as if she'd snagged it on something. But when she glanced over her shoulder to see what she was caught on, her heart nearly stopped.

For a moment she wasn't sure it was them. But who else could it be? she thought. The grinning identical faces stared at her like some kind of goofy two-headed beast. One of them had his fat paw wrapped around the strap, the purse practically in his grip.

"Hi there," one of them said. " 'Member us?"

"From Uncle Tino's garage," the one holding her purse said. "We got your car out of the mud. Remember?"

"And you didn't even thank us."

Loretta was speechless. It was the dum-dum twins, Larry and Jerry.

Back in the car Marvelli checked his watch again. Loretta had been in there exactly twelve minutes, and there had been no sign of either her or Sammy. Marvelli was beginning to worry. Sammy was a nut to begin with, and he may have picked up some new nasty habits in prison. Maybe like most cons, he didn't give a damn about anything anymore. Maybe Loretta had confronted him, and he'd decided to take her on. And, unfortunately, Loretta could be pretty pigheaded sometimes. She wouldn't back down. It could get ugly. Marvelli got out of the car. He couldn't just sit there.

He walked briskly to the front of the bookstore, forcing himself not to run. He didn't want to look conspicuous, but also didn't want Loretta to get hurt.

Inside the bookstore it was deceptively tranquil. A string quartet was playing softly over the sound system. In the café, four middle-aged women were gabbing away, sipping cappuccinos and nibbling on biscotti. Two old guys and three teenage boys were standing in front of the magazine rack, scanning the titles and slowly gravitating toward the high shelf where the current issues of *Playboy* and *Penthouse* were kept. A studious-looking girl with long red hair and wire-rim glasses was sitting at a table, gazing intently into a book. Marvelli guessed that she was about eleven or twelve. She reminded him of his daughter Nina.

He walked down the main aisle, heading toward the music department in the back, looking for signs of Loretta. He passed the New Fiction and Nonfiction sections, the Current Affairs section, Biography, History, Politics, Economics, Finance, Sociology, Myth and Religion, Health and Fitness, Beauty and Diet, Mystery, Science Fiction, Romance, Westerns, and General Fiction, peering down each aisle and disturbing some of the browsers. But there was no sign of Loretta.

Where the hell are you? he thought, getting more and more anxious. Loretta hadn't been a PO that long. She didn't know how to handle nut jobs like Sammy.

Marvelli picked up his pace, heading toward the Children's section. If Sammy did anything to her, he swore to God he'd strangle the little creep.

The Children's section was in a boxed-off corner of the store, all by itself. Marvelli stood in the Cookbook section just outside the entrance and peered in, doubting that either Sammy or Loretta would have gone in there.

Then suddenly someone cleared his throat over Marvelli's shoulder. Marvelli turned around, startled, and saw a tall, good-looking man in his early fifties, wearing tinted aviator glasses and a gray checked jacket over a black knit shirt. He was flipping through a glossy picture book called *Cakes and Pastries for All Occasions*.

Marvelli paid no attention to him. He had to find Loretta. But as he started to walk away, the man stopped him.

"Mr. Marvelli," the man said. He smiled cordially, showing two rows of perfect dental work. His voice was like velvet.

Marvelli furrowed his brows at him. *Who the hell is this guy?* he thought. *And how does he know me?*

But when the man took off his glasses and showed his light gray eyes, Marvelli nearly lost it. He knew that undeservedly handsome face all too well. The guy looked like Paul Newman with a Greco-Roman perm and a Continental makeover, haute greaseball. It was Taffy friggin' Demaggio.

Marvelli stepped forward and closed the distance between them. He wanted to rip this guy's spine out and beat him to death with it.

"Something wrong, Mr. Marvelli? You look upset about something." Taffy kept flipping pages, glancing back and forth between the book and Marvelli.

"Yeah, there's something wrong," Marvelli said. "*You.* You're what's wrong."

"Me? What's wrong with me?" Taffy grinned as if he thought this were amusing.

"You're a mob scumbag who sells cheap-crap medical supplies to hospitals. You're killing people. You killed—" Marvelli abruptly stopped himself. He didn't want this bum to think that he'd harmed Rene. That was private.

"I don't know what you're talking about, my friend."

"I'm not your friend," Marvelli said.

Taffy shrugged. "Have it your way."

Taffy was staring down at a picture of a coconut layer cake, wondering if he should just have this friggin' pest whacked or what. Veronica Springer had told him that Marvelli and his partner—whoever that was—had come out here to find Sammy. That wasn't good. Sammy had a job to do. Taffy flipped the page and saw a picture of a banana cream pie. He tilted his head to the side and frowned a little. He didn't care that much for banana cream pie.

Marvelli inched closer to him. "So what're you saying here?

You didn't sell that cheap foreign-made crap to all those hospitals? Is that what you're saying?"

Taffy kept his eyes on the pie, but he could see Marvelli in his peripheral vision. This guy better watch himself, Taffy thought. He was getting a little too testy.

"Come on, Taf. Tell me to my face. Tell me you had nothing to do with the leaky IV tubes and the hypodermic needles that broke in people's arms and the gauze bandages that weren't sterile. Come on. Tell me."

Hey, Taffy thought, *no ever died from a leaky IV tube, not that I know of.*

He casually flipped the page and found a slice of angel's food cake sitting in a puddle of raspberry sauce. *Besides,* he thought, holding back a grin, *you don't know the half of it, my friend. I'm selling to HMOs now. My stuff is showing up in something like three hundred hospitals across the country. And I'm gonna be doing more business with these HMOs once I go over to the other side and rat out my competition. I've got it all set up. I'll run it from Witness Protection with Tino as my front man.* Taffy turned the page and saw a big plate of artfully arranged butter cookies next to a cold pitcher of lemonade. *It'll be beautiful,* he thought.

"So where's Sammy Teitelbaum?" Marvelli barked.

Taffy slowly rolled his eyes toward him. He was getting annoying, this guy.

"I said, where's Sammy?" Marvelli repeated. "I just saw him come in here."

Taffy turned the page. Key lime pie. He liked key lime pie. "I don't know what you're talking about, my friend."

"Look at me when I talk to you," Marvelli said. "It's rude."

Taffy turned the page and kept his eyes on the book. Peach cobbler in a cut-glass dish. He wasn't going to bother talking to this guy. He wasn't worth the trouble.

"I said, look at me," Marvelli said.

Taffy turned another page. French apple pie with raisins in it.

"I'm asking you nice, Taf. Look at me."

Screw you, Taffy thought. He flipped the page. Little lemon tarts.

"I said, *look at me!*"

Where the hell does this guy get off talking to me this way? He keeps it up, I'll send Larry and Jerry over to work on his attitude.

"Taffy! Look at me!"

Taffy frowned and glanced up from *Cakes and Pastries for All Occasions*. The next thing he saw was the spine of a thick hardcover crashing down onto his curly head like a tomahawk. Taffy dropped his book and clutched his head, worried about his hair weave first until he felt the aftershock of the blow. Julia Child's *The French Chef Cookbook* was in Marvelli's hand.

"You son of a bitch—" Taffy started, ready to grab Marvelli by the throat.

But the commotion had drawn a small crowd, including a few little kids from the Children's section.

"Are you all right, young man?" an old woman asked Taffy.

"Did you see what he did?" one of the teens who had been ogling the centerfolds in the Magazine section said. "Totally agressive."

"Must be a real meat eater," another teen said. "Cool."

"Sir!" A big gawky clerk in a plaid shirt and a maroon knit tie wove through the crowd. "Sir!" Taffy thought the kid was talking to him until he snatched the book out of Marvelli's hand. "Sir, I'm going to have to ask you to leave the store."

"But—" Marvelli started.

"I'm sorry. Either leave now or I'll have to call the police."

The old woman reached out to feel Taffy's forehead. "Are you all right?" she asked.

The overwhelming urge to break Marvelli's legs that Taffy had been feeling dissipated like a puff of steam. The crowd was on Taffy's side. Marvelli was the bad guy.

Well, that was a switch, Taffy thought. He figured he'd milk it for all it was worth.

He held on to the closest bookshelf. "I'm all right," he said weakly. "I'll be fine."

"Sir, I'm asking you nicely," the clerk said to Marvelli, getting in his face.

Marvelli was looking past him, glaring at Taffy, who was letting the old lady fuss over him.

"Sir!"

"I'm going, I'm going," Marvelli grumbled, and stomped off.

The clerk turned to Taffy. "Can I get you anything, sir? A wet towel?"

Taffy kept his hand on his head even though it didn't hurt much anymore. "I just want to sit down," he moaned.

"Come to the café," the clerk said, staying close in case Taffy keeled over. "Can I get you something? Some water?"

Taffy groaned a little. "How about a mochaccino?"

Loretta glanced out the picture window on the second floor. She could see Marvelli standing out in the parking lot with his hands in his pockets. She wondered what he was doing out there. He should be in here, helping her, dammit.

Tweedle-Dee and Tweedle-Dum-Dum were still harrassing her, and Jerry, the meaner of the two, wouldn't let go of her purse strap. They were both wearing baggy jeans and heavy black round-toed shoes. Larry was wearing an ugly paisley-print golf shirt; Jerry was wearing a white V-neck T-shirt under a khaki zip-up jacket. She'd noticed that the expressions on their faces seemed to fade in and out, menacing one minute, blank the next. Loretta wondered if this was a congential condition, or had their mother dropped them on their heads both at the same time?

Jerry pulled on the strap. "So whattaya doing out here, lady?"

"Yeah," Larry chimed in. "You following us or what?"

Loretta kept trying to back away from them, but they stayed right with her. At this rate she was going to have her back pressed up against the plate-glass window pretty soon, and she had a feeling these two idiots wouldn't have any qualms about molesting her in full view of the parking lot. She glanced down at Marvelli again, willing him to look up at her, but her mojo just wasn't working because he didn't notice her at all.

"Why ain'cha answering us?" Jerry said. "You think we got cooties or something?"

Larry just laughed, scrinching up his eyes and showing too much tongue.

Loretta gripped her purse. If she thought she could get to her gun fast enough, she'd blow these two maggots all the way back to Self-improvement. But she had to negotiate a zipper and do a bit of rummaging before she could get to her weapon. She cursed herself for keeping all those half-used tissues in there.

"I know what you're thinking, lady." Jerry opened the flap of his jacket and showed the butt of a blue-steel automatic sticking out of his waistband. Larry lifted his shirt and showed an identical gun pressed against his hairy jelly-belly.

"You see that guy down there?" Loretta nodded down at Marvelli. "He used to be a sharpshooter in the army. He's carrying a gun, and if he sees you touch me . . . forget about it."

Loretta swallowed on a dry throat and watched their faces to see if they were buying it. The truth was, Marvelli couldn't shoot for beans and he was always forgetting to carry his weapon.

The twins craned their stubby necks and stared down suspiciously at Marvelli. It was hard to tell what they were thinking . . . or if they were thinking at all.

But they were distracted, and Loretta decided not to wait. She yanked her purse and pulled the strap out of Jerry's hand, then pulled the zipper and reached in for her gun. "Okay," she started just as she was about to whip it out. But when she looked up, there were two blue steel nine-millimeters staring back at her like vipers. She glanced sideways out the window. Marvelli was still standing there, doing nothing.

Thanks a lot, she thought. And why the hell weren't there any customers up here?

Then she remembered that she was in the Lit Crit section. No wonder no one was around.

The two doughy potato faces were focused now, and they weren't happy with her. Loretta could feel the sweat forming on her upper lip. She was at a crossroads, and she had to make a decision. Should she play their bluff and dare them to shoot her in public? Or should she play the helpless female and start crying? That went against her nature, but she had a bad feeling these two nitwits could care less if half of Seattle saw them commit a murder.

"Listen," she said, figuring she had at least three times their combined IQs, which meant she might be able to talk her way out of this. "Put the guns away. Let's talk."

Neither of them budged. It was as if they were deaf.

"Come on, guys. Don't be this way."

Suddenly Jerry jabbed his gun in her forehead as Larry simultaneously stuck his in her gut. A quick leg sweep from Larry sent her sprawling on the carpet. Together they grabbed her ankles and dragged her back into the seclusion of the Travel section. They were astonishingly fast and efficient. If Loretta hadn't been so busy being scared, she would've been impressed.

The twins dropped to their knees, one on either side of her. Jerry's gun was pressed against the side of her neck; Larry's was in her armpit.

Larry's face was grim. "You think we're stupid, don't you?" he growled.

Jerry dug the muzzle of his gun into the hinge of Loretta's jaw. His teeth were clenched. "I hate people who judge us like that."

Loretta suddenly had to pee very badly. "Easy, guys," she said, trying not to sound scared. "I never said you were stupid."

"You don't have to," Larry said. "We know."

"Yeah," Jerry snapped. "It's obvious to us." His eyes started blinking out of control, and Loretta's eyes blinked back as if his blinks were gunshots.

"You think you're better'n us," Jerry snarled. "Admit it. You do."

"No. I never said that. I never *thought* it."

"Admit it," Jerry insisted, digging the gun into her neck.

"Yeah, say it," Larry said. "Say it!"

Loretta winced. "I—"

"Hey!" Another man's voice sailed over the bookcases. "Where are you two? We're leaving."

Larry looked at Jerry, and all of a sudden their anger was gone.

"Gotta go," Larry whispered to his brother.

"Yeah." Jerry nodded.

They put their guns away, stood up, and walked off as if Loretta weren't even there. They acted as if nothing had happened.

"We're coming, Taf," Larry called out over the bookshelves.

"We're coming," Jerry echoed as they rushed out of the Travel section.

Loretta sat up, her heart still beating wildly. She was dumbfounded, but she was furious, too. She'd sworn that she'd never let anything like that ever happen to her again. She never ever wanted to be at anyone else's mercy. She squeezed her eyes shut and took deep, measured breaths. All of a sudden she felt nauseous, as if she were spinning around in that clothes drier again.

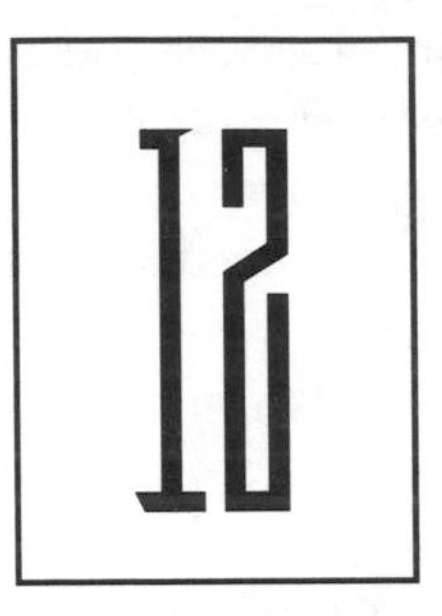

Loretta and Marvelli were back at the Grind, sitting at the var-nished maple counter that ran along one of the brick walls, rehashing their blunder at the bookstore, trying to come up with a new plan to catch Sammy. They were the only customers in the place except for a big gawky-looking guy who was hunched over one of the computers, mainlining iced caffè lattes. They stopped talking about Sammy as soon as Jennifer came over with their order.

"Here you go, Frankie," Jennifer said as she put a jumbo cappuccino and a plate of hazelnut biscotti in front of her brother-in-law.

The cup was as big as a soup bowl. Loretta looked at it with a mixture of horror and envy. She felt incredibly awful—woozy, headachy, fatigued—and she couldn't stop thinking about Larry and Jerry and their guns. She'd let it happen again, she thought. Just like that time with Brenda Hemingway. She blamed herself for not taking control of the situation.

Jennifer set down a cup of green tea in front of Loretta. "You sure you don't want some honey for that?" Jennifer asked.

Loretta shook her head. She was only drinking it because her doctor had told her that green tea was a healthy substitute for coffee. She stared down into her cup, sniffed the steamy bitter brew, and made a face. What she really wanted was coffee.

"Why don't you order a decaf?" Marvelli suggested.

"What?"

"I can see you're miserable. You won't get the jolt, but at least it tastes like coffee."

"If I taste coffee, I'm gonna want coffee—real coffee—and in no time I'll be back to square one. I've come this far; I don't want to have to start all over again."

Jennifer was nodding, holding the brown plastic tray to her chest like a stack of schoolbooks. "She's right, Frankie. I've seen some of our regulars here try to quit. Decaf just prolongs the agony. It's cold turkey or nothing." She moved a strand of her long blond hair to the side of her eye so that it caressed her face along with the rest of her hair.

Everything Jennifer did was sexy, Loretta thought. She was sexy without even trying to be. Loretta watched Marvelli out of the side of her eye. She wanted to know if Marvelli thought she was sexy.

"Lemme know if you need anything," Jennifer said as she headed back behind the counter. She was wearing khaki shorts and yellow rubber clogs. Her calves alone constituted a felony.

"So what were we talking about?" Marvelli said after he took a sip of cappuccino. When he put the cup down, he had a steamed-milk mustache.

"Finding Sammy," she said.

"Oh, yeah." He took another sip. "So what was I saying?"

"That we're screwed. We're never gonna find this guy."

"Right, right. I'm sure he spotted me at that bookstore. How else would Taffy Demaggio know who I was? Sammy's gonna do a magic act and disappear now that he knows I'm looking for him."

"So what do we do? Go home?"

Actually that wasn't such a bad idea, she thought. At least it would get Marvelli away from Jennifer.

"I don't think we should give up," Marvelli said, taking another sip. He picked up one of his long biscotti, dunked it in the cappuccino, and bit off a piece. "I was thinking maybe we should approach this from the other end."

"What do you mean?"

"If we can't catch the killer," he said with his mouth full, "then we should protect the target."

"What're you saying? That we should find Rispoli and guard him?"

"Yeah, something like that." He crunched loudly into the undunked portion of his biscotti.

"And how are we supposed to do that? Break into My Blue Heaven?" Loretta would have laughed if she'd had the energy. She picked up her tea to take a sip, but the smell drove her off before she could get it to her lips.

"There has to be a way to find that place," Marvelli said. "It must be fairly big, so a lot of people must work there. They have to have support staff, people bringing in food and stuff. All we have to do is find some blabbermouth who's been there."

"The place is supposed to be airtight," Loretta said. "That's what your friend Tarantella said."

Marvelli gave her a skeptical look over the rim of his coffee cup. "It's run by the feds, Loretta. There's got to be something wrong with it."

"Forget about it," she said. "Even if we could find My Blue Heaven, what would we do when we got there? Ring the doorbell and ask if Rispoli can come out and play? Be real."

"Hey, *you* be real," Marvelli shot back, his expression suddenly serious. "Do you realize what it'll mean if Sammy gets to Rispoli? Take that dirtbag Taffy Demaggio and multiply him by about three dozen. That's how many mob creeps like him are gonna walk because Rispoli won't be around to testify against them. Demaggio by himself is endangering the lives of thousands of people with his crappy medical supplies. These other crumbbuns are into scams that are just as bad, so if each one of them is hurting that many people, just do the math."

"But we warned the feds. We told them about Sammy. We gave it our best shot."

Marvelli was shaking his head. "That's not good enough. We are the only ones taking Sammy seriously. That means we are the only ones who can prevent Sammy from killing Rispoli."

"Don't you think you're exaggerating this just a bit? I mean, Rispoli *is* under Witness Protection."

"I keep telling you—you don't know Sammy. Rispoli should be under Sammy Protection."

Loretta shrugged and finally took a sip of her tea. It tasted as bad as it smelled. It did need honey. She picked up her cup and went over to the counter where Jennifer was stacking clean coffee mugs. "I think I'll take that honey after all," Loretta said.

"Great. What kind?"

Loretta shrugged. "I dunno. What do you have?"

"We have orange blossom, buckwheat, wildflower, clover, Tupelo—"

"Wildflower," Loretta said to keep her from going on. Honey was getting like coffee and tea—too many choices.

Jennifer slid a little brown pot with a wooden dipper toward Loretta.

Everything's so natural out here, Loretta thought as she drizzled some honey into her tea. She wondered if that included Jennifer's perfectly perky breasts.

As Loretta stirred her tea, she noticed that Marvelli had taken his cappuccino over to the gawky nerd working the computer. The guy seemed like the shy, introverted type, but Marvelli was getting him to talk. Marvelli, of course, could make conversation with a clam.

"Loretta," Marvelli called to her, "Come 'ere. I want you to meet someone."

Loretta picked up her cup and went over to them.

"This is Alan Winslow," Marvelli said. "He says he can help us out."

Alan stood up and bashfully offered his hand to Loretta. She shook it, marveling at his incredible height. He was tall enough to play pro basketball. Unfortunately there was nothing remotely athletic about him. He had pathetic puppy-dog eyes, but he was having a hard time maintaining eye contact with her. She imagined him as the biggest kid in his class, the one who grew up too fast and all the other kids picked on. She could picture him in gym class, forced to play center on a basketball team with all the jock kids dribbling around him like hornets, taunting him for not playing up to his size. Loretta knew how cruel kids could be. She'd always been the "fat girl" in school.

"Nice to meet you, Alan," Loretta said, trying to be friendly.

Marvelli hoisted his humongous cup. "Alan says he can find My Blue Heaven."

Loretta's eyes shot open as she glanced around the room to see if anyone else had come in. "Why don't you get a bullhorn, for God's sake?"

"Sorry." Marvelli lowered his voice. "Alan says he might be able to get us an address on-line. Pretty good, huh?"

"I used to work for Microsoft," Alan said to justify himself.

"I hear it's a good place to work," Loretta said. "Why don't you work there anymore?"

"I got fired."

Loretta gazed up at Alan, who obviously sensed her displeasure, then glared at Marvelli, who obviously didn't. "Excuse us for a minute, Alan," she said, taking Marvelli by the elbow and leading him away. "What the hell's wrong with you?" she hissed. "You're asking that man to do something illegal."

"Not specifically," Marvelli said.

"*Yes* specifically. You're asking him to hack his way into government files."

"We can't just sit on our hands with this, Loretta."

"We can't break the law either."

"We're not going to be using the information for illegal purposes."

"But what if Alan sells the information to someone else? Like Taffy Demaggio, for instance."

Marvelli turned around and grinned up at the tall hulking man. "Look at that face. Does he look like he'd do something like that?"

Loretta studied Alan's face. His puppy-dog eyes were melting all over her like chocolate kisses. *Oh, no,* she thought. Never pet a stray.

Marvelli whispered in her ear. "Look, we don't have many options here. Let's just let him see what he can do."

Loretta didn't like that gooey look on Alan's face, not when it was aimed at her. Unless, of course, it was somebody she wanted to get gooey over her. She glanced at Marvelli and quickly looked away.

"I don't know about this," she said, shaking her head. She noticed that Jennifer was looking at Marvelli, who was smiling reassuringly at Alan, who was staring at Loretta. *Oh, God,* she thought.

"Maybe I'll just get started," Alan said, starting to sit down. He stopped and stood up again. "Unless you don't want me to."

"No, no, no, get started," Marvelli said, holding the back of the chair for him.

"Marvelli!" Loretta warned.

"Frankie, you want a refill?" Jennifer called out from behind the counter.

"*Frank*!" This voice came from the front door, and it sounded like the screech of a mother pterodactyl. A stern-looking silver-haired woman in her late sixties/early seventies was standing on the threshold. She was holding a valise and a garment bag, and she was glaring at Marvelli.

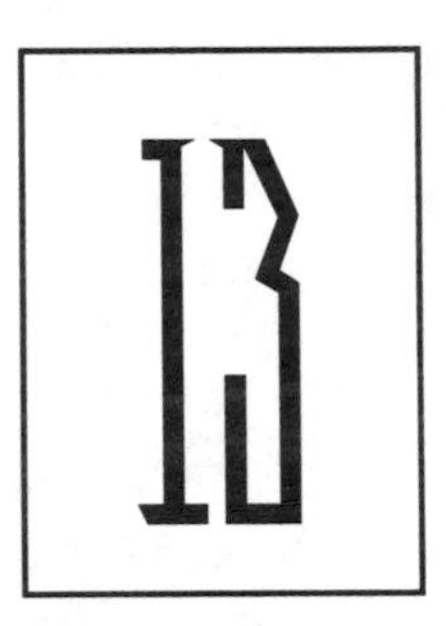

Marvelli just stared at the pterodactyl woman for a moment, waiting for his brain to process her unexpected arrival. *Annette?* he thought. Here in Seattle? It didn't make any sense. His mother-in-law was supposed to be back in Jersey, taking care of his daughter Nina.

Suddenly his gut bottomed out. Nina!

"Annette," he said, rushing up to her, "where's Nina? What's wrong?"

Annette pressed the heel of her hand against his forehead. "*Stunad'!*" she said. "Nina's fine. She's in New Hampshire at summer camp. Don't you remember anything?"

"Of course, I remember. So why are you here?"

The woman bunched her fingers and shook her hand at him. "Whattaya mean, why am I here? I'm here to visit my daughter. Is there something wrong with that?" She looked to Loretta for support. "Whatta *stunad'.*"

Loretta just smiled politely, and Marvelli wondered if she secretly agreed with Annette.

Annette closed one eye and pointed at Loretta. "Lorinda, right?"

"Loretta," she corrected.

"Close enough."

"Hi, Mom." Jennifer came over and took the valise out of her mother's hand, kissing her on both cheeks.

Annette then sandwiched Jennifer's face between her palms. "*Madonn'*, you're so skinny. Why don't you eat?"

Jennifer rolled her eyes. "I eat, Mom. I eat plenty."

"No, you don't. Look at yourself. I'm gonna cook for you. We'll freeze stuff so you can eat good till I come back the next time."

Marvelli could tell that Jennifer was biting her tongue. Everyone in the family knew that it was always best to just agree with Annette. He stood back and took in the two women, amazed that one had come out of the other. Jennifer was long and slender with delicate features. Annette was thick and squat with a broad nose and squinty eyes behind oversized bifocals. She always wore polyester stretch pants when she went out, housedresses at home—neither of which were very flattering. Her hair was the standard-issue gray lacquered-for-endurance battle-ax 'do. And despite her quick temper and whiplash tongue, Marvelli thought the world of her because she'd stuck by his wife all through her illness, moving in with them and taking care of both Rene and Nina while he was at work. In his book the woman was a saint. Bossy, but a saint.

Marvelli pictured his wife—before the cancer had struck—and he let out a silent, bittersweet sigh. Rene was nothing like her mother either. She was more like Jennifer but not exactly. She was . . . Rene.

"So are we gonna just stand here?" Annette blurted. "Jennifer, you're not gonna offer your own mother a cup of coffee?"

"Sure, Mom. What do you want? We have all kinds of coffee."

Annette threw her garment bag over a chair and took a seat. "I want an espresso with a little sambuca in it. Not too much."

"We don't have a liquor license, Mom."

"You mean, you don't keep a bottle under the counter for special customers? What's the matter with you? You have to have sambuca with espresso. Tell her, Frank."

"What?" Marvelli had been distracted, watching Alan Winslow at the computer. The guy was working away, typing and mousing like crazy. But was he finding out anything about My Blue Heaven? That's what Marvelli wanted to know.

"Frank!" Annette repeated. "Tell her, why don't you? Espresso without sambuca is like spaghetti without gravy. Am I right or what? Frank!"

"Annette, it's two o'clock in the afternoon. It's too early to be drinking."

"It's two o'clock for you," she shot back. "It's five o'clock my time. And believe me, I could use a shot of something after that flight. I thought I was gonna die."

"Why? What happened?" Loretta asked.

Annette's frown was so deep the tip of her nose almost touched her chin. "Don't ask. I don't even want to talk about it."

This was classic Annette, Marvelli thought. The world was created just to aggravate her because it consistently refused to operate the way she'd decided it should. The way she saw it, when God had created the universe, He should have consulted with her first.

"Mom, I'm gonna fix you something nice," Jennifer said as she backstepped toward the counter. "You'll like this."

"Don't bring me any cake or anything like that," she called after her daughter. "I'm on a diet."

Marvelli and Jennifer exchanged knowing glances. Annette had been on a diet for as long as they'd both known her and probably a lot longer than that. Her dieting was based on her own unique concepts of science and nutrition. Basically, if she cooked it, it wasn't fattening. If someone else cooked it, but it was Italian food, it was just a little fattening. If it wasn't Italian at all, then it was highly suspect and most likely toxic, cholesterol filled, and generally life threatening.

"Frank, whattaya standing there for? Sit down," Annette ordered. "You too, Lor . . ."

" 'retta," Loretta finished.

"I knew that," Annette said.

Loretta set her tea down on the table and took a seat, but Marvelli hesitated. He was dying to know what Alan was up to.

Marvelli raised one finger. "One second, Annette. I just gotta check on this one thing." He started walking toward Alan, and Loretta glowered at him. She didn't want to be left alone with his mother-in-law. He couldn't blame her.

As he turned away, he could hear Annette asking Loretta, "So how've you been? You married yet?"

Marvelli cringed. He didn't dare look back.

A smile was plastered across Loretta's face. She knew better than to say what she was thinking. "Nope," she said. "Not married yet."

"Don't worry, honey. You're gonna find the right guy. And pretty soon. You can trust me on that."

Loretta shot a quick glance at Marvelli, then looked away. *No,* she thought, *it'll never happen.*

Annette leaned in closer to Loretta. "You wanna know the truth?" she whispered. "I came out here for a reason. When my little girl called and told me that good-for-nothing bum Sammy Teitelbaum was bothering her again, I told myself I had to do something. I don't know what Jennifer sees in him, but it's like she's under hypnosis whenever she's around him. He always manages to win her back. But not this time, he won't. Not if I can help it."

"But how can you stop her?" Loretta said. "She's a grown woman. She'll do what she wants."

"Not if I can get her married. To someone else, I mean." Annette was nodding confidently.

"Do you have someone in mind?"

"Of course. And by the way this is the way it should be. Your parents are supposed to pick who you marry. This love stuff is way overrated. My father told me who I was going to marry, and that was that."

"You mean, you didn't love him?"

"That came later."

"But what if it didn't?"

Annette scrinched up her face and shook her head, annoyed

with the question. "That's what's wrong with you people today. You're always asking 'what if, what if?' Forget about 'what if.' Just have a little faith."

Loretta did not agree, but it wasn't worth starting an argument. "So who's the lucky guy?" she asked.

Annette looked both ways before she spoke. "Frank, of course."

"Marvelli!?" Loretta could feel the blood draining from her face.

"Sure, he's a pain sometimes, but he's the perfect husband for Jennifer. He's a good-looking son of a gun—don't you think? And he did everything for my Rene, everything. I don't know if you've noticed, but he's really lost without her. He needs someone, and so does Jennifer. They'll make each other happy. Besides, my granddaughter needs a mother, and I don't want him marrying some stranger. Nina doesn't need a stranger; she needs family."

Loretta was feeling a little light-headed. This woman was serious. She had this all planned out.

"I also want more grandchildren," Annette said. "And I don't want Sammy the schmo's little rug rats running around my house." Annette clenched her fists and shuddered. "The thought of him with my Jennifer makes my skin crawl."

Loretta stared at Jennifer making espresso behind the counter. She was gorgeous, she was young, she had a great bod, she wasn't stupid, and she looked like Marvelli's beloved Rene. Why wouldn't he want her?

Annette whispered in Loretta's ear. "They already like each other. They'd never admit it, of course, but you can tell by just watching them together. They just need a little nudge. It won't be hard to make a *mushad'.*"

"What's that?"

"A match. That's what we call it in Italian slang."

"Sounds great."

Annette squinted at her. "You don't sound like you think this is a good idea. What's the matter?"

"Nothing," she said.

Wrong, she thought. *Everything is the matter.*

"You watch," Annette said. "All I need is a week, and I'll have them together. You wanna bet?"

"That's okay." Loretta didn't want to lose twice.

"Here you go, Mom," Jennifer said, coming back to the table. She set down a small cup of espresso and a dessert plate with a cannoli on it. Loretta gazed down at the cup and the plate. The espresso smelled wonderful, and that cannoli didn't look bad either.

"What's that supposed to be?" Annette poked her finger at the pastry.

Jennifer laughed. "It's a cannoli, Mom. What do you think it is?"

"It's a Seattle cannoli. I don't want it."

"A cannoli is a cannoli, Mom. Eat it."

"No, thank you." Annette pushed the plate away and sniffed the espresso suspiciously. "You sure you don't have any sambuca?" she asked her daughter again.

Jennifer was definitely a dish, but Loretta wondered why Marvelli would ever want to have this mother-in-law twice. Of course, he already had her, so it didn't make much difference, did it?

"You want this, Loretta?" Annette asked, nudging the cannoli plate toward her.

She looked at Jennifer's figure. "No thanks," she moaned. "I'm not skinny."

"What?"

"I mean hungry."

"Oh. You sure?"

"Loretta!" Marvelli shouted from across the room. He was standing behind Alan, pointing at the computer screen. "I think we got it. I think we're in business here."

Alan gave her the puppy-dog eyes from across the room, attempting a timid smile.

Oh, great, she thought with a sigh. *My Mr. Right.*

The choppy water of Puget Sound was the color of a well-used blue-steel 9-mm automatic, which was what Loretta figured the feds would use on her and Marvelli when they figured out what they were up to, which probably wouldn't take too long.

"This is nuts, Marvelli," she said, holding on to the rail of the twenty-foot powerboat as Marvelli roared over the whitecaps, making the hull slap the surface.

"I thought you knew how to drive this thing."

"I do," Marvelli said. "I have a boat a little bigger than this back home." He was grinning into the spray, his eyes covered by wraparound sunglasses. He looked almost dashing. Loretta wanted to kick him for looking so good. He and Jennifer would make a lovely couple, she thought. Once Marvelli got out of prison.

"I'm telling you, Marvelli. This is nuts. No way in hell this will work."

"Calm down and start thinking like a feebie."

"What a frightening thought," she muttered.

She felt the leather ID wallet in her pocket, making sure it was still there. It was a genuine FBI ID issued to Special Agent

C. Gibson. Marvelli had a similar one in his pocket that identified him as Special Agent Michael Tarantella. The IDs had arrived at their hotel this morning via overnight express from Agent Tarantella. Marvelli had said that Tarantella owed him big-time for a multitude of past favors, and this only partly repaid the debt.

She rearranged her blowing hair and yelled over the rumble of the engine. "You sure these things are for real?"

Marvelli nodded and yelled back. "Tarantella said not to worry. These are real IDs. He also prepped me over the phone on what to expect when we got there."

"But he's never been there himself."

"Right. But that's good. If we seem a little awkward, that's why."

"But he told us himself that you have to be escorted to get into My Blue Heaven. Remember?"

"Not necessarily. He told me that veteran agents who have business there and who've been cleared can get there on their own. Tarantella fixed it so that we can get in. See, I knew he was holding out on us when we met him in the parking garage. He just didn't want to stick his neck out."

"I don't understand. How did he fix it?"

"He and his partner Gibson are currently working undercover in two different mob families. They need to check out some information that they've received to see if Rispoli can corroborate it. We're cleared to talk to him for as long as we need to."

"But how do we get him out?"

"We'll figure that out when we get there."

"Great plan," she grumbled.

"Positive mind, Loretta. Always gotta have a positive mind."

"Gotta have a better plan," she countered. "This is too complicated, too many variables, too many ways for things to go wrong."

"Don't make it complicated until it gets complicated. Don't anticipate."

"What're you?" she muttered. "Norman Vincent Peale?"

"What?" he yelled over the engine. "I didn't hear you."

"Never mind," she yelled back.

She looked out across the waters to the islands in the distance. Each one had thick stands of tall evergreens that grew right up to the shoreline. These islands were mostly small, and it felt as if she and Marvelli had passed more than a hundred of them since they'd left the rental dock back in Seattle almost three hours ago. She gazed up at the towering white clouds that kept crossing the sun. It was beautiful out here, she thought. They could run away and never come back, go native and live together on one of these little islands. No one would ever miss them.

Except for Annette. And Jennifer. And Marvelli's daughter. And Julius Monroe back at the office. And her family.

Loretta stared at Marvelli's profile as he stood at the helm, the wind blowing through his hair, and she sighed. *Forget it,* she thought.

She could see from the determined set of his jaw that she was wasting her time thinking about the two of them ever getting together. He only had one thing on his mind: saving Rispoli from Sammy so that Rispoli could testify against Taffy Demaggio. Marvelli was obsessed with Taffy because in his mind Taffy was responsible for his wife's death. Logically, Marvelli knew this wasn't true, but Marvelli's life had never been ruled by logic. Taffy was the evil embodiment of all the doctors and nurses and hospitals that had failed to save Rene.

Marvelli would never get over his wife, Loretta feared, and she also feared that he would eventually get together with his sister-in-law simply because she resembled Rene. It almost made Loretta feel sorry for Jennifer.

"There it is," Marvelli called out. "Up on that hill."

As they rounded a cluster of tiny islands, a bigger one came into view. It took Loretta a moment to locate the building on the landscape, it blended in so well. A long, low, sand-colored structure was built into a hill overlooking the sound. It looked more like a factory than a prison, and if Marvelli hadn't pointed it out, she would have just assumed it was a lumber or paper mill. Tall pine trees obscured most of the building, and unless you were approaching from this angle, boaters probably wouldn't even notice it at all. As Marvelli veered the boat toward the dock on the island, My Blue Heaven disappeared from view completely.

"Unbelievable," Marvelli said. "These people on the Internet are amazing. Alan Winslow E-mailed some disgruntled guy he found on a victim's rights web site, and the guy knew exactly where this place was. He even downloaded a map." Marvelli pointed to a piece of printer paper on a clipboard hanging from the dashboard. "These directions are better than the ones Tarantella gave me."

"But why would this guy on the Internet just give away such valuable information?"

"My guess is he's related to someone who was hurt—maybe even killed—by one of these finks in Witness Protection. They do tend to get away with their crimes when they agree to flip."

Loretta studied Marvelli's expression. On some level he probably agreed with the vigilante mentality. She had a feeling he wouldn't hesitate to beat the crap out of Taffy Demaggio if they met up again.

Marvelli cut back on the engine and guided the boat toward the dock. Two long piers jutted out into the water. A weathered cedar shack sat on the shore between them. Loretta was surprised at the apparent lack of security. She'd expected to find armed guards with vicious dogs, high fences topped with coils of razor wire, and James Bond speed boats mounted with machine guns. But there was none of that. Just an empty dock and a dirt path that led up the hill.

As Marvelli turned off the engine and let the boat glide up to the dock, a redheaded man with a gray mustache came out of the shack. He was somewhere in his forties, wearing jeans and a flannel black-and-red buffalo-plaid shirt over a gray T-shirt. "Howdy," he said, crinkling his eyes with a smile. He took off his Seattle Mariners baseball cap, smoothed his hair, and put it back on. "Nice day."

"Yeah," Marvelli said. "Too bad the Mariners lost yesterday. Four–zip."

Loretta had read in the paper that morning that the Mariners had beaten the Orioles 9–8, but she kept her mouth shut.

"They play the Yankees tomorrow," the man said.

"The day after that, too," Marvelli said.

The man's friendly face suddenly turned serious. He turned his cap around backward, and Loretta suddenly heard rustling in the branches on both sides of the dock. She did a double take when she thought she saw a rifle barrel receding into the foliage behind the shack.

The redheaded man opened his flannel shirt to show a badge pinned to his T-shirt. "Deputy Armistead, United States Marshals Service."

Marvelli pulled out his new ID and opened it for the man. "Special Agent Mike Tarantella, FBI."

Loretta tried to swallow, but her mouth was bone dry as she pulled out her ID and showed it. "Special Agent C. Gibbons, FBI," she said. She wished she'd sounded more natural.

"Hand your IDs to me, please," Armistead said as he walked out farther on the dock. He got down on one knee and reached out for them. "Keep your hands in sight and stay on the boat until I tell you otherwise." He took their IDs and went back into the shack.

Loretta glanced sideways, looking for more gun barrels. She didn't see any, but she was certain they were there. Her heart was thumping like a drum beat on a slave ship. She listened carefully for movement in the bushes, but all she could hear were the low waves slapping the hull of the boat.

"What's taking him so long?" she asked through clenched teeth.

"Who knows," Marvelli said.

A few minutes later, Armistead came back out. He nodded and waved for them to come ashore. His cap was turned back the right way, but his expression was still pretty grim.

The inside of My Blue Heaven looked like a very modern college dorm with lounges, game rooms, and reading rooms on the main floor. The floors were covered with blue-gray industrial carpeting, and the walls were freshly painted. All the doors were metal, painted ice blue to match the walls, and most of them had reinforced-glass windows in them.

Loretta was amazed at how quiet it was as she and Marvelli followed Deputy Armistead down a long hallway. It was definitely a federal facility, she thought. Not exactly a country club, but nothing like a state facility. That's real hard time.

Armistead led them past an open pair of double doors. Loretta peeked in and saw a very well equipped gym where a group of men in shorts and sweatpants were playing basketball while three guards in khaki uniforms watched from the sidelines. Loretta noticed that the guards weren't carrying riot sticks. How civilized.

Among the men playing ball was one black guy who handled the ball pretty well. The rest of the players were white guys who looked pretty pathetic. She assumed these were inmates and wondered if one of them was Rispoli.

"This way," Armistead said, prompting Loretta to keep up.

She picked up her pace, her pulse racing because she didn't want to blow her cover. Federal agents don't dawdle—at least not that anyone should notice.

She exchanged glances with Marvelli behind Armistead's back. He looked as cool as could be while she was sweating buckets under her clothes.

They came up to a locked windowless door. Armistead stared up at the video camera mounted on the wall. The three of them waited in silence until the door buzzed, and Armistead pushed it open. They walked into a narrow hallway with a locked mirrored picture window on one wall. There was another locked door at the other end of the hallway. Loretta was certain that there were guards behind that mirror, scrutinizing them.

That's it, she thought. *They've got a computer in there, and they've called up files on the real Gibson and Tarantella. They're looking at photos of the real agents, and they are not me and Marvelli. That's it, we're finished. We're screwed.* Best case scenario: She and Marvelli would be reprimanded and they'd lose their jobs. Worse case: They'd go to prison. And not a nice one like this.

Time seemed to stop, and Loretta feared that she'd sweat right through her jacket, giving herself away. Armistead stared at her, fish-eyed and poker-faced. She was convinced he knew. But what were they waiting for?

Suddenly the second door buzzed, and Armistead held it open for Marvelli and Loretta. They passed through into another long hallway. This one didn't have the same institutional smell that the last hallway had. She thought she could smell burnt coffee. Someone had left a coffeemaker on with next to nothing in the pot.

"Down this way," Armistead said, pointing down the hallway.

They followed him up to a stained-wood door with a red plastic nameplate in a brass holder—Ronald E. Darcy, Special United States Marshal. Loretta assumed he was special because instead of being in charge of a regional territory, he ran My Blue Heaven.

Armistead knocked on the door and opened it. A young man in a suit that was too big for him was just getting up from his desk. He had a stack of files under one arm. "Go ahead in," he said to Armistead, nodding at the inner door. "He's waiting for you."

The young man breezed out of the office, apparently in a hurry to do something. Maybe he was in a hurry to get out of the line of fire, Loretta thought. She balled her hands to hide the trembling.

Armistead knocked on the inner door.

"Come in," a voice inside said.

Armistead opened the door and waited for Loretta and Marvelli to go in first. A man in a brown suit was sitting at a mahogany desk. "Special Agents Tarantella and Gibson to see you, sir," Armistead said. He walked past Marvelli and laid their IDs on the man's desk.

The man studied their IDs for a long moment, nodding to himself the whole time. "Thank you, Armistead," he finally said.

"Do you want me to stay?" Armistead asked.

The man shook his head. "You can go."

Armistead left the room.

The man stood up and extended his hand to Marvelli, revealing his true size. "Ron Darcy," he said. Darcy was short and compact, and Loretta imagined that he might have been a gymnast when he was younger. He had straight, steel-gray hair that fell over his brow and a serious but boyish face that betrayed the fact that he was probably in his fifties.

"Mike Tarantella," Marvelli said, shaking his hand.

Loretta extended hers. "Gibson," she said with a terse smile.

Darcy flashed an equally terse smile as he shook her hand, then gave them back their IDs. "What's the *C* stand for, Gibson?"

"Charlotte," she said without missing a beat. She'd already prepared for this, even though she had no idea what the *C* did stand for.

"Have a seat," Darcy said. "So you're here to talk to Gus Rispoli?" He was grinning as if this were funny.

Marvelli nodded. "That's why we came."

"I assume you've already talked to Agent Springer about him."

Loretta nodded, praying that he wouldn't want to get into any details.

"Well, then I guess you know what a prickly character Rispoli is."

"We know," Loretta said, nodding again and getting more and more uncomfortable with this chitchat.

"Well, this is my suggestion," Darcy said, "and you can take it or not, I don't care. But from what I've seen, Rispoli is a lot more cooperative when you don't gang up on him. It's better to deal with him one-on-one. He's more comfortable with that. I'd suggest just one of you meet him initially."

Both Loretta and Marvelli were nodding. Loretta was waiting for Marvelli to volunteer. This was his idea, after all. He should be the one to go into the lion's den. Anyway, Loretta wanted to keep her involvement limited to "accomplice."

"I'll go," Marvelli finally said, and Loretta relaxed a little.

"I've noticed that he seems to trust Agent Springer more than any of male agents he deals with," Darcy quickly pointed out. "He may respond better to a woman." He was looking at Loretta.

Loretta stopped breathing. "Well, if that's what you recommend," she said, glancing at Marvelli. "Of course, Agent Tarantella is more familiar with this particular aspect of the investigation than I am. . . ." She was waiting for Marvelli to pick up on her cue, but he was just staring out the window at the great view of the sound, nodding to himself.

"What do you think, Mike?" she said. "Mike?"

"Hmmm?" Marvelli was slow to snap out of it. "What do I think about what?"

Loretta wanted to brain him. "I was saying you're more familiar with the investigation, so maybe you should go in and meet Mr. Rispoli first."

"Oh, sure. No problem."

Loretta was dying inside. Feebies don't act like this. Darcy was going to see right through them.

But Darcy was grinning at them as if he were anticipating the punch line to a joke. "You undercover people are really something," he said. "You really are a breed apart. Not like regular law-enforcement personnel at all. I don't know how you people do it."

"Neither do I," Loretta said, forcing herself not to smack Marvelli in the head.

Darcy stood up. "I'll take you down to see Rispoli," he said to Marvelli. "Agent Gibson, you can wait here if you'd like."

"Fine," Loretta said. She was anxious to get on with this thing.

Darcy came around his desk. "Make yourself comfortable . . . Charlotte? May I call you Charlotte?"

"Please."

"This may take a while," he said to her as he led Marvelli toward the door. "Rispoli doesn't warm up easily to new people. My assistant should be back shortly if you need anything. His name is Bob."

"Thanks," Loretta said as they left. She hoped Marvelli had come up with a plan for sneaking Rispoli out of here because she sure as hell didn't have one.

She scanned Darcy's office, thinking hard. Tall pines were swaying in the breeze outside the window behind his desk. The entire island seemed tranquil, almost deserted, but she was sure there were guards posted everywhere. Even if they could get Rispoli out of the building, it would be suicidal to make a run for it.

She stared at the phone on Darcy's desk and considered calling in a bomb threat or something, anything that would create a distraction. She went over and picked up the receiver, listening for a dial tone. She started pressing buttons, trying to get an outside line, but nothing worked. She knew from her days as an assistant warden that all prison phones have special codes so that sneaky prisoners can't call out.

Suddenly she heard someone entering the outer office, and she hung up the phone. Must be Bob the assistant, she thought. She quickly returned to her seat as the doorknob turned. She looked over her shoulder, expecting to see the clean-cut young man in the ill-fitting suit.

The door swung open, and what stared back at Loretta was as surprised to see her as she was to see him. He was as big as a heavyweight, with a lantern jaw and a greasy black pompadour. He was wearing jeans and a blue work shirt, the sleeves cut off at the shoulders to show off his pumped-up biceps. A broad smile slowly bisected his face, revealing wide gaps between all his top teeth.

"Hi," he said. He was carrying a vacuum cleaner and a plastic bucket full of cleaning supplies. "Mind if I clean up?" He had a soft southern accent with a lot of twang. East Texas, she guessed.

"You have to do that now?" she asked, trying not to stare at his massive chest.

"They told me to finish up before lunch."

Loretta shrugged. "Okay. If you have to."

He came in and closed the door behind him. As he bent over to plug in the vacuum cleaner, she noticed that he was staring at her. "Name's Buddy," he said.

"Hi," she said, but didn't offer hers. This wasn't the place to make friends.

"I been in for a long time," he said. "A *long* time."

She nodded politely to show that she'd heard him.

"Ain't been with a woman since I don't know when." A tongue bulge rolled across his bottom lip.

He stood up slowly to his full height, his eyes locked on hers. Loretta's eyes widened. He looked like a great big erection.

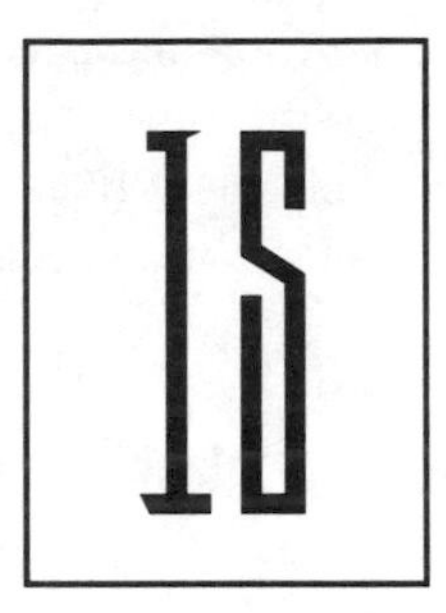

"Something I can do for you?" Loretta asked, trying to be cool.

A low, growly laugh seeped through the spaces between Buddy's teeth. His smile looked like a bear trap. His stare was unwavering.

"You want me to move so you can vacuum?" she asked.

His eyes pointed to the sofa against the wall.

Loretta's temples started to throb. Suddenly she was back at Pinewood, trapped in the laundry with Brenda Hemingway, about to be forced into that clothes drier. Her jaw was set, but her heart was screaming.

Buddy stepped toward her, dragging the vacuum cleaner by the hose like a caveman dragging his club. She immediately stood up, not wanting to be in a submissive position, but he came right up to her anyway. The top of her head was even with his chin. He dropped the hose. It hit the carpet with a dull *fwap,* flopped over, and slowly uncoiled between her feet.

"Been a long time," he mumbled. His breath was overpoweringly minty.

Loretta moved back, pushing her chair with the backs of her calves.

Buddy kept coming. "Been a *real* long time," he said. He spoke in a low purr.

"I suggest you back off, pal," she said.

He just grinned at her, showing all his spaces.

"Don't make me repeat myself," she said. "I'm an officer of the law . . . FBI."

"Ooouu," Buddy said, puckering up and blowing mint in her face. "I've always wanted to do a feebie"—his face suddenly went dead—"for all the times you people did it to me."

Loretta's blood turned to ice.

Buddy quickly flashed that big grin of his. "Just kidding, darlin'."

He stooped down and picked up the hose, standing up again real slow. Suddenly he looped the hose over her head and around her waist, pulling her so close she had to press her palms against his rock-hard chest to keep away from his face.

"Release me," she ordered, trying her damnedest not to think about Brenda Hemingway. But the more she tried not to think of Brenda, the more she thought about her, imagining the worst happening all over again.

He started nudging her over toward the couch, his black eyes glinting through the slits of his lids.

"I said, let me go," she said.

He just laughed, a deep growl bubbling up from his muscle-bound throat. "I'll let you go, darlin' . . . when I'm through." He nudged her again, this time with his groin, which was harder than his chest.

"Stop!" she said, but she hated the sound of her own voice. She sounded like a desperate female, and he was probably getting off on that.

"Come on, darlin'. Don't fight the inevitable. Y'all want it as much as I do."

"I doubt it," she said as she snatched the end of the hose and jammed the nozzle into his eye socket.

"Hey!" he squealed. "Get that thing outta my—"

"My foot's on the vacuum cleaner, pardner. Think it's got enough suction to take your eye out? Let's find out, buckaroo."

"Hey, hey! Hold on there, girlie." He let go of the hose and raised his hands to his shoulders. "Don't be doing nothing crazy now."

"Why not?" she said. "I thought men always wanted women to suck things for them."

"Not my *eye*!"

"Don't knock it till you've tried it." She kept the nozzle pressed to his eye, forcing him backward. She held it like a six-shooter, blinded by a lust for revenge. This may have been some mook named Buddy standing in front of her, but the rage she was feeling was all aimed at Brenda Hemingway.

She tapped the foot pedal on the vacuum cleaner with the top of her shoe. "How about just a little bit? Just to see how it feels?"

"No!" Buddy roared as he backed away and crashed into a wall. Three pictures fell to the floor, including a photo of the president who now had a spiderweb crack centered on the tip of his nose. "Don't do it, lady," Buddy pleaded. "I'll just go away. I swear."

"What the hell's going on in here?"

Loretta's head swiveled toward the voice that came from the doorway. Two men rushed into the room—one in a khaki guard's uniform, the other in a blue blazer, gray slacks, and a burgundy tie. The stocky guard got between Loretta and Buddy, spinning the convict around and getting him in an arm lock from behind. The other man grabbed Loretta's wrist and wrenched the nozzle out of her hand. He had a blond-going-to-gray crew cut, blunt features, and a protruding belly that hung over his belt.

"Hey!" she protested, but the man ignored her, keeping a grip on her wrist.

"Come on, Buddy. Let's go," the guard said as he steered Buddy toward the door.

Buddy didn't resist, but he did manage to give Loretta a smoldering look before he left. The message his expression conveyed flickered between "I still want you, darling" and "I want to kill you, lady."

"Do you know who that guy is?" the man in the blazer scolded, finally letting go of her wrist.

"Am I supposed to care?" Loretta was glowering at him.

"That's Buddy Henley. He's seven for seven, for chrissake."

"He's what?"

"Seven for seven. His testimony in seven consecutive trials has resulted in seven convictions. *Good* ones."

"Well, hooray for him." Loretta straightened her collar.

The man scowled at her, pointing at the doorway Buddy and the guard had just gone through. "That man is going to put away the current leadership of the Mexican Mafia. Big-time heroin dealers. Killers. We *need* Buddy."

"Don't try to make him sound like some kind of hero. He tried to rape me."

"He's no hero, but he is necessary."

Loretta did not agree, but she held her tongue. Buddy Henley was probably as scummy as all the scum he'd testified against. The only difference was he'd made his deal with the feds first. Eventually he was going to get a reduced sentence, a new identity, and a split-level in the heartland while his old muchacos were going to rot in prison like a band of mariachi cock-a-roches. She knew it was the only way to put these dirtbags away, but somehow it didn't seem fair.

The man straightened his tie and cleared his throat. "I apologize if I got a little sharp with you, ma'am." He offered his hand to her. "Carl Dibler," he said, "U.S. Marshals Service."

Loretta didn't miss a beat. "C. Gibson, FBI," she said, shaking his hand.

Dibler squinted at her. "You sound like you're from back East. You don't work out of the Newark office in Jersey by any chance?"

She nodded. "Uh-huh."

"You the only Gibson at that office?"

Loretta had no idea, but she didn't dare hesitate. "Yup," she said. "Just me."

He dropped his chin and looked her in the eye. "I worked a case once with a Special Agent C. Gibson from the Newark office. The *C* stood for Claude. He was a guy."

Loretta could feel the blood draining out of her face.

"So how can you be the only Gibson at the Newark office?" Dibler asked. He was staring at her like a state trooper who'd just stopped her for speeding.

She stared back, thinking hard, sweating more. "I guess you don't remember me, do you?" she said.

He furrowed his brow and shook his head.

"I guess you haven't heard. I'm surprised. I was the talk of the town when I came back."

He looked puzzled. "Came back from where?"

"Baltimore," she said. "Johns Hopkins? The hospital?"

"Were you sick?"

"Well, in a way, yes."

"What was wrong with you?"

"I was a woman trapped in a man's body," she said absolutely straight-faced. "I wasn't meant to be Claude. I was meant to be Charlotte."

Carl Dibler leaned away from her.

"Hey, come on, Carl. It's still me." She reached out and touched his arm, which stiffened on contact.

He lowered his voice. "You telling me you had a sex-change operation?"

She looked down and nodded. "I had to, Carl. And not just because I was living a lie. I had to do it for work," she said.

"For work? What're you talking about?"

"I had been undercover so many times as a man, I was useless. I felt like a spent bullet. There were just too many bad guys out there who knew my face. The only way for me to keep going undercover was to become someone else."

She waited for him to say something, but he just stared at her, his face blank as he tried to process all of this. Finally he tilted his head and flashed a little grin. "You know something—Charlotte, is it?"

"Yes."

"You know something, Charlotte?" He took her wrist and squeezed it hard. "I think you're full of crap." He reached under his jacket to the small of his back and pulled out a set of handcuffs.

A vein on Loretta's temple started to throb, like a worm hav-ing a heart attack. She tried to pull away from Deputy Dibler's grip, but he was too strong.

But Loretta was no pushover. Dibler struggled to position her wrist so that he could attach the handcuffs. "It's useless to resist, ma'am. You're under arrest."

"For what?"

"Impersonating a federal officer of the law, being on restricted federal property without authorization—"

"Carl," she said, suddenly relaxing her arm, "how can you do this to me?"

"Very easily," he grunted.

She reached over with her free hand and stroked his cheek. "Carl," she said. "Come on. We have history."

His head snapped back. "What're you talking about?"

"Remember that night we were together on that case?"

"What case?"

"Come on, you remember."

"You mean, Cleveland? At the motel?"

"Right." She had no idea what he was referring to, but she

had to improvise. "I remember looking at you from behind and thinking to myself, If I weren't a man, Carl Dibler would definitely be the one. Well, Carl . . . I'm not a man anymore . . ." She slowly circled his shiny pink ear with her finger.

Dibler shook his head to shoo her away. He moved back a half step but didn't let go of her wrist. "We shared a room that night. You were in the next bed, you sick son of a—"

"I never touched you, Carl. I sure thought about it, but I never acted on my impulses. I just watched you sleep." She heaved a forlorn sigh.

He dropped her wrist and moved farther away from her. "You're sick, Claude. Sick. You ought to retire before you disgrace yourself."

Loretta moved toward him and touched his sleeve. "You must have your twenty years in, Carl. We can both retire and live off our pensions. I bet you'd love Key West—"

He slapped his hands over his ears. "Stop talking. I don't want to hear it."

She gripped his shoulders, her face inches from his. "But, Carl—"

Suddenly Special U.S. Marshal Ron Darcy walked into the room, followed by Marvelli and a crabby-looking guy in faded black jeans and a blue work shirt. "What's going on, Carl?"

Dibler threw up his arms to get Loretta off him. His face was lobster red. "Nothing," he muttered as he stalked out of the room in double time.

Darcy and Marvelli stared at Loretta, expecting an explanation.

"We go way back," she said with a girlish grin and left it at that. She hated using so-called feminine wiles, but in this case she had no choice. She gave Marvelli the hairy eyeball, trying to yell at him telepathically: *Can we get the hell out of here, Marvelli? Like right now?*

"Agent Gibson," Ron Darcy said, extending his arm and drawing the crabby-looking man into their circle, "let me introduce you to Gus Rispoli. Gus, this is Special Agent Charlotte Gibson."

Loretta extended her hand, but Rispoli just deepened his

frown and looked at her as if she were offering him a handful of dirt. He was very thin with terrible posture. He had a beak nose, and his neck crooked at the Adam's apple like a buzzard's. After scrutinizing her for a few moments, he finally took his hand out of his pocket and shook hers, but very briefly as if he didn't want to touch her. His hands, feet, and head were unusually large and out of proportion with the rest of him, which made him look like a living stick figure.

"Nice to meet you," Loretta said curtly, not knowing exactly how she should respond to him.

"Yeah, hi," he croaked. He refused to look at her.

Mr. Charm, Loretta thought.

"I know you have a lot to discuss with Gus," Darcy said. "I can set you up in the conference room if you'd like. Or you can go outside and roam the grounds. You'll find benches all over."

Marvelli smiled at him in disbelief. "You're joking, right?"

Darcy shook his head. "The grounds are quite secure. You may think you're alone out there, but you're not. Far from it. Right, Gus?"

Rispoli nodded with a scowl on his face. "Shoot you down like a friggin' bug, these people," he said. He refused to make eye contact with anyone.

Loretta remembered the rifle barrels she'd thought she'd seen in the trees when they were on the dock. There were snipers and guards hiding all over this place. She glanced at Marvelli and yelled at him in her mind: *Now what, genius?*

Outside on the grounds Marvelli was still wondering what Loretta and that Carl guy had been doing back in Ron Darcy's office. As they walked down a dirt path through the pine trees with Rispoli between them, he kept sneaking glances at her when she wasn't looking. Was *that* her type? he wondered. The guy looked like a hedgehog.

As they ambled down the incline of the path, Marvelli could see the dock and their boat in the distance. It was about sixty yards away. The problem was, how do they get Rispoli on board and get the hell out of there without getting caught? Of course, he wasn't so sure Rispoli was going to want to get on. The guy kept giving them the Sicilian eyeball, which Marvelli was very familiar with. His mother-in-law was Sicilian. No people on earth are more suspicious than Sicilians. They invented it.

"So," Rispoli finally said after not talking for ten minutes, "who sent you? Taffy?"

Loretta's grim expression turned grimmer. "What're you talking about, Gus?"

"You came here to whack me, right? Taffy Demaggio must've sent you."

Marvelli said, "You seem pretty calm if you really believe that."

Rispoli shrugged and took a cigarette out of the pack in his shirt pocket. "You won't get away with it." He lit his cigarette from a book of matches and took a long drag. "They'd shoot you down before you took three steps." Smoke filtered out of his nose.

Loretta grinned, trying to keep it light. "I don't know what you're talking about, Gus. We're not here to kill you."

Rispoli stopped walking, squinted one eye, and took a long drag off his cigarette. "Right now there are at least three rifles aimed at us. You raise a finger against me, they'll make you Swiss cheese."

Marvelli scanned the pine boughs swaying in the breeze all around them. He didn't see anything unusual, but that didn't mean snipers weren't up there. He leaned toward Rispoli and whispered: "Are the grounds bugged? Electronic ears? Stuff like that?"

Rispoli scowled. "How the frig should I know? What do I look like, General Electric?"

Marvelli looked up at the trees again. An electronic ear wouldn't work through branches. Maybe it was safe to talk. He was going to have to risk it.

"Look, Gus, we're not federal agents. We're parole officers from Jersey. We're here to save your butt."

Rispoli just squinted at Marvelli. He was going to be hard to convince.

"You know a guy named Sammy Teitelbaum?" Loretta asked.

"Maybe," Rispoli said cautiously.

"Taffy gave him the contract to have you whacked," Marvelli said.

Rispoli shrugged. If he was impressed, he wasn't going to show it. "This guy gonna do it here?" he asked matter-of-factly. It was more professional curiosity than personal concern.

Marvelli shrugged. "Who knows? Whattaya think, they're gonna put it in the paper?"

The former hit man nodded. "You got a point."

"My guess is Sammy will try to get to you in transit," Marvelli said.

Rispoli nodded sagely. "Vulnerable. Yeah, that's the way to go."

The three of them looked out at the blue expanse of the sound. "A sitting duck," Rispoli said, the cigarette dangling from his lips.

His face suddenly turned stony. "How do I know you two are on the up-and-up?"

"You don't," Loretta said. "You just have to trust us."

A smile broke out under Rispoli's nose. Marvelli was flabbergasted. He didn't think the guy *could* smile. "I don't trust *nobody,*" he said.

"You're in real danger," Loretta said. "We can help you—"

Rispoli shook his head and laid a hand on her forearm to silence her. Marvelli frowned. He didn't like Rispoli touching her.

"I'm in no more danger now that I was twenty minutes ago, and I'm still breathing, ain't I?"

"Bad logic, Gus," Marvelli said. "Doesn't mean it couldn't happen."

Rispoli furrowed his brows. He was offended. "I know that. Whattaya think, I'm stupid?"

"All right, let's suppose Loretta and I are working for Taffy, and we're here to whack you. Naturally we can't do it here. But if we can get you out on the water, we could—"

"*If* you got that far. The odds aren't with you."

"If we kill you, yeah. But what if we keep you alive?" Marvelli said. "You are a very valuable asset. We could use you as a hostage. Make 'em do whatever we want or else we kill you."

Rispoli's face relaxed as he started to nod. He was enjoying this. It had been a while since he'd planned something like this, and he was getting into it. "Could work," he said with a half grin. Then the grin disappeared. "But what's in it for me?"

"A little fun," Loretta said. "You must be pretty bored in this place."

Rispoli raised his eyebrows. "You got that right. But fun ain't enough. Fun ain't all it's cracked up to be."

"How about this?" Marvelli said, thinking on the fly. "You help us get you out, then all you have to do is get away from us and you're a free man. Disappear and set up your own Witness Protection Program. You've got six more years to serve, plus if you testify in all the trials the government wants you to, you'll be on everyone's hit list."

"That's true," Rispoli said. "I'll be good for nothing when they get through with me."

Loretta was making faces at Marvelli because she didn't approve. She didn't understand that he wasn't being serious. He was just telling Rispoli what he wanted to hear to get his cooperation. No way in hell he was going to let Rispoli go free.

"So you wanna take your chances with us," Marvelli asked, "or do you wanna stay here and be Mr. Popular?"

Rispoli flicked his cigarette away and pulled out a fresh one. He was thinking it over, his eyes cast down. He lit the new cigarette, sucking in his cheeks to get it going, then took a long drag, holding it for a moment as his gaze drifted up to the sky. He slowly exhaled smoke onto the breeze. "Okay," he said.

"That's it?" Loretta said. "Okay?"

The hit man shrugged, picking flecks of tobacco off the end of his tongue. "What do you want, a debate? I thought about it enough. Let's do it."

"Great," Marvelli said, then he wiped the smile off his face in case he was being watched. "So how do we do it, Gus?"

Rispoli's eyebrows shot up, turning his forehead into a washboard. "Whattaya asking me for? I thought you had this all planned out?"

"Well, yeah, in general. We just need some help with the details."

"Ha!" Loretta rolled her eyes.

Marvelli shot her a dirty look. He needed some support here.

"I'm only asking you, Gus, because you're sort of an expert in these kinds of illegal things," Marvelli said. "I mean, we're just amateurs when it comes to breaking the law."

Loretta folded her arms indignantly. "Excuse me."

"Later," Marvelli said firmly.

"You bet, later," she said, glaring at him.

Marvelli held his tongue and glanced up at the pine boughs. This wasn't the time or the place.

Rispoli sighed in annoyance. "You say you got a boat? Is it a good one? Fast?"

"Yeah, it's not bad."

"You know how to drive it? I don't know nothing about boats."

"Don't worry. I can handle it," Marvelli said.

"That's not good enough. You gotta fly."

"I'll fly if we have to. Don't worry." But Marvelli was worried. That boat was good, but it was nothing special.

"Okay, so here's what we do," Rispoli said, starting to stroll. "We walk down to the dock. When we get near the water, we move in closer together. I'll stay behind you two to cover you." He cast a skeptical glance at Loretta. "If I can."

Marvelli didn't like people making cracks about Loretta's size, and he would have told Rispoli off in short order if he didn't need the guy so badly right now.

"They won't shoot if there's a risk of hitting me."Rispoli explained. "As you say, I'm too valuable."

Marvelli exchanged glances with Loretta as they walked down the path, Rispoli between them and slightly behind. She looked as doubtful as he felt.

As they approached the dock, Rispoli hissed into their ears. "Get closer together."

Marvelli did as he was told, touching shoulders with Loretta.

Another boat was just pulling into the dock, a sleek twenty-five-footer. Rispoli's eyes were riveted on it. "Let's take that one," he said in a low growl. "Looks faster than yours."

Marvelli wanted to bite his nails, but he kept his hands at his sides. "How do we know it's got enough gas, Gus? Ours has at least half a tank."

"Let's risk it," Rispoli said as they stepped off the dirt path and onto the planks of the dock. "I like that one better."

Marvelli avoided Loretta's glance. His stomach was in a knot. He knew this was nuts, but they'd gone too far to turn back now.

The twenty-five-footer's throaty engine sputtered out as it glided in toward the dock. On board a man in jeans and a gray sweatshirt was getting ready to throw a line. Another man at the helm was guiding her in.

"Okay," Rispoli said. "As soon as they get off, we get on. I'll untie the rope. You get down out of sight, sweetheart," he said to Loretta. "And you," he said to Marvelli, "get behind the wheel and tear ass—"

Suddenly a third person appeared on the boat, coming up from down below. It was Agent Springer, inappropriately dressed in a gray suit and black pumps. Her stare instantly went from incredulous to infuriated as she pointed an accusing finger at the three of them.

"Stop them!" she yelled.

Before any of them could react, a marksman rapelled down out of an overhanging pine tree, his M-16 assault rifle trained on Loretta, Marvelli, and Rispoli. The two men on the boat with Springer were pointing Uzi submachine guns at them. Marvelli noticed another gun barrel sticking out of another tree off to the side. An all-terrain vehicle came buzzing down the path, the driver leading with a black matte .45 automatic.

Instinctively Loretta and Marvelli raised their hands above their heads, but Rispoli calmly took one last drag off his cigarette before flicking it into the water where it hit with a hiss. "I guess that plan sucked," he said.

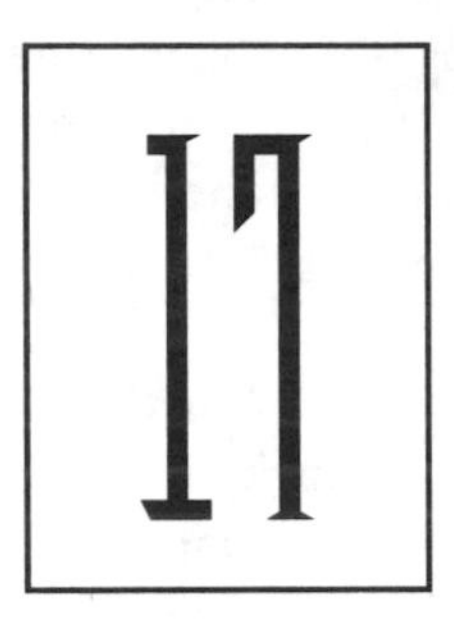

Veronica Springer felt the deck of the boat shifting under her feet as she stared at Gus Rispoli and the two parole officers from New Jersey. Her brain was racing as fast as her pulse. When she'd first spotted Marvelli and his partner, she'd wanted to kill them for having the gall to come here. She'd wanted them arrested, prosecuted, convicted, and locked up immediately. But now she was reconsidering the situation. Maybe this could be an opportunity, she thought. Maybe she shouldn't be so hasty. This could be a good thing if she steered it the right way.

She climbed up onto the dock and went right over to Rispoli, Marvelli, and his portly partner—Springer could never remember that woman's name. Springer made eye contact with all three of them. "What's going on?" she asked in a low voice.

"We're trying to escape," Rispoli said, squinting one eye against the smoke drifting into his face from the cigarette dangling from the corner of his mouth.

Marvelli whispered, "Actually we came to save him."

"He's in real danger," what's-her-name, the chubby girl, said. "None of you people would listen to us."

Springer looked at them, each in turn, then glanced at the guards and the deputies and all their guns. The only sounds were the low rumble of the idling all-terrain vehicle and the slap of the waves against the pylons under the dock.

She looked Marvelli in the eye and kept her voice down. "How'd you get in here?"

"We said we were feebies."

"How'd you pull that off?"

Marvelli didn't answer. All of a sudden he was trying to grow brains, Springer thought.

But she was the one thinking a mile a minute, looking for the opportunity, the angle. What if she hadn't arrived when she did? she thought. What if they did manage to spring Rispoli? Well, for one thing it would be a lot easier for Taffy to get to Rispoli if he were free. In fact, Marvelli and what's-her-name could lead Taffy's people right to him. This could be very good. Taffy gets rid of the main witness against him, then Taffy turns state's evidence, and she gets the kudos. This could be excellent.

Springer ignored the guards and deputies and all the firepower. "Show me your IDs," she said to Marvelli and Loretta, suddenly remembering her name.

"What?" Loretta said.

"Just show me your IDs," she said, softening her tone a bit.

Reluctantly the parole officers did what she asked. She gave the IDs a cursory glance, then handed them back. "Sorry for the misunderstanding," she said in a full voice for the benefit of the crowd.

Rispoli raised his eyebrows. Springer could see the confusion behind the parole officers' pasted-on poker-faces.

"You're right," she said softly. "Gus is in danger. I want you to get him out of here."

Springer turned to the guards and deputies. "My mistake," she announced. "They've been cleared to have Mr. Rispoli." She flashed an everything's-okay smile. She outranked all of these men, so they had to listen to her.

Slowly they lowered their weapons.

"Get going," she whispered to Marvelli. "I've got your cell-phone number. I'll call you."

Marvelli smiled at Springer and started to usher Rispoli to the rented powerboat, but Loretta didn't get it.

What's with the sudden change in attitude? Loretta thought suspiciously. *What's Springer up to?*

Loretta started shuffling toward their boat. Marvelli was already on board, helping Rispoli get on. Gus made himself comfortable on the bench along the stern of the boat. Springer was looking down at him from the dock, an odd tight smile on her face.

The guard who had arrived on the all-terrain vehicle came over and untied the lines, tossing them on board. At the helm, Marvelli nodded his thanks.

Loretta sidled up behind Marvelli. "'What's going on?" she asked.

Marvelli kept his eyes on the dashboard. "Beats me." He turned the ignition, and the engine came to life with a loud rumble.

"I don't think we should trust her," Loretta said.

"Right now I don't think we have a choice," Marvelli said. He turned the wheel and guided the boat away from the dock. Springer was still wearing that terse smile, her eyes glued to Marvelli. Loretta wondered what that was all about. Marvelli looked back at Springer and gave her an equally terse smile accompanied by a two-finger salute.

Marvelli guided the boat out into open water, then opened up the throttle and started to pick up speed. The hull belly flopped over the waves as Marvelli gave it more gas. Rispoli had his legs stretched out and his fingers linked behind his head as if he were on vacation. Sweat had formed on Loretta's upper lip, but she didn't dare wipe it away. The guards and deputies were still close enough to see, and she didn't want to appear nervous.

She went to the bench and sat down next to Rispoli, twisting her body sideways so that she could see the shore. She had a beautiful view of My Blue Heaven and the dirt path that led down to the dock. It could have been a picture postcard. She felt the sweat gathering in her armpits and hoped to God she never saw this place ever again.

But then she noticed a figure at the top of the hill, running down the dirt path. She squinted to make out who it was, but they were too far out now. She got up and took the binoculars hanging from a hook over the helm. She couldn't make out the running figure's face, but she knew right away who it was from the blue blazer, gray slacks, and the hanging beer belly. It was Carl Dibler, the deputy who'd worked with C. Gibson when she was a he. He was running faster than a man with a gut like that should.

Loretta refocused on the dock. The deputies and guards looked very agitated all of a sudden. They were pointing out over the water—at them.

"Marvelli, I think you'd better step on it," she said, keeping the binoculars to her face. She could feel a pulse thrumming through her stomach.

"What's wrong?" Marvelli said.

An alarm went off on shore that sounded like a foghorn on speed. Three seconds later an ungodly engine roar came out of the distance. Loretta scanned the water with the binoculars, frantically looking for its source, but she couldn't find it.

Rispoli picked up his head. "What the hell's that?" he barked in annoyance. The noise was spoiling his ride.

Loretta wrinkled her nose and scanned the surface of the water through the binoculars, looking for the source of the engine roar. She put down the binoculars to get the big picture, and as soon as she did, she saw it in the distance coming around the edge of the island, a metallic-blue cigarette boat. It was coming after them at top speed, lunging over the surface of the water like a giant stiletto.

"IGG," Rispoli said, leaning back and lacing his fingers around his bent knee.

"What?" Loretta was starting to panic.

"IGG," the hit man said casually. "Ill-gotten gain. Must've belonged to some drug dealer who got convicted. The government always takes the good stuff for themselves."

"Marvelli!" she yelled up to the helm. "Can't you go any faster?"

"I'm doing the best I can here," Marvelli shouted back. He had both hands on the wheel, alternately turning back to see where the cigarette boat was and looking ahead to see where he could go.

"You know what you oughta do?" Rispoli said, grimacing

against the spray. "Hang a right and hug the shore. Weave in and out of those little islands over there. Maybe we can lose 'em."

"Oh, yeah?" Marvelli said, clearly resenting the backseat driving. "You know how deep it is over there? I don't. We could run aground."

Rispoli shrugged. "Or we could get caught."

The cigarette boat was gaining on them. It seemed huge compared to their boat, a thirty-five-footer at the very least. There were two men on board that Loretta could see. The one in the passenger seat was holding a bullhorn to his face. "Stop your craft immediately," he ordered. "Cut your engines and show your hands."

Rispoli flipped him the bird.

"Don't do that," Loretta scolded. "They're mad enough."

Rispoli sneered. "You mean if I wave nice, they'll go away?"

Loretta just glared at him.

"Hey, Gus," Marvelli yelled from the bridge, "come over here and give me some advice."

"You mean I gotta get up?" he said.

Loretta grabbed him by the back of his shirt and hauled him off the bench.

"Easy! Easy!" he snapped. "I hate pushy broads," he muttered.

"I'll show you pushy. I'll push you overboard if you don't watch it," she snapped back.

Rispoli went over to Marvelli, sulking all the way.

"Come on, Gus. You're the bad guy here," Marvelli said. "Tell me what I should do."

"I told you already," Rispoli shouted impatiently. "Go over by the shore! Use them islands!"

The cigarette boat was getting closer, and the man on the bullhorn was getting louder. "Stop your craft immediately. Cut your engines. I repeat, stop your craft immediately."

The sound of automatic gunfire reverberated over the water in three-shot bursts. Loretta could see the bullets plinking into the water ten feet short of the stern. "Do what he says, Marvelli," she yelled. "Hug them islands!"

Marvelli spun the wheel, and the boat veered sharply to the right. Loretta hung on to the rail to keep from being thrown overboard. He headed for a small rocky island that was about the size of a tractor trailer. It was no more than a hundred feet from the big island. "This better be deep enough," he shouted.

Loretta held her breath, imagining them hitting rocks in shallow water, the bottom of their boat shattering like an egg, and them flying through the windshield at seventy miles per hour.

They zoomed around the little island, Loretta gritting her teeth and gripping the rail, but to her amazement nothing happened, they just kept going. She looked back to see where the cigarette boat was. It swerved around the island, barely slowing down to do it, and now they were closing in.

"Over there," Rispoli said, pointing to a cluster of even smaller islands, the smallest one no bigger than a Volkswagen Beetle. These islands were even closer to shore.

Marvelli's face was clenched like a fist, and so was Loretta's stomach. They were going to hit bottom, she was convinced. They were going to die.

Loretta looked back. The cigarette boat was charging hard. The report of the automatic gunfire carried over the surface of the water a split second after the bullets plinked into the water six feet off the starboard side. The man with the bullhorn was firing an assault rifle at them.

"I can't get in there," Marvelli grunted as he turned the wheel and skirted the islands.

"Chicken," Rispoli sneered, lighting another cigarette.

"Do you have to smoke?" Loretta complained as smoke blew into her face.

Rispoli gave her a look. "You got some scotch? I'll drink instead."

Loretta didn't bother to answer.

"I'm gonna make a run for it," Marvelli announced as he steered toward open water.

"Bad idea," Rispoli said, shaking his head.

Loretta had to agree with him. On a straight course, their boat was no match for the cigarette boat. It had taken the deputies almost no time to gain on them, and now they were just fifty feet back.

"Stop your craft immediately," the bullhorn deputy shouted. Another short burst of gunfire followed, riddling the stern this time.

Loretta dove for the deck, and Marvelli crouched down behind the wheel, but Rispoli just stood there smoking with his hand on the rail. "Bastards," he cursed under his breath.

The cigarette boat was running neck and neck with them, twenty feet off the port side. Loretta could make out the piercing eyes of the deputy behind the bullhorn. She could also see the assault rifle he was holding. She ducked when white-hot muzzle flashes shot out of the rifle and three more bullets hit the water just short of their boat.

"I think they missed," Marvelli said, but Rispoli was shaking his head no.

"They're trying to hit below the water line," the hit man said. "You're probably taking on water now."

"What's that, like shooting out our tires?" Loretta said. She was getting fed up with his matter-of-fact attitude.

Rispoli ignored her and pointed with his chin. "Take a hard right at that next buoy," he said to Marvelli. "Head back toward shore."

Marvelli objected, "We're gonna hit bottom if we go back there."

Rispoli shrugged. "Then these guys are gonna sink us. Maybe end up hitting somebody in the process."

"They won't hit you," Loretta said bitterly. "You're the one they want alive."

Rispoli smiled at her.

A skull has a prettier smile, she thought.

"Hey, you want to give up, we'll give up," Rispoli said. "But I'm not the one who's gonna catch hell over this. You know that."

Loretta looked at Marvelli. They both knew that he was right.

As the two boats raced toward the buoy, Marvelli called back to Loretta and Rispoli. "Get down and hang on to something."

The buoy was coming up fast. Three more shots zinged into

their wake, their reports following a second behind. Marvelli ignored it. He was concentrating on timing his moment.

"Last warning," the bullhorn yelled. "Stop your craft."

"Stop *this,*" Rispoli blurted, giving them the finger. "You miserable mother—"

Suddenly he was thrown forward as Marvelli abruptly cut back on the engines to make the turn around the buoy. Rispoli was whipped into a corner as Marvelli hit the throttle, and the boat roared toward shore. The cigarette boat sped past the buoy, going too fast to follow. It made a wide arc and headed after them, but by now Marvelli had gained some ground.

"Now what, Gus?" Marvelli called to the hit man.

Rispoli crawled to the helm. "Over there." He pointed to a long line of tiny barrier islands that stretched over a hundred yards. The bigger ones hosted small trees and bushes, but some were just outcroppings of gray rock or single car-sized boulders, and others barely crested the water at all, like shark fins. "Sneak in there between those two big islands," Rispoli said, pointing out which ones he meant.

"I can't go in there—"

Rispoli threw up his hands. "It's your ass, pal, not mine."

"All right, all right," Marvelli said. "But you two watch the sides. That's a narrow strait. Even if it's deep enough, I'm not sure we can squeeze through."

Marvelli slowed down as they came up to the islands, but he didn't dare slow down too much with the cigarette boat moving in fast. "Talk to me, people," he yelled as he maneuvered the boat around a cluster of boulders.

Two angry bursts of gunfire ricocheted off the rocks as he swung the boat around and just barely missed a boulder that looked like a half-submerged hippo. He cut back on the engine until it sounded like it was gargling. The cigarette boat sped up from behind but had to make a sharp U-turn to avoid the rocks. Their wake rocked Marvelli's boat, throwing it against the hippo with a sharp thunk.

"Damn!" he grunted.

Loretta peered over the side, then reached into the water and ran her hand along the fiberglass. "It's okay. No damage. Keep going."

The deputy fired another short burst, hitting rocks again. One bullet ricocheted into the bench on the stern, forcing Loretta to duck after the fact. Her heart was slamming.

"Hurry up. Get going," Rispoli yelled.

Marvelli gave it some gas and eased the boat into the narrow strait. "Talk to me," he yelled.

Loretta was on the starboard side, Rispoli port. "You've got about a foot on this side," Rispoli said.

"About four inches on my side," Loretta reported.

"How deep?" Marvelli asked.

Loretta looked down. The water was clear to the rock-strewn bottom. "Doesn't look very deep. Maybe three feet. It's hard to tell."

Three more shots rang out in rapid succession, gouging the rocks on Loretta's side. One bullet ricocheted back toward the boat and chipped off a piece of fiberglass from the hull just inches from Loretta's hand.

"Floor it!" Rispoli barked.

But Marvelli already had that idea. He pushed the throttle, and the engines growled. The boat lurched forward, fishtailing into the boulders on Loretta's side. The sound of rocks scraping the bottom of the hull made Loretta wince. The boat slowed down, straining to move forward.

"We're hung up on the bottom," Marvelli yelled.

Loretta grabbed a fish net on a long aluminum pole that was bracketed to the side of the boat and thrust it into the water, trying to push them off the rocks like a Venetian gondolier, but the pole wasn't strong enough and it just bent.

"Try singing 'Santa Lucia,' " Rispoli said sarcastically.

"Try helping," she snapped back.

He shrugged. "What do you want me to do?"

"Get out and push."

Rispoli jerked his thumb at the cigarette boat, circling the waters behind them like an angry shark. "Not with them out there shooting at us. What're you, crazy?"

Loretta saw red. "Who the hell do you think we're doing this for?"

Rispoli shrugged as if he couldn't care less.

Loretta reached over and grabbed him by the shirtfront. "Come with me."

"Hey! Whattaya think you're doing? Let go of me."

Clutching the walk-around rail with her other hand, she dragged him past the helm to the front of the boat.

"Loretta," Marvelli called out, "what're you doing?"

She ignored him and shouted in Rispoli's ear, "Jump!" She started jumping, bouncing the skinny hit man along with her. Soon they were both off their feet, rocking the boat up and down.

Marvelli didn't have to be told what to do. Whenever the prow rose and the stern dipped, he gunned the engine. The sound of churning rocks banging against the hull was painful, but little by little the boat lurched forward and slipped through the strait, finally making it into deeper water.

He rushed to a hatch in the deck, threw it open, and stuck his head in. A few seconds later he pulled his head out and slammed it shut. "No holes that I can see," he announced with a big smile. "Amazing."

As Loretta and a ruffled Rispoli returned to the back of the boat, the cigarette boat raced off to take the long way around the barrier islands.

Marvelli reached for the throttle and started turning the wheel so he could flee in the other direction, but Rispoli held up his hand. "Wait."

"What for?" Loretta said frantically. "We can't wait."

"We gotta split up," Rispoli said. "You be the decoy," he said to Marvelli.

"No," Loretta blurted. She didn't want Marvelli to get caught by himself.

"Hey!" Rispoli protested. "You said you wanted to save me. So save me. The only way to do it is to split up."

"That's nuts," Loretta said.

"Oh, yeah? Well, playing sink-the-*Bismark* is more nuts. I do not wanna get shot."

Loretta could hear the cigarette boat's engines in the distance. They'd be here soon.

"Okay, fine," Marvelli suddenly said. "You two get out and hide in the bushes. I'll be the decoy."

"But—" Loretta said. She was worried about what would happen to him.

Rispoli already had one leg over the side of the boat. "Just stick to the shore and go where their boat won't fit," he told Marvelli. "You'll lose 'em. Maybe."

He hopped over the side and into the water. It came up to his chest.

"Go ahead," Marvelli said to Loretta. "I'll meet you back at the hotel."

"Are you sure?"

"Go ahead. I'll be okay."

"I don't want you to get shot."

"I won't get shot."

"I don't want you to go to prison either."

"Loretta, will you stop talking and get out."

She hesitated, her brows knit, not knowing whether she should or not.

"Go!" he said.

She frowned and finally hopped overboard, getting soaked up to her shoulders. Rispoli had already swum to shore, which was about sixty feet away. He was dragging himself out of the water, walking as best he could over the rocks.

In the distance she could see the cigarette boat rounding the barrier islands, so she swam to the nearest island instead of trying to make it to shore. She quickly found a large bush and crouched down behind it. Marvelli revved his engines and took off. Loretta stayed down and listened for the cigarette boat. She could hear their engines gaining in volume as Marvelli's decreased. Her heart was thumping as she heard the cigarette boat approaching, wondering if they'd seen her, but it roared right by. She peered through the branches, still worried about Marvelli, but then she remembered Rispoli. It occurred to her that he might take off and disappear for good. She stayed out of sight until it was quiet.

When she was sure the cigarette boat was gone, she poked her head over the top of the bush and looked for signs of Rispoli, but he was nowhere to be seen. *The bastard was running away,* she thought. *That's why he wanted to split up. Damn!*

She stood up and waded back into the water, determined to find him so she could ring his skinny little neck. He wasn't going to get away with this, not after all they'd gone through to spring him.

She dove in and started to swim, which wasn't easy with her clothes on. They dragged her down, and by the time she was only halfway across, she was exhausted. She stopped and treaded water for a second to catch her breath.

But then she heard something in the distance, a racing engine. The cigarette boat! she thought. She looked all around to see where it was, but it wasn't the cigarette boat. It was a powerboat, not Marvelli's, speeding over the water from the direction of My Blue Heaven.

All of a sudden she was freezing. More guards and deputies, she thought. More bullets. And here she was, stuck between the barrier islands and the shore. If she started swimming either way, they'd see her. There was nowhere to go. She was just a helpless head on the water, bound to be caught.

She started breathing fast, her heart pounding. Out of the blue an image of a courtroom came into her head, a black-robed judge sitting behind the bench.

Helping a federal prisoner escape and impersonating a federal agent, she thought. *How many years do you get for that?*

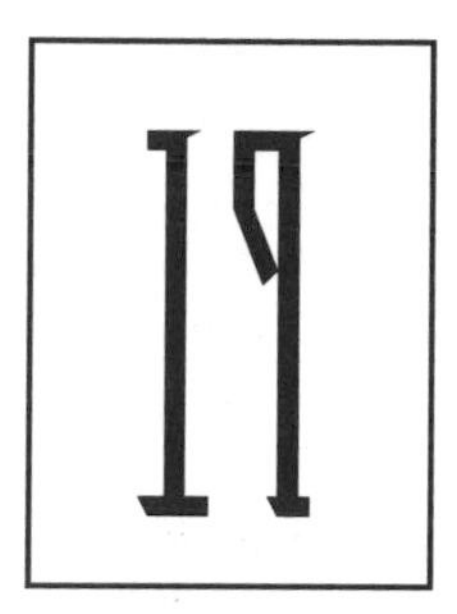

Loretta stayed low in the water, her nose just over the surface. She could see the powerboat coming toward her in the distance. It was at least a football field away, but it wasn't moving all that fast. This boat obviously wasn't chasing after Marvelli. These guys were trawling the shore, looking for signs of Rispoli and the two phony FBI agents.

Loretta knew she couldn't stay where she was, out in the open, but she couldn't decide whether she should go back to the tiny island or head for the shore where Rispoli was. The distances were about the same, and she didn't trust Rispoli to sit still and wait for her, so she decided to go to the shore. She sucked in a deep breath and slipped under the surface.

Holding her breath, she opened her eyes and took a quick look, then closed them again because the salt water stung. As far as she could see, the way was clear. No haunted shipwrecks, sharks, killer whales, electric eels, or sea serpents. She tried to swallow the lump in her throat, wishing she hadn't just thought of sharks. With her eyes closed, she imagined great whites swarming all around her.

She started to swim, letting out some air through her mouth so that she wouldn't surface. Back in high school she'd had to swim the length of an Olympic-size pool underwater on one breath in order to pass her life-guard test. But that was almost fifteen years ago, and she hadn't done it since then. She still remembered how to do it, though. Let out some air so that you don't float. Take single deliberate strokes and get as much glide out of them as you could before you took another so as to conserve energy. Don't rush. Take your time.

But her chest already felt crushed. She wanted air, and she'd just started. She took another stroke and glided with her arms tucked in at her sides, trying to calm down and settle into it. But then she thought about sharks again, and she opened her eyes to check.

That's when her thoughts shifted from sharks to another predator—Brenda Hemingway. She remembered being inside that industrial clothes drier at the Pinebrook Women's Correctional Facility. Brenda had made her strip naked, then tied her up with electrical cord. She'd poked and prodded Loretta as if she were livestock, ridiculed her for being fat—even though Brenda herself couldn't fit into Loretta's clothes when she'd tried them on. Loretta would never forget Brenda dancing around her like a voodoo queen, her feet jammed into Loretta's pumps, banging the heels on the floor tiles and making little firecracker pops. It was as if she were getting the sacrifice ready for the slaughter.

Then all of a sudden Big Brenda hauled Loretta up by an arm and a leg and stuffed her into the drier. Loretta had screamed for mercy, but Brenda just laughed at her, her big pink tongue pulsating in her mouth like a bullfrog. The drier door slammed shut with a loud ping. Instantly Loretta couldn't breathe. She was curled up in a contorted fetal position, her throat constricted. Then the drier started to move, the gears grinding hard with the unaccustomed weight. She heard the propane burners firing up beneath her. Brenda's face was outside the round glass window, peering in at her. Loretta's stomach lurched as she started to tumble. She was hyperventilating. She couldn't breathe—

Loretta's chest felt as if it were going to explode. Her pounding heart was shaking her chest. She opened her eyes to prove to herself that she wasn't in the drier, but she could tell from the depth of the water that she was nowhere near the shore. She recalled that somewhere out here there were some big boulders that broke the surface. If she could find one, maybe she could hide behind it and go up for air. But she couldn't see any boulders anywhere near her, and when she looked straight up, she saw the dark bottom of a hull haloed by the sun looming over her like Jaws.

She had no air left. She had to surface before she passed out and drowned. Her arms and legs ached as she used what little strength she had left to propel her body up through the water. She couldn't get there fast enough, and when she finally made it, she sucked in as much air as she could, inhaling the water dripping down her face, coughing painfully, her lungs on fire.

Her eyes shot open. The side of the boat was just inches from her face. She expecting someone to start yelling at her, "You're under arrest," multiple gun barrels pointed down at her head.

But there was nothing.

The boat's engine was idling loudly, which must have drowned out her coughing. She fought to control her ragged breathing and stop panting.

She listened carefully and heard two male voices above her. "You see anything?" the higher voice asked.

"Nope," the low one said. "Ain't nothing here."

"Look close. We don't find them, there's gonna be hell to pay."

"There's already gonna be hell to pay. First time anybody's ever broken out of here. Darcy's gonna get his butt reamed for this."

"We're *all* gonna get our butts reamed. Keep looking."

They fell silent for a while. Loretta stayed still, silently treading water. They must have been looking over the other side of the boat, searching the shoreline. That's why they hadn't noticed her yet.

"Come on," the low voice suddenly said. "Let's move on. There's no one here."

The engines revved, and Loretta dipped under the surface, swimming down under the boat. When she thought she was deep enough, she looked back up and saw the boat's churning propellers moving away.

But now she was in a real bind. If she surfaced, the men on the boat would spot her. She had to swim underwater to one of those boulders so she could hide. She was exhausted and her arms and legs felt like jelly, but she had no choice. She had to force herself.

She took her first strokes, and all of a sudden she thought of coffee. She craved it so much she could taste it in her memory. If she had a real cup of coffee right now, she could do this. She needed caffeine. That's why she was so exhausted and disoriented. A little coffee would give her the energy, the edge, even the sense of direction she needed to do this.

She could smell the aromas in her mind. She kicked harder, gliding forward, bubbles streaming out of her nose, hands in front of her like Superman. She was flying though the air, searching for a cup of coffee, ready to dive-bomb the first espresso bar she found. She was so fixated on getting some coffee into her veins, she forgot where she was, and when she opened her eyes, she was shocked to see a boulder looming just a few feet in front of her. She looked down and saw bottom. It wasn't that deep here; she could probably stand up.

She quickly swam around the big rock. Her feet touched bottom as she cautiously rose to the surface, sucking in air as she coughed and blinked, pushing the wet hair off her forehead. She spotted the shore and got her bearings. Staying low, she peered around the rock to see where the boat was. It was far in the distance, chugging along close to shore. She stayed put and waited until it rounded a point and was out of sight.

She pushed off and swam for shore, standing up and walking when it got too shallow to swim. Her clothes were dripping. She wondered how the hell she was going to find Rispoli and where she was going to find a big piping-hot cup of coffee so she could dump it in his lap when she found him. Her shoes squished as she walked over the rocks. Immediately she went into the woods to get out of sight. Blinking back tears, she told herself she wasn't going to cry, even though she was right on the verge of it.

"How the hell did I get here?" she grumbled.

Everything had gone wrong. She'd just lost the government's most important witness against the mob. She and Marvelli were in deep doo-doo now. For all she knew, Marvelli was probably getting torpedoed to kingdom come right now, and if he wasn't, they'd eventually catch him and throw him in jail, and his sister-in-law Jennifer would come by to visit him, and he'd be so lonesome and vulnerable, he'd end up marrying her in one of those jailhouse ceremonies with periodic conjugal visits. And Loretta would probably end up back at the Pinebrook Women's Correctional Facility, sharing a cell with Brenda Hemingway.

She wrung out her hair and slapped her arm where a monster mosquito was helping himself to a transfusion. A second mosquito landed on her other arm, and she shook like a golden retriever to get them off, cursing them under her breath.

Then suddenly she smelled something that wasn't her wet clothes or the clean scent of pine. It was smoke, cigarette smoke. She trudged through the brush, trying to locate the source, walking under branches and swatting mosquitoes the whole way. When she came to a clearing, she found the smoker. Gus Rispoli was sitting on a bed of pine needles, leaning against the tree with his fingers linked behind his head, his ankles crossed, the ever-present cigarette dangling from his lips. Seven damp cigarettes were lined up by his side on a rock in the sun.

He raised one eyebrow. "So where were you?" he asked. "I've been waiting."

Back in Seattle Marvelli knocked on the door to Loretta's hotel room.

"Who is it?" Loretta called through the door.

"It's me."

He heard the bolt being thrown, but no one opened the door, so he let himself in. He did not find happy campers inside. Loretta was sitting on the bed, Rispoli at the table. They were both glaring at him. Loretta was still in the same clothes she'd gone swimming in, and she was scratching some whopper mosquito bites on her arms and neck. There was a particularly angry-looking bite on her cheek. Apparently she didn't trust Rispoli to behave while she took a shower.

Gus Rispoli was sitting at a table littered with foil and cellophane wrappers from candy bars, a stick of beef jerky, a cinnamon Danish, and a couple of packages of peanuts, as well as two empty Heineken cans and several nip bottles of Johnnie Walker Red. Most of the junk food he'd only tasted and left uneaten, but the booze he'd drained to the last drop. He didn't look drunk, though, just cranky.

"How come she says I can't get no room service?" Rispoli griped.

Loretta answered before Marvelli could respond. "I already told you, you can't. Don't ask again."

He ignored her and looked to Marvelli. "How come? All's I want is a steak and some coffee."

Loretta raised her voice. "I said no room service. You'll tip them off that we're up here."

Rispoli made a face and waved her off in disgust. He was used to first-class service whenever the feds took him out of My Blue Heaven.

"How're you guys doing here?" Marvelli asked. "You okay?" He hoped to clear the air a little.

"Oh, we're just peachy," Loretta said sarcastically. She grabbed some fresh clothes and headed for the bathroom. "I'm taking a shower," she announced, and slammed the door behind her.

Marvelli and Rispoli looked at each other.

"Hard woman," Rispoli said.

"Not really," Marvelli said. "Not when you get to know her."

"I don't think I wanna get that close."

Marvelli just shrugged. Whatever.

"So how'd you get rid of them guys in the cigarette boat?" Rispoli asked.

"I took your advice and hugged the shore. They thought they had me cornered in this little bay a couple of miles from where I left you off, but I managed to squeeze through a strait where they couldn't fit. I ran like hell and lost them before they could catch up."

"See? I told you," Rispoli said.

Marvelli could see that he was the kind of guy who had to be right all the time.

"See?" Rispoli repeated. "I was right. Wasn't I?"

"Yeah, I guess you were." Marvelli took off his jacket and hung it over an empty chair.

Rispoli shook one of the beer cans to see if there was any left. There wasn't. "So how about that room service?"

"Don't bust my chops, Gus. Loretta already told you."

"Aaahh, that's a load. How's that gonna tip anybody off that I'm here?"

"Hmmm?" Marvelli wasn't paying attention. He was listening to the sound of the shower through the bathroom door, thinking about Loretta shampooing her hair. He liked her hair, especially when she wore it loose.

Rispoli was getting steamed, waiting for an answer. "I said, how's a friggin' steak and a pot of coffee gonna give me away? How?"

"Let's not take any chances, okay, Gus? Sammy hits you, I may as well shoot myself for what the feds'll do to me."

Not to mention Loretta, he thought.

"So who's this Sammy kid again? I don't think I ever heard of him." Gus was posturing. After him, there were no hit men worth mentioning. According to him, they were all street punks.

"Sammy Teitelbaum," Marvelli reminded him. "He's connected with Taffy Demaggio."

"Directly connected?" Rispoli seemed skeptical.

"No, through Tino Mazelli. The bookie from Newark?"

"Yeah, yeah. I know him. He's a flea. And those two nephews of his should've been abortions if you ask me."

You're right about that, Marvelli thought. He glanced at the bathroom door and remembered how Larry and Jerry had hassled Loretta. More than hassled. The sons of bitches would've raped her if they'd had the chance. He clenched his jaw, a flash of pure hate blinding him for a split second.

Rispoli was shaking his head, his eyes crinkled tight. "This Sammy Teitel—whatever his name is. I don't know if I know him. He got a nickname or something?"

Besides Dirtbag? Marvelli thought.

"No, I don't think he's got any nicknames," Marvelli said. He heard Loretta turning off the shower.

Rispoli shrugged as if Sammy didn't matter. "So how about that steak?" he asked again.

"Change the tune, will ya, Gus? You're not getting any room service, so just stop asking."

"So what'm I supposed to do? Live off peanuts and Ding Dongs? Forget about it. I need nourishment. I got low blood sugar. I gotta eat real food, not this crap." He brushed the wrappers onto the floor.

Marvelli glanced down at the mess on the carpet. "I suppose you think you're getting maid service, too? Think again, Gus." Marvelli stared Rispoli in the eye until he bent over and started picking up the wrappers.

"There, you happy?" Rispoli snarled. "Maybe I should cook, too. It's probably the only way I'm gonna keep from getting sick around here."

"You're breaking my heart, Gus," Marvelli mumbled as he listened to Loretta moving around in the bathroom. He imagined her combing out her long wet hair. "So, Gus, tell me. If you were Sammy, and you were planning to whack a guy in your position, how would you do it?"

"How the hell should I know?"

"You're a hit man, Gus. You must have some ideas."

Rispoli rolled his eyes under his overhanging brow, like the crab that he was. "Why the hell should I tell you?"

"Why? Because it might help us keep you alive."

Us, too, Marvelli thought, glancing back at the bathroom door.

"Depends," Rispoli grumbled.

"Depends on what?"

"How the customer wants it done."

"The customer being Taffy, you mean."

"Taffy or whoever. Some guys want it done neat; some guys like it messy, lots of blood and suffering. Some guys make special requests."

"What kind of requests?"

Rispoli glanced at the bathroom door, then leaned in close to Marvelli and whispered. "Body parts cut off and stuck in the vic's mouth, up the—"

Marvelli interrupted before he could go on. "I get the idea. So how would Taffy want you done?"

"Messy. He's a sick pup, that Taffy. He'll want it to hurt. Bad."

"So how would he do it? Hire a bunch of guys to barge in and beat the crap out of you?" Marvelli glanced at the door, wondering if he should get up and double lock it.

Rispoli shrugged. "Maybe."

"You seem pretty calm about it."

The hit man shrugged again. "A guy'll do it any way he thinks he can get away with. Me, I would never do it in a hotel if I could avoid it."

"Why not?"

"Too many people around. You're gonna do three people messy, you're gonna make noise. Can't be helped. Even if you're quiet, the vics never are. They cry, they scream, they carry on. . . . *That's* what makes it messy."

Marvelli nodded, feeling a little queasy. He was trying hard not to think about a team of hit men breaking in to this room and doing a job on him, Loretta, and Rispoli. And Loretta wasn't even dressed, he thought. No telling what they'd do to a naked woman, the sick bastards. He wondered if Sammy was really that sick. He could be, Marvelli thought. Besides, in the heat of the moment people do unspeakable things. And if those people are getting paid for it, they'll really go to town.

He stared at the bathroom door. It was too quiet in there, he thought. "Loretta?" he called out. "You okay in there?"

"What?" she yelled through the door. "I can't hear you."

"Never mind," he yelled back a little louder. He looked at Rispoli and lowered his voice: "Somebody told me once that the real pros won't kill women. Is that true?"

Rispoli gave him a look, annoyed with such a stupid question. "If you're getting paid to kill someone, you just do it. Doesn't matter who it is. Some guys'll do their friggin' mothers if the price is right."

"Yeah . . . that's what I thought." Marvelli's stomach was doing backflips. "Tell me something, Gus. What if—?"

Suddenly the cell phone in Marvelli's pocket started to ring. Marvelli took it out, pulled out the antenna, and pressed the answer button. "Hello?"

"Mr. Marvelli." That's all the person on the other end said, his oily voice oozing out of the phone. Marvelli recognized the voice immediately. It was Taffy Demaggio. But how the hell did he get Marvelli's number? From Tino maybe? Marvelli just listened, waiting for Taffy to state his business.

"Short and sweet," Taffy finally said. "Here's the deal. I've got two lovely ladies here with me. One's named Jennifer. The other one's Annette. Outstanding women, both of them. If you'd like to see them again, you give me Gus, and we'll make an exchange."

Marvelli's face was hot, and his throat was tight. Exactly who was holding them? he wanted to know. Jerry and Larry? God forbid.

"You don't have to answer now. Take a few minutes and think about it. I'll get back to you." Taffy hung up.

Rispoli's brow was furrowed. "What'sa matta? You look like a ghost. Who was that?"

"Taffy," Marvelli said. His hands were shaking.

"Crap!" Rispoli said, bouncing out of his chair. "We gotta get outta here. Fast. Taffy must know where we are."

"You may be right." Marvelli stood up, too. "But where should we go?"

"What do you mean, where should we go? You're running this show here. Don't you have any other safe houses in this town, a backup team, stuff like that?"

Marvelli shook his head.

"You gotta be kidding me." Rispoli was stunned. He was being protected by amateurs.

"Okay, okay, don't panic." But Marvelli was panicking. Larry and Jerry with Jennifer and Annette? Oh, God! And what about Taffy? He was no angel when it came to women. He'd strangled that woman in upstate New York.

Rispoli ran to the little refrigerator and grabbed some beer nuts and beef jerky, stuffing them into his pockets. "Okay, let's go," he said, slamming the refrigerator shut and heading for the door.

"Wait a minute, wait a minute," Marvelli said. "I have to think."

The bathroom door opened halfway, and Loretta popped her head out. Her hair was wet, combed straight back. She only had a towel wrapped around her.

"What's going on out here?" she said with a disapproving frown.

"Come on! We gotta go," Rispoli said. He was waiting by the door, practically jumping out of his skin.

Loretta looked at Marvelli. "What's he talking about?"

Marvelli was trying to keep it together, but all he could think about was Taffy's beastie boys coming through the bathroom window and jumping Loretta from behind. "We gotta go, Loretta," he said. "Come on. Hurry up."

"Go? Go where?"

Marvelli wrinkled his brow. "That's a good question." He looked to Rispoli. "You got any ideas?"

The hit man rolled his eyes.

"Greetings," Alan Winslow the computer nerd said. He was holding his apartment door open, trying his best to be friendly, but he was having a hard time making eye contact. "Welcome to my humble abode."

Loretta sighed as she walked through the door with Marvelli and Rispoli in tow. She was already regretting that they'd called Alan.

When they were all inside, Alan just stood there, looking big and gawky, like Chewbacca with a shave. Loretta took in the apartment, which was a third-floor walk-up a few blocks from Volunteer Park. It was a cramped and cluttered two-bedroom that looked like the kind of place where mad bombers hatched diabolical plots in the movies. Books were jammed haphazardly into the built-in bookshelves that ran along one wall of the living room. Two bone-dry spider plants hung from rusty nails over the windows where they'd been rotisseried to death in the full sunlight that poured through the dirty glass. The gray velveteen couch was tattered and dusty, the cushions flat from overuse. It looked like elephant roadkill. There were newspapers and magazines all over the floor, as well as coffee cups—dozens of them, their bottoms stained with the dried sediments of what they'd last held. Alan apparently just left them wherever he finished his coffee, and some of them looked like artifacts from a mummy's tomb. Loretta peered through a doorway into one of the bedrooms and noticed three computer screens burning brightly. Two long folding tables and a tall rack of chrome baker's shelves were crammed with electronic equipment. Alan had more computer stuff in there than an air-traffic-control tower.

Loretta studied Alan's profile as Marvelli tried to make chitchat with him. Maybe Alan really was a mad bomber, she thought.

"Hey, thanks for taking us in," Marvelli said to Alan.

"Sure, no problem. It's great to have company." He snuck a glance at Loretta, and she saw him doing it, which made her very depressed. She knew a crush when she saw one.

"This is Gus," Marvelli said, drawing Rispoli into the conversation and purposely leaving his last name out.

"Hi, Gus," Alan said.

Rispoli just grunted, his eyes darting around the living room. He was probably checking the place out, looking for something he could steal.

"I figured out the sleeping arrangements," Alan said eagerly. "You guys can take my room. I'll sleep on the couch. And there's a futon in the computer room that you can use . . . Loretta." His voice trailed off as he said her name, too bashful to say it out loud. Loretta imagined him pivoting on his big toe with a bouquet of daisies in his hand as he looked at the ground and tried to work up the nerve to tell her what was in his heart.

Oh, God, spare me, she thought, feeling both guilty and repulsed at the same time. Alan was a sweet guy, but come on, he was no girl's fantasy.

Alan took a tentative half step closer to her. "They won't bother you," he said. "They don't make any noise."

"Excuse me?" She couldn't figure out what he was talking about.

"My computers," he said. "They only make a little noise, just when they're backing up, that's all. But I'll turn them off if you want."

"No, no, that's all right," she said. He was letting her sleep with his prized possessions. Maybe this wasn't such a good idea. No telling what sexual fantasies he'd have thinking about her being in the same room with his beloved computers. And he'd just be a few feet away, sleeping out here on the dead elephant. This was a bad arrangement, she decided. Why not put Rispoli in with the motherboards, and she and Marvelli could share Alan's room? That would be nice.

Fat chance, she thought, smirking to herself. Never in a million years. First of all, they couldn't let Rispoli out of their sight. And second, she and Marvelli—

She let out a long sigh. It wasn't even worth thinking about.

Suddenly Loretta detected the scent of fresh coffee, and she imagined a coffeemaker dripping out its hot nectar into a clear glass pot. She wanted a cup so badly. The fatigue she was feeling wasn't as bad as it had been, and she wasn't having headaches anymore, but she still had the cravings, especially when she smelled it. Staying here was going to be a problem if Alan mainlined the stuff.

Rispoli wandered off into the computer room, and Alan looked very concerned, following right after him. He obviously didn't want anyone touching his computers.

When they were out of the room, Loretta whispered to Marvelli, "Is this gonna work out?"

He shrugged. "It's got to. Where else can we go?"

"How about another hotel?"

He made a face and fluttered his hand. "Too risky. I thought about going to Jennifer's apartment, but Taffy probably knows where that is. She's listed in the book."

Loretta nodded in agreement. "Anyway, how would we have gotten in?"

"I've got a key."

"You've got a key to her apartment?" Loretta tried to be nonchalant about it.

"Yeah, Jennifer gave it to me. You know, just in case."

"In case of what?" Loretta asked.

"You know, an emergency."

What kind of emergency? Loretta wondered jealously. Jennifer was definitely after him—Loretta was convinced.

Through the doorway, Loretta could see Alan showing Rispoli how his computers worked. Alan was sitting at one of the long tables with Rispoli standing over his shoulder. The hit man looked curious but skeptical.

"What're you—I mean, we—gonna do about Jennifer and Annette?" Loretta asked.

Marvelli shook his head. "I don't know. If we go to the police and tell them the whole story, the feds could get wind of it and come after us. But Taffy is a ruthless SOB. If we don't do something, then Jennifer and Annette might get . . ." He didn't have to say the rest.

"How about if we offer him a deal?" Loretta suggested.

Let him keep Jennifer, she thought.

"What kind of deal?" Marvelli seemed dubious.

"Tell him we'll make the exchange. Jennifer and Annette for Rispoli. That's the only way to flush out Sammy."

"But what about *him*?" Marvelli nodded toward Rispoli. "We can't use him as bait. He'll be dead the minute they see his face."

Loretta shrugged. "We'll just have to figure something out so it doesn't get that far."

"Talk like that makes me nervous, Loretta. I'd rather have a definite plan."

"You got one?"

"No, but I think—"

Suddenly Marvelli's cell phone rang. His eyes widened as he pulled it out and stared at it for a moment without answering it.

Loretta felt a bolt of panic shoot through her stomach. She wasn't worried about them screwing up; she was afraid of what might happen if this all worked out and they ended up saving Jennifer. Would the whole experience drive her closer to Marvelli, her big hero?

Marvelli flipped the phone open and pressed the answer button. "Hello," he said abruptly.

Loretta pulled on his wrist and put her head next to his so that she could listen in. She could feel his hair against hers.

"Mr. Marvelli. I think we should talk."

"So talk, Taffy," Marvelli said.

"In person, I mean."

"Why?"

"Because I like to deal with people face-to-face."

"How do I know you're not trying to set me up?"

"You *don't* know."

"Then why should I meet you?"

"Because you like these lovely ladies I've got here with me and you'd like to see them again."

Marvelli didn't answer. "Where?" he asked.

"The aquarium."

"Where's that?"

"I dunno. Down by the water somewhere. Ask around."

"When?"

"Half an hour. Don't make me wait."

"How—?"

Taffy hung up.

Loretta looked Marvelli in the eye. She was worried. "You're not gonna go, are you?"

"Do I have a choice?"

She didn't want him to go. The twins would be there. Sammy Teitelbaum, too. She was afraid of what they might do.

Marvelli called through the doorway into the computer room. "Alan? How do I get to the aquarium from here?"

Before Alan could answer, Rispoli rushed back into the living room. "You gonna go out?" he asked. "Bring me back something to eat. A steak sandwich. Well done."

Loretta got in his face. "Cool it, Gus."

He frowned and looked hurt. "But I'm hungry. Ain't you ever gonna feed me?"

Loretta closed her eyes and counted to ten before she murdered him. Her headache was back. She needed coffee so bad.

Special Agent Veronica Springer stood in the watery shadows of the walkway that encircled the Seattle Aquarium's four-thousand-gallon tank. She was watching Marvelli, who was standing below her in front of the tank, scanning the crowds of tourists as they ogled the fish, anxiously looking for Taffy Demaggio. Behind him, a school of silvery tuna abruptly changed direction, then changed direction again as a snaggled-toothed, eight-foot tiger shark glided into their path. The shark's eyes were empty and emotionless.

As Springer watched Marvelli, her stomach churned acid. She was thinking about Taffy and how dumb he was. Kidnapping those two women was a monumentally stupid move. She could've killed him when he'd told her about it. She was so upset, she felt like eating something, *anything*.

But it was nervous eating that had gotten her into trouble before and made her as big as a house. She quickly reached into the pocket of her blazer for her diet pills and shook one out of the bottle, popping it into her mouth and swallowing it dry as she started walking toward Marvelli.

So stupid, she kept thinking to herself. Incredibly stupid.

Wavy blue-green light slithered across the carpeting as she moved closer to Marvelli. She slowed her pace, wondering how she should handle him. Thank God she just happened to call Taffy when she did, and thank God he'd told her about the women and meeting Marvelli. These women must be good-looking, Springer assumed. Why else would Taffy agree to stay put and let her handle this mess? If the women had been dogs, he would've come himself and really screwed things up. This was one time that she was grateful that Taffy's brains were in his pants.

"Officer Marvelli," she said, coming up behind him.

He whipped around and stared at her, obviously confused by her presence here.

"I happened to be driving by when I saw you coming in. Where's Rispoli?"

He kept staring at her. That stony Italian look of suspicion was petrified on his face. They all had it—Taffy, Rispoli, Marvelli, all of them.

"What do you mean, you were just driving by?"

"I've been waiting to hear from you," she said firmly. "Where's Rispoli?" Always trump indignation with more indignation. Don't let him feel that he has an issue, and don't back down.

"What, were you following me?" he said. "How'd you know I'd be here?"

She stared him in the eye. "I want to know where Rispoli is."

He didn't flinch. "I'm supposed to be meeting Taffy Demaggio here. You been talking to him?"

Acid rampaged through Springer's stomach like white water. Deny, she told herself. Don't back down.

She lowered her voice. "If you don't tell me where Rispoli is right now, I'm putting you under arrest."

"Oh, yeah? I'd like to see you try."

Testosterone, she thought, *the spaghetti sauce of the Italian male sausage.*

"Where is Rispoli?" she repeated. She unbuttoned her blazer as if she were going to go for her gun. She had to call his bluff.

But Marvelli was unmoved. "Demaggio's got my sister-in-law and my mother-in-law. Where are *they*?"

"How should I know?"

He just stared at her. He didn't have to say that he believed she knew exactly where the women were and that she was in cahoots with Taffy. Which was true, but so what? Marvelli was a minor player in this opera. He didn't matter. She kept telling herself that. Marvelli was a spear carrier; she was the diva. He had to shut up; this was her aria.

"Look," she said, "you seem to be under some kind of misconception that I'm in league with Taffy Demaggio—"

"You saying you're not?" he interrupted.

"You're damn right I'm saying I'm not," she shot back. "Now, if you want my help in getting your relatives back, you had better change your tune and stop insulting me."

They stared at each other with venom in their eyes, neither one willing to back down. All of a sudden she began to feel a little more awake. The diet pills were kicking in.

Neither of them said anything. She wasn't sure what to throw at him next. Her stomach was in agony. Out of the corner of her eye, she could see that tiger shark circling the tank again. *Priorities,* she kept thinking. She had to get her priorities straight. Marvelli and his tubby partner were nothing to her. They were expendable. They were just a nuisance. She had to get rid of them.

But how?

The shark was gliding very slowly. Springer glanced at its eye. There was nothing there, no emotion, no intention. That's how she had to be, she decided. Focused, lethal in and of herself.

What was the goal? she asked herself.

Killing Rispoli so that Taffy flips, and get the credit, she thought.

But how do we do it?

Let Taffy handle it. He has his people on it. That's his part of the deal.

But what about Marvelli and what's-her-name?

Use them.

How?

Let them take the rap.

How?!

Rispoli's their responsibility. If he gets killed under their watch, they should take the blame. In fact, they probably will take the blame because Taffy's hit man is Marvelli's brother-in-law. It'll look like a conspiracy, a family affair. The parole officers from New Jersey conspired with Sammy Teitelbaum to kill Rispoli.

Why would they do that?

Money. Why else? Sammy offered them cash for Rispoli's whereabouts. It makes perfect sense.

She thought about it for a second. *If Marvelli and his partner take the rap for Rispoli's murder, that takes the heat off Taffy.*

Just one problem, though, she thought.

"Where's Rispoli?" she asked Marvelli.

"Where's Jennifer and Annette?" Marvelli responded.

The tiger shark slid by. It was just three feet away. Springer didn't dare break eye contact with Marvelli to look at it, but she could feel the shark looking at her. She took it as a sign of support.

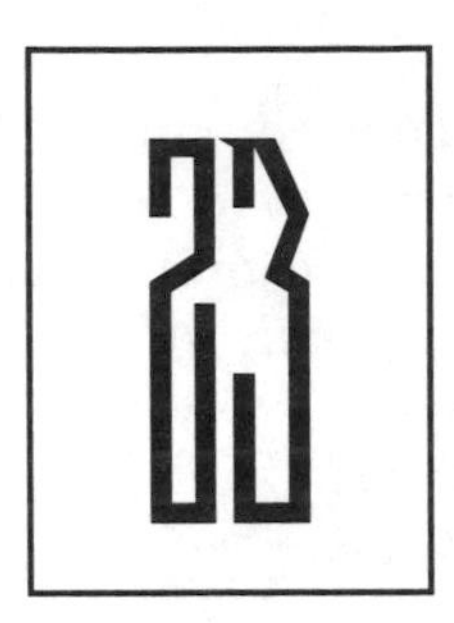

Loretta glanced at her watch, then gazed at the oversized computer screen in front of her. She was in the computer room at Alan Winslow's apartment. Alan was sitting next to her, working the keyboard. Rispoli was on the futon, lying on his back with his eyes closed and his fingers linked over his belly.

The computer screen was a patchwork quilt of open widows, so many that Loretta couldn't focus on any one of them. None of it made any sense to her. "I thought the Internet was supposed to be fun," she said to Alan.

Alan's face fell. "Y-y-you're not having fun?" he stammered.

"Well . . . I mean, what is all this?" Loretta realized that he was trying to impress her, and she didn't want to hurt his feelings, but this was incredibly boring. She sighed, wondering why all the Mr. Wrongs were attracted to her. But she felt bad thinking that because Alan was decent enough—he was just . . . boring.

No offense, Alan, but I can do better, she said to herself. *I can definitely do better. I hope.*

She glanced at her watch again, wishing Marvelli would get back soon. She wished a lot of things about Marvelli, but right now she just wished he'd save her from Alan's guided tour of the Net.

Alan moved the mouse, clicking here and there, closing windows and opening new ones. "Let me show you something really neat. Have you ever used Java?"

She just looked at him. "Yes. Once upon a time. A long time ago." She could've used a cup of java just to stay awake.

"Well, you'll like this," Alan said eagerly. "I mean, I think you will. I mean—"

"Hey!" An unfamiliar voice from the doorway startled them both. A scrawny guy in his late twenties with bad posture, a buzz cut, and black horn-rimmed glasses with tinted lenses was standing in the doorway. He was holding two big black automatics, one trained on Loretta and Alan, the other on Rispoli, who was fast asleep on the futon.

Loretta recognized him right away. It was Sammy Teitelbaum. *Oh crap!* she thought.

"Hands where I can see 'em," Sammy said. "You know, just like in the movies."

Worry lines scored Alan's forehead. "H-h-how'd you get in here?" he demanded.

"Through the door," Sammy said. "You ought to get a better lock."

"This is Seattle, not N-N-New York," Alan complained.

Sammy shrugged. "*C'est la vie,* baby."

"So how'd you find us?" Loretta asked. She wanted to get him talking before he killed all three of them. Her gun was in a fabric holster Velcroed to her ankle under her pant leg. If she had any hope of getting to it, Sammy would have to be distracted. Of course, with him carrying two guns, she'd have to drop him in one shot or suffer the consequences. She was a good shot, but she wondered if she was good enough. "How'd you know we were here?" she asked, consciously keeping her hands in her lap.

"I've been following you and Frankie since you first got here," he said with a proud grin. "I was waiting for you two at the airport."

"Congratulations. You're very conscientious," she said.

"Thank you." He seemed genuinely grateful for the compliment even though she didn't mean it that way. "You know, I even followed you out to My Blue Heaven."

"We didn't see anyone following us," Loretta said.

"Well, actually I was already there waiting for you. In a sailboat."

Loretta's eyes shot open. Springer! she thought angrily. That little bitch. She's been feeding him information.

"Who told you where My Blue Heaven is?" Loretta demanded. "A woman FBI agent named Springer maybe?"

Sammy shrugged. "Never heard of her. Taffy told me where to go."

And Springer must've told him, Loretta thought. That dirty little so-and-so.

Rispoli stirred from his sleep and sat up on his elbows. Sammy's head snapped around as he honed in on his primary target. Rispoli glared up at the young hit man, blinking his eyes to get them to focus. He was still half-asleep and grouchier than ever. "What the hell you gonna do with those things?" he grunted. He sounded like a frog from the Bronx.

Sammy glanced at his guns, thrown by the question. "What do you think I'm gonna do? I'm gonna blow you away."

"You're gonna blow your nose, that's what you're gonna do."

Sammy was insulted. "What're you talking about?"

Rispoli made a sour face. "What the hell's wrong with you? You don't bring guns like that to a hit. You'll make so much noise, the cops'll be here in no time."

"You don't know what you're talking about. You gotta show power when you do a hit. You gotta establish dominance. Show the person who's getting whacked that you mean business, that you're not gonna take any crap."

"You mean you talk to 'em?" Rispoli was totally disgusted with Sammy. "What kind of person are you? You never talk to 'em. You bring a little gun—a twenty-two or a twenty-five—and you just shoot 'em. Period. No talking."

"I'm talking to you now, ain't I?" Sammy said.

"Which just goes to show what a jerk you are."

"Oh, I'm a jerk? I'm holding a gun on you, and I'm the jerk. This just goes to show what kind of an idiot *you* are. No wonder Taffy wants you dead."

Rispoli pressed his lips together and shook his head. "What the hell's wrong with you? You *never* mention the client's name, not when there's other people around." He pointed at Loretta and Alan. "Now you gotta kill them, too. You know that, don'tcha?"

"I know that. What do you think, I'm stupid? I'll get to them." Sammy shook one of his guns at Loretta and Alan, who cringed and covered his face with his arms. Loretta stayed still, conscious of her hands in her lap and the gun on her ankle. Her heart was hammering in her chest, but she wasn't showing it.

"So whattaya waiting for?" Rispoli yelled. "We gonna talk all day, maybe have a little tea party? Come on, get on with it. I hate people who drag their asses."

Sammy's teeth were clenched. Rispoli was getting under his skin. "I'm not dragging my ass, old man."

"Who you calling old? Me? I'll kick your ass any day."

"Oh, yeah?" Sammy took an abrupt step toward Rispoli, jabbing his guns into the space between them.

Loretta decided it was time to act. While Sammy was focused on Rispoli, she reached down for her gun, pulling up her pant leg and ripping the Velcro apart as she swiveled around in the desk chair at the same time.

But the Velcro was stronger than she expected, and she fumbled with the holster. Suddenly she felt cold steel pressing into her scalp.

"Bad move," Sammy said. "Take off the gun and throw it in the corner. And don't try anything dumb."

She had no choice but to do what he said, bending over and sliding the gun along the hardwood floor until it banged against the floorboard.

"Now sit up straight," he ordered, "and put your hands on top of your head."

She sat up and linked her fingers over her head. Sammy was standing over her, his arms stretched as far as they could, one gun on Loretta, the other on Rispoli. His nostrils were flaring, and his bare arms were tight and sinewy as he whipped his head back and forth, making sure neither of them did anything strange. Out of the corner of her eye, she saw Alan. He was so jittery he looked like a blur.

Loretta tried to control her breathing so she could calm down and talk straight. "Sammy," she said, swallowing hard, "can we talk about this for a minute?"

He shook his head and flashed a tight grin. "I'm afraid not, honey bunny."

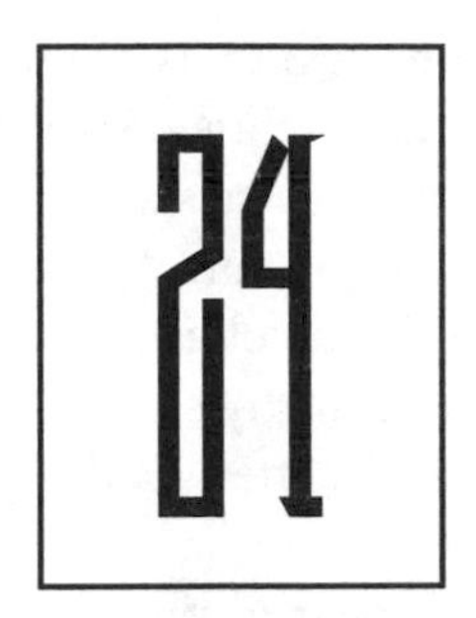

"Come on, Sammy. Just hear me out," Loretta said.

Sammy's arm was ramrod stiff, the gun motionless in her face. "No-o-o-o-o," he said, dragging it out as if he were blowing a smoke ring. The guy was as nutsy as Marvelli had said.

"Whattaya talking to him for?" Rispoli shouted. "He's a dummy."

"Will you shut up!" Loretta snapped. "You're just making this worse."

Sammy grinned, looking at Rispoli sideways. "Nyah, nyah, nyah-nyah, nyah," Sammy taunted, happy to see his target being reprimanded.

"I just want to tell you one thing," Loretta said to Sammy, stalling for time.

"I don't want to hear one thing," Sammy replied. "I don't want to hear *any* things. Not out of you."

Alan was still sitting next to Loretta, his trembling hands clenched over his head.

"Hey, you wanna see something really neat?" Sammy asked him. "Get on-line and find www dot samtheman—that's all one word—dot com."

Alan gulped. "What's that?" he asked.

"My web site."

"You've got a web site?" Alan asked in disbelief.

"Hey, why not? I've got a business. I've got to advertize." Sammy wiggled one of his automatics at Alan. "Go ahead. Get on-line. WWW dot samtheman dot com."

Alan swiveled around in his chair, got on-line, and typed out the address. After a minute Sammy's web site started to materialize on screen. "Had Enough?" the headline said. "Why Not Just Eliminate Your Problem(s)?"

A picture of a coffin appeared under the headline.

Alan scrolled down to the text. "Have it your way," it said. "I'll do it any way you want. Your wish is my command. Custom work is my specialty. Competitive rates and all work is guaranteed. Disappearances available upon request for an additional fee. If you're finally fed up, contact me at samtheman@firewall.com."

Alan's hands were rattling the keyboard he was so nervous.

"Real killers don't take out ads," Rispoli grumbled from across the room.

"Oh, yeah?" Sammy widened his eyes at Rispoli. "I've gotten jobs off that web site. Good ones."

"You wouldn't know a good one if it bit you in the ass."

"This is a good one," Sammy replied smugly.

"Yeah? How much is Taffy paying you?"

"Plenty."

"How much?"

"Thirty grand."

"Ha! Chump change!" Rispoli said. "When I was working, I didn't leave the house for less than fifty." Loretta was shocked to see Rispoli so happy. She didn't think that face was capable of smiling.

"Yeah, but there are bonuses with this one," Sammy said.

"Bonuses? What bonuses? What's he giving you? Blue Cross and Blue Shield?"

Sammy started to reply, then changed his mind. He relaxed his face and just shrugged. "Believe what you want to believe, old man. No matter how you cut it, your time's up. Meter expired." He squinted one eye and sighted down the barrel of the automatic aimed at Rispoli.

"Wait!" Loretta blurted.

"Why?" Sammy asked calmly, his attention still focused on Rispoli who was glaring at his executioner like an unrepentant crab.

"You don't know the whole story, Sammy."

"I don't need to know any more stories. I *am* the story."

Loretta was breathing hard. Sammy was going to do it. She glanced at her gun on the floor against the wall, but it was too far away.

"Say good-bye, Gus," Sammy said with a chuckle.

Loretta glanced at Alan, but he wasn't going to be any help. He was shaking like a garbage bag full of Jell-O.

Sammy lowered his barrel and took aim at Rispoli's chest, carefully picking his spot.

"Wait!" Loretta shouted. It was time to play her ace. "Taffy's got Jennifer," she said.

Sammy froze for a second, looking from Rispoli to Loretta. Slowly he lowered the gun on Rispoli and raised the one aimed at Loretta, turning his head around to face her. The look of contained rage on his face was terrifying. "What're you talking about?"

Loretta forced herself to get the words out coherently. "Taffy Demaggio kidnapped your wife and your mother-in-law—"

"*Ex*-mother-in-law," Sammy corrected.

"Taffy wants Gus," she continued. "He wants to trade the women for him. You can't kill him, Sammy."

Sammy's face was suddenly an awful shade of gray, and Rispoli was laughing so hard he almost rolled off the futon. "Some contract," Rispoli said between snorts. "Taffy's trying to screw you, my friend. He trades for me, then he kills me himself, and there goes your payday, Sammy-boy. I hope you haven't spent those thirty Gs yet." Rispoli was laughing so hard he could hardly speak.

But Loretta stayed focused on Sammy's face. The man was crestfallen, but he wasn't putting down his guns.

"Look, Sammy," she said, piecing together a plan on the fly, "let's work together on this. We'll help you get Jennifer back. Annette, too. Just put the guns away."

Sammy's hands were limp, but his fingers were still on the triggers. Loretta wasn't even sure that he'd heard her.

"Jennifer," he breathed with a catch in his voice. "My Jennifer . . ."

Loretta's heart went out to him, but all she could think was that if Sammy rescued Jennifer, she might get back together with him and stop buzzing around Marvelli. It was a hell of a thing to think right now, but she couldn't help it. She didn't want Marvelli getting together with Jennifer.

"Hey! Hey!" Rispoli barked. "You, Mr. Hit Man, snap out of it. You ain't gonna save your wife with tears, big boy."

Sammy could barely raise his voice above a whisper. "What're you saying?"

"What I'm saying is, if we put our heads together, maybe we can take care of this Taffy situation. If you're for real, that is, which I'm not yet convinced of."

Sammy was squinting, trying to understand. "You saying we should do Taffy?"

"Sure. Why not? He ain't doing me any good alive. And who knows what he's doing with your wife? You know how he is with broads."

"Shut up!" Sammy shouted. "Just shut up!"

Rispoli showed his palms in conciliation. "No offense, pal. But you obviously know what I'm talking about."

Sammy's teeth were clenched, and his brow was beaded with sweat.

"So whattaya think?" Rispoli said. "You wanna do it or not? It's up to you."

"I . . ." Sammy scratched his head with the butt of one of the automatics. "I don't know. I need to think."

"Yeah, well, don't think too long," Rispoli said. "Taffy's not gonna sit still waiting for you."

Loretta wished Rispoli weren't so blunt. Sammy still had his fingers on those triggers.

Sammy was kneading his temples with the butts of his guns. "I wish I had a cup of coffee," he moaned.

"I'll make a pot," Alan quickly volunteered, springing up from his seat.

"I'll go with you," Rispoli said ominously, getting up from the futon. "Just in case you decide to call nine-one-one." He followed Alan out of the room.

Sammy flopped down onto the futon, his face crumpling as if he were about to burst into tears.

Loretta felt awful for him. She wanted to do something for him, but she didn't know what.

"Jennifer," he moaned. "Jennifer."

"They're making coffee," she said, not knowing what else to say.

"Jennifer," he whispered desperately, his eyes squeezed shut.

A lump formed in Loretta's throat as she blinked back tears of her own. "And make some decaf, too," she called out to the kitchen. She needed something.

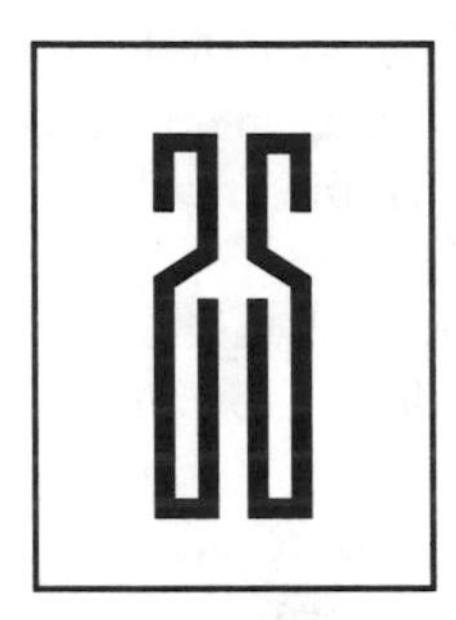

Marvelli was still stewing over Special Agent Springer showing up at the aquarium as he climbed the worn marble steps to Alan Winslow's apartment. He was convinced Springer was dirty, but how dirty? Was she just doing the typical fed thing, trying to run the show so that she could take all the credit in the end? Or did it go deeper than that? Could she really be working for Taffy? And if she was, why?

Marvelli rounded the bannister and headed for Alan's door at the rear of the building. He knocked twice out of courtesy, then twisted the knob and let himself in. There was no one in the living room, but he could hear voices coming from the computer room.

"No, no, no," he could hear Gus Rispoli saying. "That's crap. It'll never work."

"Sure, it will. All we need is a good strong tranquilizer, like the stuff they use on rhinos, and an umbrella. You put the tranquilizer in a syringe and attach it to the end of the umbrella. When we see Taffy out on the street, we stick him in the butt with the syringe, and in two minutes he'll be out like a light. I'm telling you, this works. Back in the seventies, an East German spy used poison in an umbrella to kill this British guy. In London I think it was. I read about it in a book."

"You know what you can do with your damn books, don't you?" Rispoli snarled.

Marvelli walked through the doorway and his eyes shot open when he saw Sammy. He thought he'd recognized that nutball's voice.

Marvelli instinctively reached inside his jacket for his gun but felt nothing but hip. His gun was in the trunk of the rental car. He never liked carrying a weapon and seldom did. Besides, he was a lousy shot.

"Loretta!" he said in a stage whisper as he pointed at Sammy. "That's him. Get your gun."

Loretta waved him off. "It's okay," she said. "Calm down."

Marvelli gave her a look. What did she mean, it was okay? It wasn't okay. It was Sammy!

"Hey, Frankie, how ya doing?" Sammy stood up and extended his hand. "It's been a long time." He took Marvelli's hand and started pumping it.

Marvelli looked at Loretta. "Where am I? The Twilight Zone?"

"Yeah, I know," Sammy said. "It's weird, isn't it? I mean, I was supposed to be killing this guy over here"—he jerked his thumb at Rispoli—"and now we're working together. Life is strange, isn't it?"

Marvelli tightened his grip on his ex-brother-in-law's hand. He wasn't going to let him go.

"Hey, chill out, man. You're hurting me. I work with that hand." Sammy tried to pull out of Marvelli's grip, but Marvelli was too strong.

Marvelli's expression was grim. "Somebody explain to me what's going on," he said.

"Excuse me." Alan popped his head in through the doorway. "Regular or decaf?" he asked Marvelli.

"What?"

"Coffee? You want regular or decaf? Or would you rather have tea?"

Marvelli shook his head in confusion. "I don't know. Regular."

"Milk and sugar?"

"Sure."

"You got it. I'm just gonna run down to the bakery and get some tarts. They make great tarts. I already told everybody else." Alan raced out into the hallway and out the front door.

"Tarts?" Marvelli looked at Loretta. "What the hell is he talking about?"

"He was raving about the tarts," she said matter-of-factly. "Best tarts in the world. Raspberry, lemon, and pecan."

"Pecan?" Marvelli loosened his grip on Sammy's hand. He loved pecan pie.

Sammy yanked his hand away, working his sore fingers and knuckles. "I forgot how strong you were," Sammy muttered. "Anyway," he said, "why don't you sit down, Frankie? Maybe you can help us out here. We're trying to figure out the best way to get Jennifer and Annette back. We thought about using Gus here for the trade, just the way Taffy wants. Gus could hide a little gun on his body and then take out Taffy soon as he gets the chance. Only problem is, Gus doesn't like that idea."

Rispoli was shaking his head. "I ain't sticking no gun up my butt, I don't care how small it is. Anyway, it won't go down the way you think. Taffy's got no intention of ever giving those women back. They've seen him. They're witnesses. They gotta go."

Marvelli stopped breathing for a second. He knew Rispoli was right.

Sammy was unfazed by logic. "So the other thing I was figuring," he said, "we kidnap Taffy and use *him* for the trade."

"You wanna kidnap Taffy?" Marvelli said in disbelief. "What're you, crazy? That's against the law. We can't let you do that." He looked to Loretta for support, but she was looking up at the ceiling, making like she wasn't hearing any of this.

"Don't be a friggin' boy scout, Marvelli," Rispoli croaked. "Taffy's a dangerous character. You know that."

Marvelli did know that, and that's what was worrying him. Taffy wouldn't think twice about killing Jennifer and Annette. "All right," he said, "hypothetically, even if we did look the other way, how would you find Taffy?"

"That's the big problem," Sammy said, nodding gravely. "Where the hell is he? You got any ideas?"

Go ask Agent Springer, Marvelli thought bitterly, but he held his tongue. He had to talk to Loretta about this alone.

"We figure Taffy's staying at one of the nicer hotels downtown," Sammy said. "That's his style. He wouldn't hole up in a motel outside of town or anything like that. That's not Taffy."

"Right," Rispoli added. "Taffy always goes first-class all the way."

"That doesn't narrow it down very much," Marvelli said. "There are plenty of nice hotels in Seattle. What we need to do is lure him out."

"How?" Rispoli was skeptical.

"With something he can't resist." Marvelli plopped down on the futon next to Rispoli. "Does Taffy have any passions, a hobby, anything like that? Is there something that's guaranteed to get his attention?"

Rispoli and Sammy responded simultaneously: "Broads."

"Oh," Marvelli said. "Well, I guess Seattle's got a lot of them, too."

"Marvelli!" Loretta scolded.

"You know what I mean, Loretta. If Taffy wants a woman, he'll find himself one."

Just as long as it's not Jennifer, he thought, already getting angry. After all, why wouldn't he go for Jennifer? She's young and beautiful . . . and he's got her right there. Marvelli's jaw muscles tightened. The bastard better not touch her.

"Taffy likes a certain kind of woman," Rispoli said. "He's pretty particular about that." He was looking at Loretta.

"Oh, yeah, you're right," Sammy chimed in. "I forgot about that." He was looking at Loretta, too.

"What?" she snapped. "What're you looking at me for?"

"Taffy likes his women with meat on the bone," Rispoli said. "Hefty."

"Yeah," Sammy said. "He really digs the big, beautiful ones. But flashy. You know what I mean?"

"Yeah, he likes 'em all dolled up," Rispoli said.

Marvelli's gaze bounced back and forth between Loretta and the two hit men. He knew what they were getting at, and he didn't like it.

The hit men were still staring at Loretta, sizing her up.

"It wouldn't take much," Sammy said. "Just a little . . . jazzing up."

"Bait," Rispoli said ominously. "We need good bait."

Loretta looked to her partner for support. "Marvelli?"

But Marvelli didn't say anything. He knew what they were aiming at, and he didn't approve. But the alternative was even less appealing. What if Taffy decided to try a skinny girl for a change? The thought of Taffy forcing himself on Jennifer turned his stomach. That was Rene's little sister, for God's sake. He couldn't let that happen.

"Come on, Loretta," Sammy said with a con man's smile. "Whattaya say?"

Rispoli looked at her with watery hound-dog eyes, his arms spread out, palms up.

"No," she said, shaking her head. "Forget it."

Marvelli felt that he should be defending her, but he kept his mouth closed. He was worried about Jennifer and Annette, and he had a feeling Sammy and Rispoli were right. This might be the only way to lure Taffy out. He hated the thought of Loretta doing something she didn't want to do, but she was tough and she could take care of herself. Jennifer and Annette couldn't.

"Come on," Sammy coaxed. "It could be fun."

"Forget it," she said, raising her voice.

"It'll be easy," Rispoli said. "No big deal."

"Yeah," Sammy said. "Nothing major. Just a little more makeup, do your hair a little different, some heels, a sleazy outfit—"

"No, I said." She was adamant.

Marvelli was about to intervene when the front door opened, and Alan clomped into the room, carrying a white paper bag. "Anyone want a tart?"

Loretta bared her teeth at him.

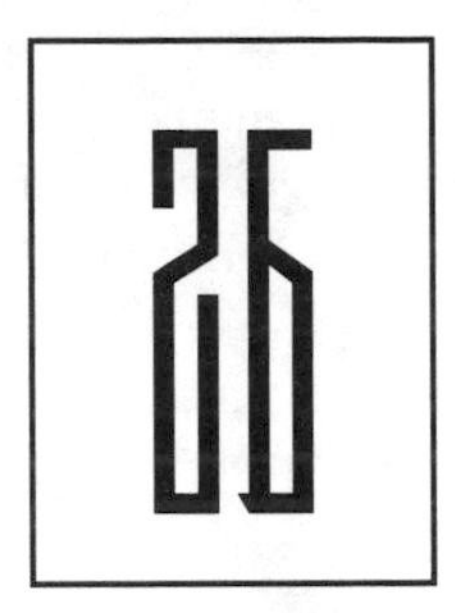

Rispoli called out from the back of the beauty parlor. "She won't do the nails."

Sammy was in the waiting area with Marvelli. "Frankie, she's gotta do the nails," he whined. "Go talk to her."

Marvelli was sitting in a canvas director's chair that didn't quite fit his frame. The salon, which was called the Mane Event, was down the street from Alan Winslow's apartment. It was a very "girly" place with lots of plants and open Chinese fans hanging from mauve walls. Marvelli felt very uncomfortable being here even though Loretta was the only customer except for a little old lady under the dryer helmet. The old lady hadn't moved in a while, and Marvelli wondered if someone should check on her, see if she was still breathing. The two beauticians, Gayle and Tina, were both out back working on Loretta under the strict supervision of "Mr. Gus."

Rispoli came out into the waiting area. Both he and Sammy were staring at Marvelli, expecting him to do something, but Marvelli just shrugged. "What do you want from me? I can't force her." He went back to flipping through the pages of an old *Cosmopolitan*, looking at the pictures of the models.

Sammy pulled the magazine out of his hands. "You don't understand," he said. "The nails are essential. She's got to do it."

"Long and red with the little pictures on them," Rispoli said.

"Take it up with her," Marvelli said, snatching up a copy of *People* from the glass-topped coffee table in front of him.

"You don't get it," Rispoli said, taking the chair next to Marvelli. "This is necessary. Taffy likes *flashy.*"

"*Very* flashy," Sammy said, pulling up another chair. "She's gotta have the nails to get his attention."

Rispoli grabbed Marvelli's forearm. "Listen to me. You know how Taffy got his name?"

Marvelli shook his head.

"When he was a kid, he worked on the boardwalk in Atlantic City, at a candy store that specialized in saltwater taffy. He worked there until he was, like, twenty-five because he liked to make time with the fat broads who came in to buy candy. That's a fact."

"Gimme a break, will ya?" Marvelli said, opening the magazine.

"Tell him about Big Mo," Sammy said.

Rispoli nodded. "Back in those days, he used to hang out with this three-hundred-pound stripper named Big Mo. Her real name was Maureen. Hair, heels, lips, nails—the whole number. Taffy was gaga over this woman. She had him by the nose."

"So what happened?"

"She went on a diet," Sammy said. "Lost half her body weight."

"And Taffy dropped her like a friggin' stone," Rispoli said.

Marvelli resented their telling him this story. Loretta was nowhere near three hundred pounds. She wasn't even two hundred—he didn't think.

"Go talk to her," Rispoli urged. "Tell her to do the nails."

Sammy leaned forward and laid his hand on Marvelli's knee. "This may be the only way to get Jennifer and Annette back. You lost Rene, man. We can't let that happen again." There were tears in Sammy's eyes.

Marvelli heaved a big sigh. He knew how Sammy felt. The guy was a schmuck, but he really did care for Jennifer.

"Talk to Loretta," Sammy pleaded. His voice was choked. "Please?"

Marvelli dropped his head to his chest and let his body go limp. He did not want to deal with this. This whole thing was a stupid idea; he didn't know how these two mokes had convinced him that it wasn't. He felt guilty that he had pressured Loretta into going along with it. But the look on Sammy's face was killing him. The guy was breaking his heart and busting his balls at the same time.

"All right," Marvelli finally said, tossing the magazine back onto the coffee table. "I'll talk to her. But no guarantees. She can be stubborn."

"Yeah, tell me about it," Rispoli muttered.

Marvelli ignored the sarcasm and started toward the back of the beauty parlor. He glanced at the old lady under the dryer, expecting her to stop him from entering the inner sanctum, but she didn't. She was asleep, her shoulders rising and falling ever so slightly with her breathing. Still, he walked gingerly, hesitating with every other step. It felt funny going back there, as if he were going into a women's room.

He passed several empty barber chairs and avoided looking at himself in the mirrors. When he got to the back of the salon, he found the two hairdressers. Gayle, a pretty but emaciated blonde, was sitting at the manicure table, filing her own nails. Tina, a striking redhead with an incredible body and a prize-fighter's nose, was standing behind Gayle, her hip cocked and her arms folded under her unavoidable breasts.

"Your friend's not cooperating," Tina said, making it clear that she was losing her patience.

Gayle look up at Marvelli and pouted. "She looks great, but she won't let us finish. It's a shame, too, because we're almost done."

"Where is she now?" Marvelli whispered.

Tina pointed with her head toward the back. "She's in the john."

"Let me talk to her alone," Marvelli said.

The women shrugged and headed toward the front of the salon.

"Why don't you check on the lady under the dryer?" Marvelli called after them. "I think she's done."

Well done, he thought.

Loretta was just coming out of the bathroom. "What the hell do *you* want?"

Marvelli's jaw dropped. "Loretta?"

"What?" she snapped.

But he was speechless. He couldn't believe what he was seeing. Her dirty-blond hair had been highlighted or something, and it was . . . big. It was as if it had been inflated. Her brows had been shaped, and she was wearing two shades of purple eyeshadow, with lots of mascara. Her lips were ruby red, shiny, and moist. She was wearing a sleeveless black blouse, buttons open to show a hell of a lot more cleavage than Marvelli had ever seen before. A tight tan skirt came up to the middle of her thighs, which made him wonder what would happen when she sat down. Stylish black platforms with very high heels gave her at least two or three inches on him. She walked up to him, but he leaned back so he could take in the whole package. He couldn't believe it. She looked . . . incredible.

"Stop staring, Marvelli," she growled. "It's just me."

"I—" He cleared his throat. "I know that." But he'd never imagined that Loretta could look so sexy. He'd never thought of her that way.

"So what do you want? Do *you* want me to do my nails, too?"

"Well, I . . . they say it'll help. But what do I know?"

Yeah. Do the nails, he was thinking.

"I don't want claws," she said. "I feel ridiculous as it is." She flicked at her big hair as if it were an alien creature sitting on her shoulder.

"Why don't we sit down?" Marvelli said. His shorts were getting tight. He sat down at the manicure table and crossed his legs, hoping to readjust things down there.

Loretta took Gayle's seat. "I only agreed to do this for one reason: to nail that snippy little witch Springer."

Marvelli nodded. God, was he horny. He hadn't been horny like this in a very long time. "Well," he said, "why don't you get your nails done so you can scratch her eyes out?"

"Never," Loretta spat. "That's how girls fight. I want to punch her lights out."

"Okay." Marvelli nodded. He shifted in his seat. His shorts were getting tighter.

She leaned in closer to him and suddenly softened her tone. "Do you really think the nails will make a difference? Be honest."

"Well . . ." He shrugged. "Sammy and Gus say yes. They say Taffy's particular." It was true, they had said that, but Marvelli felt guilty telling her to do it. *He* was the one who wanted to see her with killer nails.

"All right." She sighed. "I'll do it. I've gone this far." She flicked at her hair again.

Marvelli couldn't stop staring at her.

"Veronica Springer," Loretta grumbled to herself, shaking her head.

"What about her?"

"Nothing," she said. "Just talking to myself."

"Oh."

"You haven't got any aspirin, have you?"

"Aspirin? No. You got a headache?"

"Yes," she said. "I thought I had gotten past my coffee withdrawal symptoms, but I guess I haven't yet. Unless it was the hairspray that gave me a headache." She hunched her shoulders and flicked at her hair again. He wished she'd stop doing that. Her hair was very sexy.

"Why don't you go get the mousse girls so we can get this over with?" she said. "I'll bet they have aspirin someplace here."

"Right," Marvelli said. But he didn't want to get up. Not with what he had in his pants.

He spun around in his seat. "Gayle? Tina?"

"Coming," one of them called from the front of the salon.

Marvelli slunk out of his chair like Groucho Marx, staying low and keeping his back to Loretta. "I'll wait out front," he said, but as he hurried away from her, he couldn't help but look back. He dug his hands into his pants pockets, trying to make more room.

Suddenly he thought of that guy in the Bible who looked back and turned into a pillar of salt.

Marvelli was sitting behind the wheel of his rented green Taurus, staring out the windshield at Loretta across the street with her new hair, nails, and heels and all that leg showing as she took her time strolling down Sixth Avenue, checking out all the fancy shop windows. Sammy was in the passenger seat, cracking open pistachios and dropping the shells on the floor. Rispoli was in the backseat smoking. Marvelli drummed on the steering wheel, making it thrum. He didn't like this one bit, none of it. It had been a stupid idea from the start.

This was the fourth place that they'd tried. The two "criminal geniuses" had picked these places based on their proximity to the better downtown hotels. Their assumption was that Taffy wouldn't stray too far from his base of operation. But it was twilight now, and there was still no sign of Taffy. Marvelli was convinced that this was just a big waste of time. They weren't going to find the bastard, not this way.

"How come we don't have a wire?" Rispoli suddenly croaked from the backseat. "It would be better if she were wearing a wire."

Marvelli sighed in exasperation, trying to hold his temper. "I told you already, Gus. I don't have those kinds of toys. I'm a parole officer, not a feebie."

Sammy nodded in agreement as he popped another pistachio into his mouth. All his fingertips were stained red.

"Why didn't you get the white ones?" Marvelli asked him testily. He was fed up with Sammy, too.

"The red ones taste better," Sammy said.

"No, they don't," Marvelli said. "They taste the same."

"I don't think so," Sammy said. "What do you think, Gus?"

"About what?"

"Pistachios. Which taste better? The red ones or the not-red ones."

"How the hell should I know?" Rispoli snapped. "I don't eat them things."

"Why not? You don't like 'em?"

"Too much damn trouble to open."

"Yeah, but they're good."

"Who the hell cares?" Rispoli said.

"Enough with the pistachios!" Marvelli shouted, his eyes starting to cross. He was trying to concentrate on Loretta. He was worried about her. What if Taffy did show up, and he had those two retards Larry and Jerry with him? They knew her. What if they recognized her through all that makeup?

Sammy held out the bag of pistachios to Marvelli. "You want some?"

He shook his head. "No thanks."

Sammy's eyebrows shot up. "What're you, sick?" he said. "I've never seen you refuse food."

Marvelli ignored him and kept his eye on Loretta. He couldn't stop thinking about her, thinking about her the way she was now, and that was making him mad. They'd been working together for almost six months now, and he'd never thought of her that way. But as soon as she got a makeover, he suddenly got the hots for her. Was he really that shallow?

Across the street Loretta moved on to the next shop, a fur store. He watched her eyeing the full-length mink coats. He was getting grouchier by the minute, but he wasn't sure why.

The interior of the car had become very quiet, so much so that Marvelli could hear Rispoli drawing on his cigarette.

All of a sudden Sammy heaved a heavy sigh and broke the silence. "I love her," he said with a catch in his voice.

Marvelli's first impulse was to backhand him between the eyes with a closed fist, but then he realized that Sammy wasn't talking about Loretta.

Sammy looked at Marvelli. "We *are* going to get Jennifer back, aren't we?" A tear clung to the bottom of his thick black eyeglasses. He was asking for hope.

"We'll get her back," Marvelli assured him, even though he had some serious doubts himself.

Cigarette smoke swirled in the space between Sammy and Marvelli, doing a slow tango.

"Last time I saw her," Sammy said. "I told her I wanted to get married again. She didn't say no."

"Did she say yes?" Marvelli asked.

"She didn't say no."

Marvelli pressed his lips into a noncommittal smile and shrugged.

"You don't know what it's like, Frankie." Sammy was staring blankly out the window. "You had Rene, and you two had been together forever. Plus, you were both so cool about things. What I mean is, you're a real-life tough guy, Frankie, and in a lot of ways so was she. But with me and Jennifer, it's different. We run hot, man. Real hot."

"What the hell're you talking about?" Rispoli grunted.

"I love her. That's all there is to it, Gus. I'm just . . . comfortable with her. I'm not like that with anyone else. I mean, when I see her, the rest of the world just dissolves. She's the only one I can see, the only one who matters. It's like I don't need anybody else. I'd be perfectly content if she were the only person I ever talked to again. You know what I'm saying?"

Marvelli nodded. He understood exactly what Sammy was saying, and he wondered if he could ever feel that way about someone again. Loretta maybe, he thought.

But the word Sammy had used—"comfortable"—stuck in his mind. He actually was comfortable with Loretta. But was comfortable enough? Shouldn't there be something more? Like passion? And not the kind that starts in your pants.

"I know Annette hates my guts," Sammy said. "I mean, she used to tell me to my face all the time. I know she doesn't want me and Jennifer getting back together. But so what? She doesn't understand how I feel." He turned to Marvelli. "Maybe you could talk to her for me. She likes you."

Marvelli rolled his eyes toward Sammy and didn't say what he was thinking. Annette would hire a hit man to keep Sammy away from her daughter.

"Maybe you ought to get things straight with Jennifer first," Marvelli said. "Worry about Annette afterward."

"Yeah, but Jen listens to her mother. I mean, she was the one who spoiled things between us the first time."

Marvelli kept his mouth shut. *Hanging out with wiseguys had nothing to do with it, huh, Sammy?* he thought.

Marvelli glanced at Loretta and wondered what Annette would think if he got involved with her. Not much, probably. Annette was pretty negative, and she didn't like anyone who wasn't already related to her—preferably by blood. It was a Sicilian thing.

"Whatever it takes, I'm gonna get Jennifer back," Sammy mumbled. "I don't care. I love her."

"Hey, you two," Rispoli rasped. "Snap out of it. Over there." He pointed with his cigarette.

Out in front of the fur shop, Loretta was frozen where she stood. She was staring at Alan Winslow, who was walking tentatively toward her, about twenty feet away.

"What the hell's he doing here?" Rispoli sputtered angrily.

Alan was decked out in his nerdy best, pocket protector and all. His body language was unmistakable. Even though his shyness made him hesitant, taking two steps, then stopping for a second before he started again, he was leading with his groin as if he had a bloodhound down there.

Loretta's body language was pretty clear, too. Her fists were on her hips, and her knees were locked. Marvelli couldn't make out her face very well at this distance, but he could sure imagine the expression. Fierce and forbidding. Don't even get near me, buster.

But with Loretta decked out the way she was, the hound dog in Alan's corduroys could not be scared off the track. He smelled something very enticing, and he wanted a closer look. Probably wanted to touch, too. Marvelli knew just how Alan felt because he felt pretty much the same way himself.

"Crap!" Rispoli hissed. "We got more trouble."

"What?" Marvelli said.

Rispoli pointed with his smoldering cigarette again. "Over there. On the corner."

Marvelli zeroed in on the fancy jewelry store on the corner. Standing in front in a dark suit was Taffy Demaggio. He was staring at Loretta and Alan.

Marvelli could feel butterflies fluttering in his chest. He let out a long, slow breath. "Oh, boy," he said.

“Loretta?” Alan had stars in his eyes as he approached her. He had a white bakery box in his hand.

“What’re you doing here, Alan?” She glanced sideways at the green Taurus, hoping one of them would come over and escort Alan away.

“Bear claws,” he said, holding up the box. “There’s a place down here that makes great ones. You want one?”

“No thanks.” Actually she wouldn’t mind having a little nosh because she hadn’t had dinner yet, but a sweet pastry would only make her want a cup of coffee even more than she already did. Her head was throbbing from caffeine deprivation.

He inched a little closer, and she backed toward the fur store’s doorway. She had to get rid of him.

“Loretta, you look so . . . different,” he said.

Yeah, like a hooker, she thought sarcastically.

“I . . . I like your new look. I really do.”

Oh great, she thought. *Just what I need right now. A lovesick puppy.*

She didn’t have much sympathy for him because he was staring at her cleavage, not her face. *So typical,* she thought. *Men are all the same. Even the geeks.*

"Don't you have someplace to go, Alan?" she asked, trying to give him the hint.

"Me? No, not really. I can hang out. If that's okay with you, I mean." He was doing that guy thing, tiptoeing around what he really wanted so that if she rejected him, he could make like he never really wanted to hang out with her in the first place. Marvelli did that all the time, and she hated it. Not that she could ever figure out what he *really* wanted. The only thing she knew for sure was that it wasn't her.

"Alan, why don't you go home?" she said. "I'm sort of busy here."

"Oh . . . Well, I could just keep you company. I'm not doing anything right now. I could even help you. If that's okay."

"No, Alan, it's not okay. I told you—"

"Excuse me." A tall, very tan man in a dark blue European-cut suit suddenly appeared at Loretta's side. She hadn't heard him coming. "Is this person giving you trouble, miss?" he asked.

In the shadows of the storefront, it took a second for Loretta to realize that this was Taffy Demaggio. His voice was surprisingly warm and deep. She'd expected a dese-dem-and-dose kind of a guy, but he wasn't that way at all. He was well built with a trim waist and a broad chest. She guessed that he was in his early fifties, but he had a full head of thick salt-and-pepper hair. He also had black-olive eyes that crinkled and sparkled. She glanced down at his hands, which were clasped in front of him. Amazingly he didn't even have a pinky ring.

Alan was glaring at him, two hot little eyeballs under one straight eyebrow. "I'm not giving her any trouble, mister. I *know* her."

"Alan, why don't you go home?" she said, hoping he would just go without a fuss. She finally had Taffy on the line; she didn't want to lose him.

"I think I'd better stay," Alan said stubbornly. He was going to defend her honor.

She rolled her eyes. *Oh, please,* she thought.

"Listen, my friend," Taffy said, flashing a menacingly perfect set of teeth, "the lady has made her wishes clear. Now I suggest you honor those wishes and take off. Immediately." Taffy leaned into him and reinforced the point with his body. Taffy had the stance of a light heavyweight; Alan was a great big marshmallow. Despite the age difference, Taffy was the hands-down favorite.

Alan looked to Loretta for support, but she couldn't cut him any slack, not in front of Taffy.

"Go, Alan," she said dismissively, hiding the fact that she felt bad for him.

"You heard the lady," Taffy said. "Go, Alan." He flashed his perfect teeth.

Alan looked like he was going to cry. " 'Bye," he mumbled to Loretta as he turned and quickly walked away, the bakery box dangling by his side from two fingers.

Loretta turned to Taffy. "Thanks," she said. "I just moved here because of him." She nodded toward Alan. "I didn't know he'd turn out to be such a jerk."

Taffy shrugged sympathetically. "I'm sorry to hear that."

"Say, you wouldn't know of any good restaurants around here, would you? I want to celebrate."

"Celebrate what?"

"The end of Alan."

Taffy laughed. "Well, I'm not from around here myself, but I think there's a good Italian place near here. In fact, I was on my way there right now. I realize you don't know me, but I'd appreciate having some company. I don't like eating alone in restaurants."

"Me neither," she said.

"So would you like to join me?"

Loretta just looked into his eyes. His soothing voice was like the warm, sweet taste of hot fudge. She waited, watching his shining eyes. They didn't wander down to her cleavage or anyplace else for that matter. He was waiting for an answer.

"If you don't want to," Taffy said, "I understand. I apologize for asking."

"No," she said quickly. "I would like to." She knew he was a mobster with a long résumé of serious crimes, but he was charming as hell, not at all the greaseball that Marvelli had described. Besides, she was supposed to be luring him in.

"It's just on the next block" he said. "We can walk." He extended his open hand to indicate the way.

Loretta grinned, and she didn't have to pretend.

"That was great," Loretta said as she dabbed the corners of her mouth with her napkin. The remnants of two lobsters littered their tomato-sauce-stained plates and a large discard bowl in the middle of the table. Taffy had ordered lobster fra diavola for two.

"I'm glad you liked it," Taffy said. He was looking into her eyes, his elbows on the table, fingers linked on his chin. His eyes were still crinkling and twinkling.

The restaurant was old-style Italian—dim lighting, minimal decor, white tablecloths, and flickering candles in green-tinted glass holders on every table. The room seemed to absorb sound, so that even though there were at least thirty other people having dinner around them, Loretta felt that their conversation was their own.

"This place is a real find," Loretta said. "Have you been here before?"

Taffy shook his head.

"Did someone recommend it?"

He shook his head again. "I have a rule whenever I go traveling. I get the phone book, and I look for restaurants called Michael's. Every town seems to have one, and they're always good. I've never been disappointed. I don't know why, but it always works out that way."

"I'll keep that in mind," she said.

"You do that. Who knows? Maybe I'll run into you sometime."

She shrugged and grinned. "Maybe."

She picked up her champagne flute and took a sip. He had ordered a bottle of Cristal, which she'd heard was better than Dom Perignon, but of course she'd never tasted either so she couldn't say. What she could say was that the Cristal was divine, and even though what was left in her glass was a little warm, it was still great. Everything about the meal was great. Even Taffy, she had to admit.

She wished she could build up a little animosity toward him, but it was very difficult. Marvelli would have a cow if she knew what she was thinking, but she really had no reason to hate Taffy. She'd never seen the results of his hospital-supply scam or any of his other criminal enterprises. All she saw was a very courteous gentleman who'd treated her to a scrumptious dinner at an elegant restaurant. Sure, this was shallow thinking, and she knew it, but she hadn't been taken out on the town like this in a very long time, and occasionally a person needs this kind of thing. Marvelli had never taken her out, except for pizza, and they always went dutch. Besides, it was Marvelli and the two hit men who had wanted her to get done up like a bimbo. Okay, fine. If that's what they wanted, then she got to take the bimbo perks. It was only fair.

"You ready for dessert?" he asked.

"Gee, I don't know. . . ."

"Have you ever had zabaglione?"

"No, what's that?"

He closed his eyes and waved his head as if he were getting light-headed. "It's the best. It's a custard that they make right at the table layered with fresh strawberries. You have to try it."

"You don't have to twist my arm."

"And coffee? Maybe cappuccino? Espresso with some sambuca in it?"

Espresso with sambuca sounded awfully tempting. And she was also tempted to have *real* espresso, the high-octane stuff. She'd been feeling crappy ever since she'd given up caffeine, and this really was the perfect meal. She couldn't top it off with just a decaf. She reached for her champagne glass and drained it. *Hey, why not?* she thought. She could quit again tomorrow.

"Espresso sounds good," she said. "Make mine a double."

Taffy smiled, crinkling his eyes even more. "You got it, sweetheart."

Taffy gave the waiter their dessert orders. "Zabaglione for both of us and two double espressos with sambuca. In fact, why don't you just bring the bottle."

The waiter, a poker-faced young man with sleepy eyes and a tiny mouth, nodded. "Anything else, sir?"

"Not right now," Taffy said.

After the waiter left, Taffy poured out the last few drops of champagne into Loretta's glass. "Go ahead. Finish it," he urged.

"Okay," she said with a cute little shrug.

He deliberately maintained eye contact with her because he knew broads liked that. It made guys seem sensitive. If she only knew what he was thinking. He had a boner for her like a Louisville slugger. This woman was nice, he thought. She reminded him a lot of Cathy Dunne, the one who couldn't take a little rough sex. Poor kid. It was too bad about her. Maybe he did get a little carried away.

But Loretta here looked a lot hardier. He was willing to bet she could take it. That night with Cathy had been absolutely incredible, and he was thinking maybe he could recreate it with Loretta. She definitely looked like she could take it. He'd try to be more careful this time.

Of course, strangling Cathy was sort of what made it incredible. That made it *special.*

The waiter returned, pushing a cart filled with ingredients—eggs, cream, sugar, lemon, and fresh strawberries in a white ceramic bowl. A wire whisk sat in a large copper mixing bowl. Without a word, the waiter went to work, cracking eggs and pouring in ingredients.

Taffy raised his eyebrows to get Loretta's attention. When she acknowledged him with a smile, he smiled back.

"You're gonna *love* this," he said.

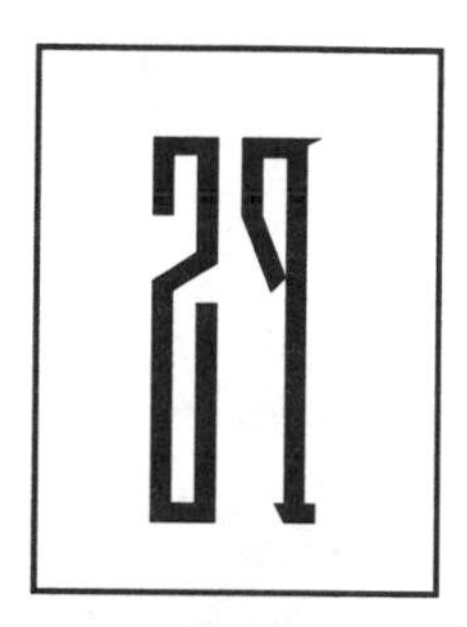

The green Taurus was parked across the street from Michael's Restaurant. Marvelli was behind the wheel, holding a pair of binoculars to his face, peering through the quaint leaded-glass windows at Loretta and Taffy laughing and eating zabaglione, having a great old time. Taffy kept putting his hand on Loretta's forearm to emphasize whatever it was he was saying to her.

The son of a bitch better keep his hands to himself, Marvelli thought, *before I go in there and ram his arm down his throat and pull it out his—*

"Hey, Frankie," Sammy interrupted, "gimme the binoculars. I wanna look."

"Nothing to see," Marvelli grunted. "They're just eating."

"What're you so grouchy about?"

Rispoli piped up from the backseat, "He's jealous, stupid."

"Who? Frankie?" Sammy threw his arm over the seat back and turned around to face Rispoli.

"Why, sure!" Rispoli said. "He's got a thing for this Loretta girl. Can't you see that?"

"I don't have a *thing* for Loretta," Marvelli said, keeping the binoculars on his face.

"You don't think you do, but you do," Rispoli said.

"You're crazy," Marvelli said. "We just work together."

"I got eyes," Rispoli said. "I can see what's going on."

"There's nothing going on. You saw nothing." Marvelli was getting mad.

"That's the whole point," Rispoli said. "I've been watching you two together, and that's what I see, nothing. You both go out of your way to do nothing, and *that* tells me there's something there."

"What the hell're you talking about?"

"It's what I don't see that tells the story. You two are too careful with each other. It's like you're both afraid to get too close because you'd be jumping each other's bones if you let your guards down."

Marvelli caught Rispoli's eye in the rearview mirror and glared at him. He was too damned perceptive.

"You're dreaming, Gus," Marvelli said, forcing a grin. "Loretta's just my partner."

Rispoli sucked on a cigarette. "Yeah, sure."

"Hey! Hey!" Sammy said, getting all excited. "They're coming out. Look."

Marvelli didn't need the binoculars to see Loretta and Taffy coming out the front door of the restaurant. Taffy held the door open for her and put his hand on the small of her back as she walked out. Marvelli squinted to see the expression on her face. She didn't seem to mind having a low-down murdering scum-thief-bastard's hand on her.

"Come on," Marvelli said, grabbing the door handle. "Let's grab him."

"With pleasure," Sammy said as he reached for his door.

But from the backseat Rispoli grabbed them both by the shoulders. "Wait," he said, the cigarette dangling from his lips.

"What for?" Sammy said, trying to pull away from Rispoli's grip.

"Too many people here," Rispoli said. "Let's wait and see where he takes her."

"Yeah," Sammy said, instantly changing his tune, "maybe he'll take her back to where he's keeping Jennifer."

Rispoli shrugged. "You never know."

Marvelli held his tongue, doing a slow burn as he watched Taffy and Loretta strolling down the sidewalk. Taffy still had his hand on her back. Marvelli was seeing red. He didn't want Taffy taking her anywhere. He reached for the key in the ignition.

"No," Rispoli said. "Let 'em walk a little. If we get too close, Taffy'll spot us."

Not if I run him over first, Marvelli thought. But he let go of the ignition key.

"This way," Taffy said as he guided Loretta down a side street off the avenue. "I want to show you something."

"What?" Loretta asked.

"You'll see."

So will you, she thought. *As soon as Marvelli, Sammy, and Rispoli get here.* If *they get here. What the hell were they waiting for?* she wanted to know.

She didn't dare look over her shoulder and risk making Taffy suspicious.

"Did you enjoy dinner?" he asked.

"Very much," she said, looking into his eyes. Her cheeks ached from smiling so much, and she wished he'd get his goddamn hand off her back. She'd reconsidered her initial impression of him. Taffy was smooth, but he was just like all the rest. He put up a good front, but no man is that perfect, which only said to her that he just wanted what they all wanted, except that he wanted it a lot more. Why else would he act so wonderful?

The streetlights were spaced farther apart on this street. They walked long stretches in near darkness. All the shops were closed, and there were no residential apartments on the upper floors. There were no other pedestrians either.

Come on, guys, she thought. *Now's the time.*

"You know, Loretta, I think you're a very special person," Taffy said.

She couldn't quite make out his expression in the dark, but he was making her nervous now. "You seem pretty special yourself," she said, working hard to maintain a tone of playful flirtation. "So where are we going?"

"It's a surprise," he said. His eyes twinkled in the dark.

"What kind of surprise?"

"A good one."

"How do you know I'll like it?"

"I think I know what you like."

"How could you know? We just met."

"You liked what I ordered at the restaurant, didn't you?"

"Yeah . . ."

"Then trust me."

As they approached the next streetlight, she could see his face better. It was heavily outlined by the shadows, like a wooden mask. He didn't look so smooth anymore.

"You can trust me," he said. "You do know that, don't you?" The shadows moved across his face as they walked.

"I guess," she said noncommittally.

Come on, guys, she thought. *Let's go.*

They passed under the streetlight and strolled back into the darkness. He had moved closer to her. His hip was touching hers, and his hand was still on her back. She could feel him slowing down.

Oh, no, she thought. She knew what was coming next.

They slowed down to a crawl, and suddenly he moved in front of her, entwining his arms around her lower back. His face was inches from hers. She laid her hands on his chest, ready to push him off if she had to.

Come on, guys! Hurry up! She was yelling in her head.

She resisted his embrace, but his hands were locked around her. "I'll bet you're a good kisser," he purred. She could feel the rumble of his voice in her chest.

She laughed nervously. "I think you're getting a little ahead of the game," she said.

Come on, guys! Take him now, please!

"No, I can tell about these things," he said, pulling her closer. "I'll bet you're a dynamite kisser."

"I don't know about that," she said, keeping her tone light as she tried to push him away. Unfortunately he was stronger than she'd thought, and he wasn't taking the hint.

Now, guys! Before I put his eyes out.

"Let me just see if I'm right," Taffy said. "Just one kiss."

In your dreams, she thought. *Just one kiss was like saying, I'm just gonna have one cookie.*

"I don't think this is good idea," she said as she struggled to keep him off her.

But he could not be dissuaded. His lips were rummaging around in the dark, looking for hers. She turned away to avoid him, but he was persistent.

"Enough!" she finally said.

But he wasn't listening. He wasn't about to give up.

Marvelli! she thought. *Where the hell are—?*

Suddenly she felt something next to her cheek between their faces, something cold and hard and metal. She jumped, suddenly realizing that someone else was standing right there.

"What the hell—?" Taffy said. He let go of her and moved back a step. "What do you think you're doing?"

But when he moved away, light from the next streetlamp suddenly illuminated the short dark figure. Loretta's heart stopped. It wasn't Marvelli, and it wasn't Sammy or Rispoli. It was Special Agent Veronica Springer, and she was holding a silver 9mm automatic in Loretta's face.

"Bad choice, Taf," Springer said under her breath. Her eyes were rivetted on Loretta. "You picked the wrong cutie-pie this time."

Taffy was pissed. "What the hell're you talking about?"

Springer twisted the gun barrel into Loretta's rouged cheek. "Nice look," she said sarcastically.

Loretta didn't have a comeback. She wasn't breathing.

"Shall we stroll?" Springer asked. It wasn't a question.

Moonlight shimmered over the harbor as Loretta clopped across the wooden dock in her high heels. She could hear the distant whoosh of traffic on Alaskan Way. She could also hear the footsteps walking right behind her. She glanced over her shoulder and saw Taffy and Agent Springer, both with their guns out. With the end of the dock straight ahead, Loretta was convinced they were going to make her walk the plank.

All things considered, that might be the easy way out, she thought.

The dock was lined with pleasure boats of all sizes and varieties, but none of them seemed to be occupied. Even if they were, Loretta didn't dare try calling out for help. If Agent Springer didn't gun her down, Taffy surely would now that he knew who she really was. Neither of them had any compelling reason to keep her alive.

"Take a left," Taffy said gruffly. "Right here."

"Here?" Loretta asked, pointing to a tugboat moored to the dock. It had a barn-red pilothouse with polished brass fittings that shone in the dark and curtains over the portholes.

Much too pretty to be a working boat, she thought. Must be a houseboat.

"Go aboard," Agent Springer ordered flatly.

When Loretta hesitated, trying to see where she was going in the dark, Taffy jabbed her in the back with the barrel of his gun. "Hurry up!" He stepped aboard right after her and went to the door to the pilothouse. He knocked five times, slow and deliberate. Then Loretta heard a bolt being thrown on the inside. The door swung open, and pale yellow light spilled onto the deck as if it had been heaved from a bucket.

"In," Taffy said, jabbing her with his gun again.

"All right! I'm going!" she snapped, annoyed with the prodding. But before she went in, she looked down the length of the dock for signs of Marvelli, but there was no one.

Jerk! she thought. A sinkhole suddenly opened up in the pit of her stomach as she realized that she was all alone out here. No one was going to rescue her. For some reason Marvelli had abandoned her.

She stepped inside and squinted as her eyes adjusted to the light. Seated at a butcher-block kitchen table were the twin nitwits, Larry and Jerry, both with their guns conspicuously jammed into their waistbands like a couple of pirates. Annette and Jennifer were also at the table, but they weren't tied and gagged the way Loretta would have expected them to be. A yellow legal pad was at the center of the table, pens scattered all around. A mammoth bucket of fried chicken was on the kitchen counter, at least half of it still left, along with leftover coleslaw, mashed potatoes with gravy, and biscuits. Loretta looked closer and saw that the four of them were playing hangman. They stared up at her with empty faces as if they hadn't been expecting company.

"Hey, look who's here," Jerry said, suddenly enthusiastic.

"How ya doin', Loretta?" Larry said. "Long time no see."

Dumb as doo-doo, Loretta thought.

The two women seemed to be unharmed, although Annette's hair was so frazzled it looked as if she'd just gone through electroshock therapy. Jennifer's long, lovely locks, on the other hand, looked perfect. In fact, she looked great, which just aggravated the hell out of Loretta. The woman could be held hostage and still manage to look beautiful. Who did she think she was? Patty Hearst? It wasn't fair.

A sour expression was fermenting on Annette's face. "Loretta?" she said, both skeptical and condemning. "What did you do to yourself?" She painted the air with her hand. "You look like a *putan'*!"

"What's a *putan'*?" Loretta asked. It didn't sound like a compliment.

"A whore," Taffy said with a weird grin on his face.

"In Italian," Agent Springer clarified as she slammed the door shut and threw the bolt.

"You used to be such a nice girl, Loretta," Annette scolded. "What happened?"

"It's a long story," Loretta said, not wanting to get into it right now. She had her eye on Springer, who was moving around the room like a nervous cat, staring blankly at the bucket of chicken on the counter. The gun was in her right hand; the other hand was a closed fist, and she was shaking it as if she were shaking dice.

"Let us go," Loretta said to Springer. "You're in enough trouble as it is. Don't make it worse."

Springer shook her head as she shook her fist, still pacing, still staring blankly.

Loretta pointed at Taffy. "If you help him kill Rispoli, then you'll be charged with murder, too. You know that."

Springer kept shaking her head. "No," she muttered. "Won't happen that way." She seemed to be talking to herself.

Taffy's voice boomed through the pilothouse. "Then how *will* it happen?"

Larry and Jerry were frozen, eyes wide, like little kids who were afraid they were in trouble. Annette was glaring at Springer, waiting for her to answer Taffy's question. Jennifer was staring at Springer, too, but the look on her face was blank resignation.

"Just let me think," Springer muttered, shaking her fist furiously. "I'll figure it out. Just let me think."

Taffy snatched her wrist and pried her hand open. Two little white pills bounced to the floor. Loretta knew what they were. Diet pills.

Taffy stepped on the pills and crunched them under his shoe. "Don't overheat your brain, sweetheart," he said. "I've already got it all figured out."

Everyone was waiting for Taffy to explain when Jennifer's voice suddenly cut through the silence. "You're going to kill us," she said evenly. "That's what you're gonna do."

Taffy grinned. "Very good," he said. "At least there's one broad here who's got half a brain." He looked at Larry and Jerry. "And who would've thought it would be the bimbo?" Taffy started laughing, and the loyal twins joined in to be polite even though they didn't understand.

But then Taffy stopped laughing. He gave the twins a grim look, and immediately they stood up and pulled out their guns, flanking their boss. They were facing Loretta, Annette, and Jennifer with guns leveled.

"So where do you stand?" Taffy asked Springer, who was off to the side, looking frazzed and jittery, her eyes darting back and forth between the three women and the food on the counter.

"Oh, go on and have a piece," Loretta said sarcastically. "You're too skinny anyway."

Springer's eyes snapped like a whip as she shifted her gaze and stared into Loretta's eyes. Slowly she raised her gun and pointed it at Loretta's chest. The FBI agent moved her position so that she was in line with the men, facing the women. "This is where I stand," she said in a low growl.

Loretta's stare didn't waver, but she was screaming in her head: *Marvelli! Where the hell are you?*

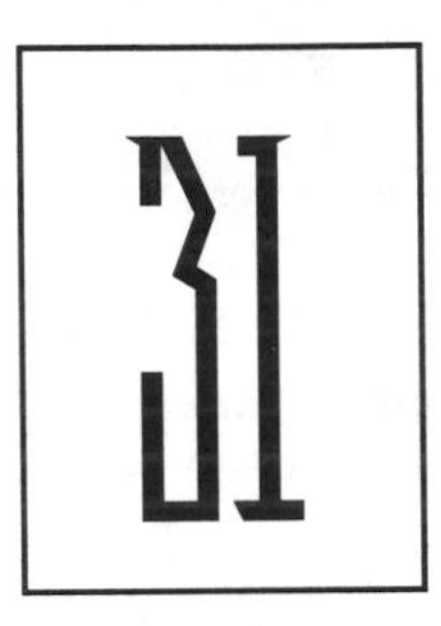

Four muzzles were staring at Loretta, Jennifer, and Annette, but the only one that was shaking was Agent Springer's. She was trying to concentrate on the murders at hand, but that bucket of chicken on the counter kept distracting her. She wanted to eat so bad it hurt.

"Why don't you just take your pills?" Loretta asked. "Don't you have any more?"

"Shut up!" Springer screamed. She closed her eyes and took a few seconds to get her temper under control. "Just be quiet," she said slowly and evenly.

But Loretta was feeling reckless. Maybe it was the double espresso she'd had at the restaurant. Caffeine was pulsing through her veins like electricity.

"Go ahead, have some chicken," Loretta taunted. "It's probably fried chicken. Bet you haven't had fried food in a long time."

But instead of getting angry, Springer calmly reached for the bucket and held it out to Loretta. "Why don't *you* have a piece?" Springer said. "You and fried food must be old friends."

Loretta narrowed her eyes. "What'd you say?"

"Or what is it they say about cops? They never met a doughnut they didn't like?" A mocking smile curved one end of Springer's mouth. She shook the bucket as if it were Loretta's dog bowl. "Go on, have some."

Loretta's eyes were popping out of her head. She wanted to grab the little witch by the throat and cram thighs, wings, and drumsticks down her gullet.

"Loretta, calm down," Annette warned.

"Shut up, lady," Larry said.

Jerry put in his two cents' worth. "Yeah, shut up."

"Everybody shut up!" Taffy shouted. When it was quiet, he looked directly at Loretta and continued. "Now, here's what we're gonna do. We're gonna walk out across the dock to another boat, a nice big cabin cruiser, and we're all gonna take a nice cruise. When we get out where no one can see us, we're gonna do you girls the old-fashioned way."

"You mean you're just going to shoot us?" Jennifer asked.

Taffy shook his head and looked down at her feet. "Cement overshoes. It's a more natural way to go. And very traditional."

Springer gave him a grim look as if she didn't approve.

"First Miss Jennifer," Taffy said to Loretta, "then Annette, and you last. *After* we finish our date." He was staring at her cleavage.

Loretta frowned. "What're you talking about?"

"Think about it, sweetheart. A man pays for dinner, he expects a little something in return." He was grinning from ear to ear.

Loretta was livid. "You rotten son of a—"

Suddenly there was a knock on the door, and Taffy's smarmy expression instantly drooped. "Put your guns away," he whispered, sticking his little automatic in the side pocket of his suit coat. Springer put hers back into her shoulder holster. Jerry and Larry stuck their guns in their waistbands at the small of their backs and faced the door.

"Who is it?" Taffy called out.

"Frank Marvelli. I'm alone."

Loretta's heart started to pound.

"I got a message for you, Taffy," Marvelli said through the door.

"What is it?"

"Open the door first."

Taffy signaled to the twins to check the windows. Larry and Jerry tiptoed to separate portholes, peered out, then tiptoed back to Taffy.

"He's alone," Larry whispered, but he looked dubious.

"He's wearing just a T-shirt and his pant legs are rolled up to his knees," Jerry said. He looked at his brother. "I think he's trying to tell us he isn't carrying a piece."

Larry shrugged. "He has a cell phone in his hand, though."

Taffy thought about it for a moment, then nodded at the door. "Let him in. But keep him covered."

The twins pulled out their guns, and Larry threw the bolt. "It's open," he said, and stood back, his gun ready.

The door swung open, and there was Marvelli in a black T-shirt that showed off his muscles, his jeans rolled up to his knobby knees. Both hands were up where they could be seen, and in one he was holding his cell phone. He scanned the room quickly, then Loretta caught his eye. *What the hell are you doing?* she wanted to scream at him. *You're going to get yourself killed!*

Jerry slammed the door shut.

Taffy sneered at Marvelli with undisguised contempt. "So what's the message?" he asked.

Marvelli held out the cell phone.

Taffy didn't want to take it. He didn't trust this Marvelli as far as he could spit. He didn't trust anybody.

He glanced at Veronica Springer, who was just standing there like she wasn't part of this. Taffy didn't trust her either. He could see it in her prissy little cat face. She was figuring out how to distance herself from this. She was bailing out, the little witch.

Marvelli shoved the phone at him. "Take it. It's for you."

Taffy looked right and left at the twins by his side, making sure they were in place in case Marvelli tried something funny, then he glanced at Loretta poured into that skirt just the way he liked it, wishing he'd never seen her in the first place. Finally he took the phone. "Hello?"

A raspy voice was on the other end. "Let 'em go, you miserable bastard."

"Rispoli? Is that you? Where the hell are you?"

A mocking laugh turned into a smoker's cough. "I'm where you ain't gonna find me. That's where I am."

"But you're near here. I know it." Taffy had stomach cramps. Rispoli was cunning and he was cold, the best hit man there ever was. If he was anywhere nearby, no one was safe.

Springer sidled up next to Taffy and leaned in close so she could hear the phone. *Just like a goddamn cat,* Taffy thought.

"So talk to me, Gus," Taffy said. "What do you want?"

"I told you what I want," Rispoli yelled. "Let 'em go. All of 'em."

"And what do *I* get out of this?"

"I won't testify against you, that's what you'll get."

"And what's my guarantee?"

"You want a friggin' guarantee, go to Sears."

"I'm just supposed to take your word for it. What're you, kiddin'?"

"That's the deal. Take it or leave it."

Springer was staring at him, waiting to see how he played this, but her face told him nothing. She was no help whatsoever.

"And what happens if I don't accept your terms?" Taffy asked Rispoli.

"You'll see." Rispoli hung up.

"Now what?" Springer said. All of a sudden she seemed nervous.

Taffy wanted to slap her.

"What the hell's going on?" Taffy said, flinging the cell phone back at Marvelli. "What's Rispoli talking about?"

Marvelli caught the phone, but he was so mad he could barely speak. He couldn't stop thinking about the shoddy medical supplies Taffy had sold, wondering how many people had died because of them, wanting to believe that Taffy was at least partially responsible for his wife's terrible suffering before she'd died. He glanced at his mother-in-law and sister-in-law, trying to avoid looking at Loretta. He felt guilty thinking what he was thinking about Loretta. He should still be in mourning for Rene, he felt. But Loretta was on his mind.

Taffy started shouting: "So whattaya think you're gonna do to me? You think I'm worried about Gus Rispoli? Forget about it. And as for you two"—he pointed at Loretta and Marvelli—"you're just pimples on my butt. You're nothing."

Marvelli wanted to coldcock him, but Larry and Jerry had their guns out, and they weren't smart enough to have second thoughts.

"And you," Taffy said, shaking his fist at Loretta, "I never thought a woman like you could ever betray me like this."

"I didn't betray you," Loretta said. "I was never on your side."

"Oh, yes, you were," Taffy said, pointing to his temple and smiling like a snake. "In my mind you were. In my mind we were like spoons in a drawer. I was all over you, doing the nasty. Doing things you would never imagine in your dirtiest dreams. Making you squeal like a—"

The cell phone flew across the room and beaned Taffy in the head. Marvelli lunged right after it, going for Taffy's throat. He'd heard enough. No one should ever dare talk to Loretta that way.

Marvelli grabbed Taffy by the lapels and wrestled him to the floor. Taffy smashed him across the face with his forearm, but Marvelli didn't feel a thing. As they tussled on the floor, Marvelli fought to get both hands around Taffy's throat, determined to strangle him.

But the twins were on top of Marvelli in a flash. Jerry grabbed him by the collar and hauled him off Taffy while Larry jammed the barrel of his gun between Marvelli's nose and cheek.

"Do him!" Taffy screamed. His face was scarlet.

"No!" Loretta, Jennifer, and Annette screamed in unison.

"I said, do him!" Taffy ordered, getting up on his elbows. "Now!"

"Okay, Taf," Jerry said, sticking his gun on the other side of Marvelli's face. He looked at his brother. "On three," he said. "One, two, thr—"

Shots rang out, but not from Larry's and Jerry's guns. The twins hit the floor, followed by Springer and Loretta. Annette and Jennifer stayed on their feet, clutching each other and screaming, but they could barely be heard over the barrage of automatic gunfire. The metal door on the other side of the pilothouse was sprouting bumps. The gunfire stopped, and the door burst open, sprung on its hinges.

"Kiss the floor, you mothers!" Sammy was standing in a swirl of gunsmoke, an AK-47 assault rifle in his hands. When he realized that everyone was already on the floor, he seemed a little disappointed.

Taffy scowled at him. "What're you? Rambo?"

Marvelli was furious. "What the hell's wrong with you, Sammy? You could've killed someone."

"Well . . . that's what I do, right?" He noticed Larry and Jerry slowly squirming on the floor, positioning themselves to make a move. Sammy waved the muzzle of his rifle in their faces, giving them a good sniff of burnt powder to remind them who had the firepower here. "Throw your pieces in the corner, boys," he ordered. But when they didn't move fast enough, Sammy jabbed their scalps with the AK-47. Two automatics instantly clattered into the corner near Loretta, who was just getting to her feet.

Marvelli caught Loretta's eye, and she gave him a tight nod. She knew what he was thinking: *Grab the guns.*

But as Loretta started to bend down, Springer suddenly got to her knees and pulled her gun, extending her arm so that it was just a few feet from Jennifer's face. Her hand was shaking, but at point-blank range she didn't have to be steady. Jennifer cringed, but she didn't make a peep.

Springer's glance shot around the room, finally settling on Sammy. "If you like your wife's face, don't do anything stupid. Taffy," she said, "get up. We're out of here."

Taffy got off the floor. "Finally you have a good idea."

Springer got up and moved behind Jennifer, putting the gun to the back of her head. "Move," she ordered. "You're coming with us." Jennifer was too scared to object.

But as Taffy headed for the door, he suddenly stopped in front of Loretta. "This is for what could have been, honeybuns." He grabbed the back of her head and ground a kiss into her lips. "Believe me, you would've liked it," he breathed in her face. "*Ciao,* babies," he said with a smart-ass grin, and followed Springer and Jennifer out the door.

Marvelli stared at Taffy's departing back, his eyes bulging. His head was ready to explode.

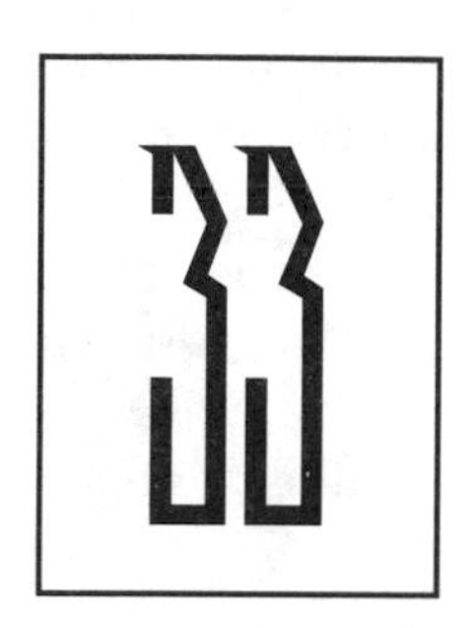

"Loretta!" Marvelli yelled.

She didn't have to be told; she was already reaching for the twin's automatics, tossing one to Marvelli and keeping the other.

He jumped to his feet. "Keep these two right here," he said to Sammy, pointing down at Larry and Jerry.

Sammy already had the two prone brothers at bay, but he looked like he was going to cry. "But what about Jennifer?" he wailed.

"Don't worry about her. I'll handle it," Marvelli said, then he turned to his mother-in-law. "Annette, go find a phone and call nine-one-one."

Annette threw up her hands in exasperation. "And what should I tell them?"

"Just tell them what happened and tell them to send some men. A lot of men."

"Okay. If that's what you want," she said, but she sounded dubious.

Marvelli went up to Loretta. "You all right?"

"I'm fine," she said. "Come on, let's go." She seemed annoyed that he'd bothered to ask, but he was worried about her. He wanted to know if Taffy had done anything to her, but he knew better than to ask. Loretta's bark was as bad as her bite.

They went to the doorway together, Marvelli putting his back to the doorframe as Loretta cautiously peeked outside, leading with her gun. She always went first because she was the better shot.

"It's clear," Loretta said. She burst through the doorway with Marvelli right behind her.

They rushed off the tugboat and started running down the dock.

"Crap!" Loretta snarled.

"What?"

"You try running in heels."

"I used to all the time."

"What?"

"You remember when platforms were popular for men? John Travolta? Disco?"

Loretta gave him a look. "You weren't a PO back then. What were you running after?"

"I was running *away*. From cops mostly. I was a pretty bad kid."

"Gimme a break, Marvelli."

The dock led them to a parking lot where they scanned the cars for signs of Taffy and Agent Springer. In the middle of the lot, a lone figure waved to them frantically. It was Rispoli standing next to the open driver's door of Marvelli's green Taurus. Rispoli got in, started the engine, and burned rubber, racing around the lot to meet them.

"Where ya been?" he yelled as Marvelli opened the passenger door and got it. Loretta jumped into the backseat. "They're gonna get away, for cryin' out loud."

Loretta leaned in between the front seats. "You saw them? Taffy and Springer?"

"Of course I saw them," Rispoli said. "They just left. Black Mercury Marquis. She was driving."

"Fed-mobile," Marvelli and Loretta said simultaneously.

"Maybe we can still catch 'em," Rispoli said.

He floored the accelerator, and the car shot off like a rocket, shutting Marvelli's door for him. The Taurus screeched around the parking lot and headed for the street. Marvelli caught a glimpse of the speedometer as they bounced over the curb. Rispoli was doing sixty, and they weren't even out on the street yet.

Loretta was ricocheting around in the backseat like an atomic particle. "Take it easy, will you?" she complained.

"Take it easy later," Rispoli grumbled. "I got a man to whack."

Loretta and Marvelli exchanged knowing glances. Rispoli was out to get Taffy, but they couldn't let that happen. As much as Taffy deserved it, murder was still murder, and they were officers of the law. But Rispoli was the expert in tracking people down, so they weren't about to put a fly in his ointment now. Marvelli knew very well that you don't tell a Sicilian what he doesn't want to hear, then expect him to help you out anyway. It just wasn't in the genes.

"Look out!" Loretta screamed as Rispoli ran a red light.

The hit man didn't hear her; he was on automatic pilot. He fishtailed around a corner and made a beeline for the entrance ramp to Alaskan Way. The engine was straining to keep up with the driver's demands. At the top of the ramp, Rispoli shot out into traffic without even looking. Marvelli clutched the sides of his seat and watched Rispoli's feet. He kept the pedal to the metal and ignored the brake completely.

They were whizzing past cars in a kaleidoscopic blur of headlights and taillights. Marvelli checked the speedometer again. They were doing over a hundred.

Marvelli's head was pressed against the headrest. He could feel G-forces. "Gus, don't you think we ought to slow down a little before we—"

"Thar she friggin' blows!" Rispoli shouted. He was pointing up ahead, smiling with mean glee, which made Marvelli very nervous. Rispoli smiled like the Grinch.

A shiny black Mercury was weaving in and out of traffic at breakneck speed.

Rispoli shook his head in disappointment. "Where the hell's the cops? They never see this stuff when it happens."

"Feds go to school to learn how to drive like that," Loretta pointed out.

"That ain't how you do it," Rispoli snarled. "That's dangerous. *This* is how you do it."

He slipped into the fast lane and floored it, coming up fast behind a white Porsche.

"Look out!" Marvelli shouted.

But Rispoli was unaffected. The front bumper of the Taurus kissed the Porsche's rear bumper with a not-too-gentle clunk. Instantly the Porsche jumped out of the lane, and Rispoli zipped past him.

"See? That's how you cover ground. You take over one lane. Make it yours." Rispoli was satisfied with himself, but Marvelli was starting to get hungry. He always got hungry when he was nervous.

Rispoli soon pulled up neck and neck with the Mercury. Springer was driving, her face scrunched and intense. Taffy was in the passenger seat, holding on to the dashboard. When he looked past Springer to see who was driving as crazy as they were, Rispoli gave him the finger. "Die, you dirty mother—"

"Watch the road," Marvelli yelled.

Suddenly Springer braked hard and veered into the slow lane, letting Rispoli pass. She cut her speed in half and pulled up behind a trailer truck.

"She's gonna get off," Loretta shouted. "She's gonna take the next exit."

"I know that," Rispoli muttered as he hit the brake and swerved into the middle lane, trying to wedge his way into the slow lane. Horns blared and tires screeched. He bullied his way in with less than fifty feet to spare before the exit. There were four cars between them and the Mercury. He took the exit, speeding up instead of slowing down, driving in the breakdown lane and passing cars on the right.

Springer accelerated, too, passing cars on the ramp. By the

time they got to the bottom, there were still three cars between the Taurus and the Mercury.

The Mercury took a right at the bottom of the ramp, then the first left, beating the oncoming traffic by jumping ahead just as the traffic light turned green. Rispoli was determined to keep up, so he flashed the headlights and blew the horn, aggressively playing chicken with the cars coming toward him. He made his way through, but several other cars had gotten between him and the Mercury.

"I can't even see them," Loretta said. "Where'd they go?"

"You lost 'em," Marvelli said, looking at Rispoli. But when Rispoli's thin lips turned into a devilish grimace, Marvelli knew he had said the wrong thing.

"I never lose anyone unless I wanna lose 'em," Rispoli hissed. He turned the wheel sharply to the left and pulled into a driveway that led to a warehouse. But instead of pulling all the way in, he cut the wheel right and drove up on the sidewalk.

"Get outta my way," he yelled out the open window at the pedestrians as he sailed along. A grungy gang of teenagers yelled back, intent on holding their ground, but when they saw that the green Taurus wasn't going to stop, they were forced to dive onto the hoods of parked cars as if they were diving into a mosh pit.

Deep hoarse belly laughs erupted from Rispoli. Marvelli thought about all the reports he was going to have to file when this was all over. Unless he got killed in an accident first, which was a definite possibility. He glanced over the seat back at Loretta. "Why don't you put on your seat belt?" he said.

She gave him a funny look. "It's a little late now."

"No, you listen to him," Rispoli said as he picked up speed and started passing the cars in the street who were stuck in traffic. "Put on the belt. Just in case."

"Just in case of what?" she asked.

He gunned the engine and the car surged forward.

Marvelli's eyes widened. Rispoli was going to jump the curb at the corner, even though it was a narrow squeeze between the traffic-light post and a newsstand. "Gus! You're won't fit!" he yelled, bracing himself against the dashboard.

"You never know," Rispoli rasped. "I may get lucky." He gave it more gas, leaning on the horn to warn the pedestrians.

"Stop!" Loretta screamed from the backseat.

But it was too late. The corner was coming up fast. Marvelli was certain the space was too narrow for them to fit.

Suddenly he was hurled forward only to be caught by his seat belt. He could hear the sound of crunching metal, but the air bags had inflated and he couldn't see anything for a moment. The car jerked to a halt. On the passenger side the light post had shaved off the front fender. Newspapers and magazines were scattered all over the driver's side. A very angry Pakistani man wearing a *USA Today* apron was pounding on the windshield with his fists. Marvelli looked over the seat back, worried about Loretta. She was lying on the floor.

"Loretta!"

"I'm fine, I'm fine," she growled, picking herself up.

Rispoli pointed through the windshield. "They're getting away."

The accident had gridlocked the entire intersection, but Springer and Taffy had abandoned their car and were hightailing it up a side street on foot.

"Go get 'em," Rispoli urged. "Hurry up. Go."

Loretta immediately shouldered her door open and got out, but Marvelli hung back. "Aren't you coming, Gus?"

Rispoli shook his head. "Too tempting."

"What do you mean, 'too tempting'?"

"With Taffy it's personal now. A hit should never be personal. That's how you screw up. I wanna keep my record intact." A funny little smile lifted the corners of the hit man's mouth.

Marvelli understood. "And you wouldn't want to screw up your deal with the government by doing another hit after you supposedly turned over a new leaf, right?"

"Yeah, that might have something to do with it, too."

"Marvelli!" Loretta was on the other side of his window. "Come on. Let's go."

The Pakistani man was pounding on the roof with both fists. Rispoli rolled down his window three inches. "Enough!" he barked at the man, then he turned to Marvelli. "Get going. Hurry up."

Marvelli kicked the mangled door until it finally opened.

Rispoli laid a hand on Marvelli's elbow. "Just one thing before you go. Shoot for the body first—the chest is best. Knock him down, then follow up with a second shot to the head. And be quick. That's how you do it."

Marvelli was puzzled. "I'm gonna arrest them, Gus. What do you think I'm gonna do?"

Rispoli put a vise grip on Marvelli's forearm. "No, you listen to me," he yelled. "First the knockdown, then the kill shot to the head. That's how you do it. That's how Taffy'll do it to *you*." Rispoli's eyes were glistening. He was dead serious.

"They're splitting up," Loretta called back to Marvelli as they dodged around honking cars stalled in traffic. Taffy and Springer were up ahead on opposite sides of the street, making tracks. "You take Taffy," Loretta said. "I'll take Springer."

"Sounds good to me," Marvelli said as he leaped the curb and sprinted down the sidewalk after Taffy.

Loretta headed for Springer, but she was worried about her partner. He had a gun in his hand, but he was more likely to shoot himself than Taffy. Marvelli couldn't shoot for beans.

Springer was rounding the corner at the end of the block, and Loretta knew she'd better get moving or she'd lose the little witch. Fortunately, even though Springer was small, she wasn't very fast. It had probably been a while since she'd had to pass the FBI endurance test at Quantico.

Loretta was running in the street alongside the jammed traffic, heading for the corner, when suddenly a hand grabbed her forearm and stopped her in her tracks.

A bearded, middle-aged man driving an old beat-up white Cadillac leered up at her through his open window. He was looking her up and down, assessing the goods. "Hey, sugar, you wanna party?"

Loretta pointed her gun in his face. "You want a hemorrhage?"

The man let go immediately, and though she wanted to smack him for assuming she was a hooker just because she was dressed that way, she ran off after Springer, not wanting to waste time.

She ran on her toes because of the high heels, but when she reached the corner, she decided to kick them off and run barefoot. Springer was already at the end of the block about to cross the street, so Loretta poured on the steam, pushing her moussed and sprayed tresses out of her face, praying she didn't step on any broken glass.

"Stop!" she shouted at Springer. "You're under arrest!" But Springer was too far away to hear, and anyway a pill-popping feebie with a major-league attitude problem who was about to face multiple felony counts wasn't going to come along quietly, not to a lowly parole officer from New Jersey.

Loretta came up to the corner and watched for a break in the traffic so that she could run across. She stepped off the curb and forced a red Jeep Cherokee to slow down. The driver cursed at her and blew his horn. She paid him no mind and kept her eye on Springer's neat cap of blond hair. The block ahead was a short one, and Loretta could see Springer turning left at the next intersection. Loretta was getting winded, but she willed herself on. She wished she hadn't had so much champagne and that she'd had a little more espresso. Her caffeine buzz was wearing off.

When Loretta turned the corner at the end of the block, she noticed the street sign. She was on Pike Street. She looked ahead and saw crowds of people strolling the sidewalks, wandering in and out of an array of different buildings. A mishmash collage of colorful signs—some classy, some outlandish—hung from the facades of the buildings. There were signs for food stalls, fruit and vegetable stands, meat markets, fishmongers, flower retailers. She'd never been here, but she'd heard about this place. It was the Pike Place Market.

A little blond head ducked into one of the first buildings in the market. Loretta wasn't even sure if it was Springer, but she ran anyway. She wasn't about to let her get away because it would give Springer time to set up an alibi for herself. Springer was dirty, through and through, and Loretta was determined to expose her.

Loretta muscled through the crush of tourists at the entrance to the building. She pushed through the glass doors and was immediately stunned by what she saw. It was like a carnival inside, a tornado of sights, sounds, smells, and faces. And blondes. There were blond women everywhere. How was she ever going to find Springer?

Suddenly she heard a scream echo across the high ceilings.

"Look out!" a man at the edge of the crowd yelled. "She has a gun!"

Loretta assumed this person was talking about her because she had the automatic in her hand, but then a skinny nervous-looking woman pointed at her and screeched. "Oh, my God! The prostitute has a gun, too! Call the police!"

The people in the immediate area scattered, but most of them hardly took notice. But there were also people scattering farther down the hallway. *They must be running from Springer,* Loretta thought.

Loretta dashed down the hallway and down a short flight of steps. She spotted an alarmed old gentleman in a white suit and a Panama hat. He nodded at the nearest shop, pointing with his eyes. Obviously he feared for his life and hoped that Loretta would spare him if he indicated where the other woman with the gun had gone.

"Thanks," Loretta said as she went into the shop, gun pointed up. The space was big, almost as big as a supermarket. She wasn't sure exactly what they sold here until she took a good whiff. Exotic aromas tingled her nose. She scanned the signs at the top of each aisle: Spices, Herbs, Oils & Vinegars, Condiments, Tea, Coffee.

The overpowering smells were making her light-headed. "Where are you, Springer?" she shouted. "Throw down your gun and come out right now."

Suddenly a stampede of footsteps came out of nowhere as at least a dozen customers and staff bolted out of the aisles, running past Loretta and out of the store, giving her a wide berth. None of them was Springer.

"Springer!" she hollered. "Where are you?"

All of a sudden the store was so quiet Loretta could hear the fluorescent lights buzzing. She glanced back at the old gentleman in the white suit by the entrance. He just shrugged, eyes wide. She turned back to the aisles.

"Springer," she shouted into the silence, "where are you, dammit?"

Marvelli couldn't believe this. He'd followed Taffy into the Tattooed Walrus Brew Pub, but now he couldn't find him. The place was packed with kids, the pierced-eyebrow crowd, and most of them were on the dance floor, stomping to the wails and shouts of a particularly bad grunge band up on stage. It was made up of the usual two guitars, bass, and drums, and Marvelli didn't think much of them—big volume, little talent, zero fashion sense. But what was really bothering Marvelli was how Taffy could have disappeared in here. A guy in his fifties dressed like a Guido from Newark should stick out like a sore thumb in this place. Maybe Taffy had ducked out a back door, Marvelli thought. But how did he get through the sardine-can crush on the dance floor? It would definitely take more than a couple of minutes to do that.

The room was dark and cavernous, with random spotlights sending splashes of blue and yellow light across the bare brick walls. The bar itself was a battered and scarred dark-wood antique, and Marvelli imagined crusty old sailors getting plastered here a hundred years ago. Behind the bandstand there were four huge copper vats, almost two stories high, and each one had a hand-painted sign on it: Walrus India Pale Ale, Stinky Feet Pilsner, Bob's Brown Ale, and Get Shorter Porter. Marvelli couldn't imagine how that music didn't curdle the beer.

The band abruptly ended the song they were playing and went into a huddle. It seemed like they were trying to figure out what to play next. Marvelli thumbed the safety on his gun, which was jammed into his waistband. He wasn't about to use it in here. He waded out into the crowd, searching faces and looking for signs of Taffy's salt-and-pepper blow dry among the cropped candy-colored cuts and the multiple piercings.

A skinny kid with short bleached-out hair and dark roots wearing a ripped white V-neck T-shirt stared at him as if he'd just arrived from the moon. "Hey, man, who are you supposed to be? Like John Travolta?"

Marvelli narrowed his eyes. "Excuse me?" Coming from someone else, he would've taken that as a compliment.

The skinny kid laughed through his nose and stared at Marvelli's clothes, which were just his normal work clothes—a black-and-white check sports jacket over a black T-shirt and pressed black jeans. "I mean, like, come on, dude," the kid said. "You're so . . . seventies."

"And what's wrong with that?" Marvelli asked, trying hard not to take offense. The seventies were a very good time for him. He'd met Rene in the seventies.

"No, no, no, don't get me wrong," the kid said. "I think it's cool . . . but it's, like, weird." The kid was looking past Marvelli.

The band started playing again with a high-impact blast that could've passed for a car crash. The kid was alternately grinning at him and looking past him. Finally Marvelli turned around to see what he was looking at. A girl with a nose ring and streaks of blue in her straggly brown hair was grinning at him mischievously.

"Hi," she said, shouting over the music.

"Hi," Marvelli said, trying to figure out what these two were up to.

But then suddenly Marvelli felt his knees buckling as he was lifted up off his feet and hoisted over the crowd on his back.

"Hey!" he yelled.

"Relax, dude," the skinny kid shouted. "This'll do you some good."

"No, it won't. Put me down."

"Easy, dude. Just go with it."

"This isn't funny," Marvelli yelled. "Put me down!"

But there was no stopping the momentum as dozens of hands held him aloft, passing him over a shifting sea of arms and heads. Marvelli didn't like the feeling of being out of control, and he started to panic. He had to get down. He had to find Taffy, arrest him, get him in cuffs. Then he had to go help Loretta. She could be in trouble.

"Put me down!" he hollered.

But no one was listening. It was doubtful that they could even hear him over the band. The crowd jostled him up and down, jerking him this way and that. The hands on his back felt creepy, like bugs crawling all over him.

"Put me down! Come on!" he yelled at the top of his lungs. *"I'm afraid of heights! Put me—! Hey!"*

Marvelli reached across his body to feel for his gun, but it wasn't there. It was gone. It must have fallen out.

Oh, crap! Marvelli thought. Somewhere in this crowd of kids was a loaded automatic. He imagined them using it to pierce themselves.

"Put me down!" he shouted. *"Please!"*

But as he started drifting toward the band with his arms outstretched and his legs pinned together, he lifted his head and spotted Taffy, who was looking right at him. The mobster was behind the band between two of the copper beer vats. There was a look of determination in his eyes and a silver automatic in his hand down by his side.

Marvelli was carried closer to the bandstand, closer to Taffy. He struggled and tried to fight the hands holding him up, but it was no use. Taffy grinned as he raised his gun hand.

"Put me down!"

Taffy's arm was outstretched, his silver automatic a gleaming point of light in the shadows of the beer vats. Unfortunately, Marvelli was the only one who seemed to notice.

He struggled and flailed. "*Put me down! Come on!*" But he'd given himself a sore throat from yelling, and his voice was hoarse and weak.

Taffy stepped out from behind the vats and muscled his way past the band, shoving the bass player to the floor. The band stopped playing, one instrument at a time, as each member finally realized that the old guy on stage was carrying a gun. The drummer played solo for almost a full minute before he noticed. The crowd saw the gun, too, and they abruptly dropped Marvelli to the floor, moving away from him as if he were poison. Taffy stood at the edge of the bandstand, pointing the gun down at Marvelli. Blue footlights streaked Taffy's face. It looked like he was wearing war paint.

Sitting on the floor and leaning back on his hands, Marvelli stared up at Taffy, his heart slam-dancing in his chest.

This is it, Marvelli thought. *The bastard killed Rene, now he's gonna kill me.*

Taffy's arm stiffened. He was taking aim.

"Mexican standoff, dude!" a voice boomed through the room. The skinny kid with the bad dye job was standing behind Taffy, holding the lead singer's mike in one hand, Marvelli's gun in the other. His arm was outstretched, the gun three feet from Taffy's head.

"This is cool," the kid said into the mike. "It's, like, seventies night at the Walrus. Burt Reynolds versus John Travolta. Cool."

Taffy's face turned to stone. "I'm not kidding around here, son."

"You are really great, man. I mean, like, you're perfect." The kid was grinning. He thought this was an act. "Okay, Burt," he said, "like, drop the gun, man." The kid advanced on Taffy and actually stuck the gun in Taffy's ear. "Come on, dude. Move."

Taffy moved two feet to the side and stumbled over the lead guitarist's wahwah pedal, but he wasn't letting go of his weapon. The expression on his face was pure malice. His fist was white around the butt of the gun.

"Get away from me, son."

"No way, man. Like, I've got the upper hand now."

"No you don't."

"What do you mean—? Hey!"

Taffy batted the kid's hand away, and the gun flew across the stage, hitting one of the copper vats with a loud clang. He raised his gun and leveled it on the kid's chest at point-blank range.

Taffy's gaze sharpened to lethal pinpoints. "Say good-bye, son."

"Hey, good line, man." The kid was still grinning. He was totally oblivious to the danger he was in. He looked to Marvelli. "Isn't Travolta supposed to be the good guy in this thing? Isn't he supposed to, like, win?"

Taffy sneered at him. "What the frig are you talking—?"

A ruckus from the back of the bandstand suddenly distracted Taffy. He turned toward the noise, but it was too late to react. The drum set was charging him.

"Hey!" he shouted.

The drums kept coming, plowing into him and knocking him

off the stage. Marvelli stood at the edge of the stage, looking down at the mobster sprawled out on the floor. Marvelli was holding the bass drum on his hip, using the crash cymbal as his shield. He had managed to sneak around to the back of the stage while Taffy was busy with the skinny kid.

Taffy was dazed, his eyes out of sync, but he was waving the gun in the air, looking for a target. "Marvelli!" he yelled. "Marvelli!"

"What?"

"I'm gonna kill you, you bastard. I'm gonna—"

The drums landed on top of Taffy and shut him up immediately. Marvelli grabbed a solid-body electric guitar from a nearby stand and leaped off the stage, ready to clobber Taffy with it, but Taffy was out cold. Marvelli took the gun out of his limp hand.

"John Travolta beats Burt Reynolds. Pretty cool, wouldn't you say?" The skinny kid was back at the mike. "Okay, next round. How about Travolta versus Marsha Brady? Any volunteers?"

Marvelli shook his head and sighed as he knelt over Taffy and pulled out his handcuffs.

Loretta walked slowly down the spice aisle, leading with her gun, her eyes darting left and right. The store was dead quiet, but she could feel Springer's hostile presence. The woman had had it in for Loretta from the moment they'd met, and now Loretta knew her dirty little secret. If Springer was carrying a gun, which was pretty likely for an FBI agent, Loretta would be her prime target.

And Marvelli, Loretta thought, creasing her brow. Springer would want him out of the picture, too. *Over my dead body,* she thought.

As she moved down the aisle, Loretta caught glimpses of the bottles, boxes, and bags of spices that filled the racks: Anise, cumin, curry, garam masala, thyme, sage, rosemary, oregano, mace, cardamom, paprika, white peppercorns, pink peppercorns, black peppercorns, sea salt, kosher salt, chili powder, allspice, nutmeg, dill, tarragon, basil, and bay leaves as well as dozens of other spices she'd never even heard of. It got her to thinking of witches and the ingredients they boiled up in their cauldrons—eye of newt, balls of bullfrog, and all that stuff—and she imagined that Springer was someplace in the store, mixing up some kind of concoction that she could use against her and Marvelli, a potion that would make them both disappear forever.

Well, at least we'd be together, Loretta thought.

Loretta came to the end of the aisle and cautiously made the turn into the next aisle, the coffee aisle. Open burlap bags of coffee beans stood up at attention all the way down the aisle on both sides, like footmen in a royal coffee court. The smells went right to her head. It was gaseous caffeine. She could feel the jangling start in her veins, like little tambourines, traveling down her forearms all the way to her fingertips, rounding her scalp and zipping down her spine. The buzz intensified and started to feel like a radioactive glow emanating from her entire body. She felt like a hundred-watt lightbulb.

She scanned the stenciling on the burlap bags. Colombian, Mexican, Breakfast Blend, Sumatra, Tanzanian Peaberry, Kona, Jamaican Mountain Blue, Guatamalan Antigua, Mocha Java, Espresso, French Roast, Chicory, Vanilla, Amaretto, Almond, Hazelnut. How could she ever give all this up? What was she thinking when she'd decided to quit? Who in their right mind gives up coffee?

She spied a sack of chocolate-covered espresso beans, and she started to swoon. Chocolate and coffee *together,* the staples of life.

Just a couple, she thought. *For energy. I'll leave some money at the cash register.*

She reached out for the sack, her fingertips swirling through the dark shiny beads as she admired how they caught the light. She started to close her fingers on a fistful, already anticipating the taste, when suddenly the whole sack toppled forward and spilled onto the floor in a dark brown splash. Loretta instinctively backed away as the beans buried her feet. Her first thought was that she was going to be blamed for this.

But then the next sack suddenly toppled over. And then the

one after that. And then the next one, and the next, and the next. They fell over like dominoes, spilling so many beans the white tile floor was completely covered.

A lone figure appeared at the end of the aisle, and Loretta instantly assumed the three-point stance—feet apart, gun extended in both hands. She stared across the coffee-bean desert, and Special Agent Springer stared back at her. Their faces were as grim and determined as gunslingers.

Springer was holding a blue-steel revolver, but she raised both hands above her head in surrender. She pitched the gun into the coffee beans far out of reach. "I'm not armed," she said, but she seemed too calm, calm to the point of being smug.

"You're under arrest," Loretta said as she waded through the beans.

"Me? What for?"

Loretta almost laughed out loud. Springer knew right well what she'd done. "Kidnapping," Loretta said, "conspiracy to commit murder, extortion—"

Springer cut her short with a disinterested shrug. "That's your word against mine."

"Mine and Marvelli's and Gus Rispoli's."

"Oh, yes, three stellar citizens," Springer said sarcastically. "Two parole officers and a convicted murderer. Whose word do you think will count for more? You three or a special agent of the Federal Bureau of Investigation?"

"You seem pretty sure about that."

Springer just shrugged.

"I'm still going to arrest you," Loretta said. Her finger was tight on the trigger. She was struggling to keep a lid on her temper.

Springer was shaking her head. "You're not here to arrest me, Loretta. You're here to punish me." She reached across her body and suddenly tore the breast pocket off her own blazer. Then she tore open her blouse, ripping all the buttons off.

Loretta frowned. "What the hell are you doing?"

Springer mussed up her hair. "You're out for revenge, Loretta. That's why you tracked me down. That's why you made this big mess." Springer waved her hand over the coffee-bean dunes. "This is a *personal* thing."

Loretta just stared at her. Yes, she hated Springer's guts, but she would never go on a rampage against anyone. She preferred to savor her vendettas.

"You just don't like me," Springer said with a smirk as she kicked off one shoe and sent it sailing up the aisle where it landed with a crunch. "You hate me for a lot of reasons. You hate me because I lost weight and you can't."

"That's a lie."

"You hate me because I'm a fed and you're just a lowly PO." Springer pulled out her shirttail and ripped it.

"You think this is gonna work?" Loretta said. "People are gonna believe I beat you up just because I didn't like you? Dream on, toots. This won't wash."

"My word against yours, sweetie."

"You're dreaming. It doesn't make sense. Your logic adds up to nothing."

Springer grinned. "The big reason you hate me is because your heartthrob Marvelli has tight shorts for me instead of you."

"You're dreaming," Loretta repeated, but her heart was beating fast. How did Springer know how she felt about Marvelli?

Springer laughed. "Fat girl pining away for her hunky partner loses out to the cute little blond fed. This kind of thing happens to you all the time, doesn't it? But this time you just couldn't take it anymore. This time you snapped." Suddenly Springer banged her head hard against the corner of the stainless-steel shelving. She felt her temple and smiled when she saw blood on her fingers.

Tears welled in Loretta's eyes, but she was determined not to cry. She wasn't going to let this nut case get to her. What Springer had said wasn't true. Marvelli had no feelings for either of them.

Springer stood on her toes and pulled down an electric coffeepot from a high shelf, carefully using her unfolded French cuffs to hold it so as not to leave any fingerprints. She turned out her knee and smashed it against her inner thigh, then did it again. She was making bruises.

"You're nuts," Loretta said, astounded by what she was seeing.

Springer grinned and shook her head. "Self-preservation. It's an art." She checked her head wound to make sure it was bleeding enough. "Now the way I see it, you have two choices. Either you can stick around and take the rap for beating me up and all the other illegal stunts you pulled since you arrived in Seattle. Or you can take off right now. Run. Hide. Maybe you'll get lucky. Maybe you'll find another stud muffin like Marvelli at some truck stop out in the middle of nowhere. You can settle down and be the trailer park queen of East Overshoes, Arkansas."

"Nobody's gonna believe you. You know that."

"Oh, if I stick to my story, they will. I'm a fed, after all, the best of the best. They'll eat it up with a spoon when I explain that you and Marvelli were in cahoots with Sammy Teitelbaum—Marvelli's brother-in-law no less—and that Sammy was giving you a cut of the fee that Taffy was going to pay him for the hit on Rispoli."

"You're unbelievable," Loretta said with a wry grin, but inside dread was filling her chest as she realized that Springer could actually pull this off. Loretta and Marvelli had conned their way into My Blue Heaven to get Rispoli out, and the connection between Sammy and Marvelli did look bad.

Springer smacked herself in the shin with the coffeepot. "And then," she said, "when I tell them that Marvelli seduced me—well, it was closer to rape actually—I'll get all the sympathy in the world."

"Forget it," Loretta shouted angrily. "No one who knows Marvelli will believe that."

Springer shrugged. "My word against his." She examined the cut on her shin, then tossed the coffeepot aside.

Loretta's hands were sweaty. She was struggling not to pull the trigger. From this distance she could plug the witch easy, drop her where she stood, then rush up and empty her load into Springer's frozen excuse for a heart.

"You gonna shoot me, Loretta?" Springer asked. "Fantastic.

It'll just make my story all the more plausible." She started to chuckle. "But you know something? I really don't think you have the guts to do it. I mean you have a gut, but you don't have the guts. Maybe that's why Marvelli preferred me over you."

Loretta's eyes bulged. Her jaw was tight, and her head was throbbing. She squinted down the barrel of the automatic, intent on putting one right through Springer's tight little abs. Gut shots were supposed to be the most painful.

But then she stopped herself and thought about it. *This is just what the little witch wants,* she thought. *She* wants *me to hurt her. I'm not gonna do it.*

Suddenly Loretta tossed her gun into a open sack of white-chocolate-covered espresso beans. Shuffling through the field of coffee beans, she skated up the aisle, her eyes locked on Springer's.

"What're you doing?" Springer said. She dropped the smarmy grin and took a step back.

Loretta started shaking her head. "It's what I'm *not* doing. I'm not playing your game, honey."

Springer took another step backward, wincing as she stepped barefoot on stray coffee beans.

"What's the matter, Springer? You look like you're in pain. Why don't you just take a few more diet pills? That'll make everything all right. It always does, doesn't it?"

"I don't know what you're talking about."

"Sure, you do. When things get tough, and you're nervous and aggravated, and all you want is a bag of chocolate-chip cookies, you take a couple of pills and presto! you're fine again. No appetite. Ready for anything."

"I don't take pills." Springer was moving away faster, trying to run, but the self-inflicted coffeepot blows were more damaging than she'd thought, and she was hobbling in pain. She retreated into the tea aisle where hundreds of glass apothecary jars held loose tea blends in various shades of brown, green, and yellow.

Loretta stayed on her trail. "I saw you taking your pills the first time we met, Springer. But I don't blame you. Someone in your situation doesn't need to be fat on top of everything else."

"What do you mean, 'everything else'?" Springer snarled over her shoulder.

"Same old story: Hard-as-nails career woman trying to survive in a boy's club. You know you'll never be one of the guys, but you'll never be anyone's sweetheart either. Caught between a rock and hard place with a glass ceiling on top. I don't blame you for popping diet pills like M&Ms. A woman like you has to hang on to every advantage she has. I mean, what are you? Forty-something? You still look all right for your age."

Springer shook her head as she hobbled backward down the aisle. "Save your breath. That's not gonna work with me."

"No wonder you're attracted to Marvelli. A good-looking guy, at least ten years younger than you—what's not to like? He'd make a good trophy husband. You could show him off at feebie cocktail parties in D.C."

Springer turned her back on Loretta and struggled on, rounding the tea aisle and stumbling back into the coffee aisle.

Loretta followed her. "Of course, it's not exactly the same for a woman," she said. "People would look down on you. To them, being with Marvelli would be like picking up a hustler. Very unseemly for a federal agent. It would definitely hurt your career."

Springer dragged her injured leg through the spilled coffee beans.

"You might do better with Taffy Demaggio," Loretta suggested. "More age appropriate. Besides, you're already in bed with him. May as well show him off to all your colleagues."

"No!" Springer screamed as she wheeled around and faced Loretta. Her face was drenched in sweat. She was like a trapped animal, her eyes wild, darting all around. "You're wrong!"

Springer's gaze was fixed on one of the burlap sacks that hadn't toppled over. Loretta followed her gaze to the sack full of white-chocolate-covered espresso beans. Her automatic was sitting on top. Springer lunged for the gun, tipping over the sack as Loretta dove into the beans. But Springer snatched up the weapon first and held it out in both hands, feet planted ankle deep in coffee beans.

Loretta skidded to a stop on the tile floor, her hands splayed out in front of her for protection.

Springer was blinking back tears, her mouth a strained clown frown. "It'll still be my word against yours. I'll say it was self-defense. They'll believe me. I know they will."

"I don't think so." A man's voice came from the end of the aisle.

Loretta glanced past Springer. Marvelli's scruffy FBI pal Mike Tarantella was coming down the aisle, making ski tracks in the coffee beans. He had a big black 9-mm aimed at Springer's back.

"Put the gun down, Springer," he said.

She glanced over her shoulder and was about to bolt when suddenly another man dove between the coffee sacks on the open shelving and grabbed her around the ankles. Tarantella moved in fast to assist, kneeling on her gun hand and taking the weapon away. In no time the men had her handcuffed and back on her feet.

"Come on," Tarantella said as he took her by the elbow and led her toward the front of the store.

Springer didn't resist, but she looked sullen and resentful, glaring at Loretta as she passed.

The other man dusted off his pants as he came up to Loretta. He was compact and barrel-chested, bald to the crown of his head with a hanging nose shaped like a hot pepper. He reached for her elbow, and she automatically shrugged him off.

"You'll have to come with me, Ms. Kovacs," he said firmly. "We have some questions for you."

"How do you know my name?" she asked indignantly.

He flashed a tight grin. "Your reputation precedes you. Come on, let's go."

She shrugged him off again. "Who are you?" she demanded.

His gaze bored into hers. "Special Agent C. Gibson," he said. "Your alias."

Loretta's face fell. "Oh . . . Well . . . thanks for the loan, I guess."

"Don't mention it."

"You don't seem very upset about it."

"Oh, I'm pissed, but not about that."

"What are you pissed about?"

"You not shooting Veronica Springer when you had the chance. Tarantella and I heard the whole thing. You should've shot her. We would've backed you up."

"Really?"

"Absolutely. Anything to get rid of that backstabbing harpy."

"Oh . . . I wish I'd known."

Gibson shrugged. "What can you do?"

Loretta pressed her lips together and shrugged.

"So shall we go?" he said.

"I guess."

They headed for the front of the store together.

Suddenly she stopped. "My partner. Frank Marvelli? Do you know if he's all right?"

Gibson raised his eyebrows and shook his head.

She grabbed his elbow and rushed him along. "Come on, let's go. Quick!"

The next day Loretta was back at the Grind, staring at swirls of steam rising from a double espresso—caffeinated. It was late in the afternoon, and the overcast sky sent a peculiar glare through the plate-glass windows. A motley assortment of luggage waited in a ragged line by the front door. She was sitting with Marvelli, Annette, Jennifer, and Sammy at a round oak table. They were jabbering away about something, but Loretta wasn't listening to any of it. She hadn't even touched her espresso, which Jennifer had provided on the house. She felt too weird. She was thinking maybe she shouldn't have had espresso with Taffy the other night. Maybe she should have stayed on the wagon. But it wasn't just caffeine that was bothering her.

"Loretta? *Loretta?*"

She gradually snapped out of it when she realized that Jennifer was talking to her. "Sorry," she said. "What did you say?"

Jennifer hooked her hair behind her ear and flashed a smile worthy of a toothpaste commercial. "I just wanted to know if you wanted a piece of cake or something."

Loretta shook her head. "No thanks." She glanced at the

dirty plate in front of Marvelli. He'd already polished off a slice of Mississippi mud pie, a blueberry scone, and a piece of linzer torte. He'd said that he was eating now because he didn't want to have to eat the food on the plane, but she knew him better than that. When the meal was served, he'd end up eating his own, hers, *and* Annette's.

Loretta picked up her cup and brought it to her lips, but she couldn't bring herself to take a sip. Staring through the swirls rising from her cup, she watched Jennifer as she came back around the counter with a piece of marbled cheesecake for Marvelli, who accepted it gratefully. She studied Jennifer's eyes as Jennifer watched Marvelli eating. The woman seemed a little too attentive, a little too . . . something. Sammy had picked up on it, too—Loretta could tell from the expression on his face. Sammy was hovering between suspicion and becoming really ticked off.

Annette was leaning back in her chair with her arms folded, ordering her daughter to bring Marvelli more coffee, more cake, more this, more that. It was as if she were training Jennifer in how to serve Marvelli.

Loretta took a tiny sip of her espresso. The taste spread out on her tongue like battery acid. She put the cup down and pushed it away. She eyed Marvelli's cheesecake, wanting just a little bite to kill the taste in her mouth, but she knew she shouldn't, not after that big meal with Taffy.

She shifted her position and crossed her legs, and suddenly she noticed Alan Winslow sitting at one of the computers on the other side of the coffee bar. He must have been staring at her because he was blushing now. She waved to him, and he gave her a tiny wave back, then quickly looked away, embarrassed to have been caught.

She imagined Alan's apartment, recalling the computer room and how Gus Rispoli had made himself comfortable on the futon. Yesterday Special Agents Tarantella and Gibson had escorted Rispoli back to his old digs at My Blue Heaven. From what Loretta had been told, Rispoli would face no additional penalties for his little getaway. He was too valuable—and too cranky—to risk losing his cooperation.

Taffy was under arrest and being held without bail until prosecutors here in Seattle and in New Jersey worked out their jurisdictional problems, trying to figure out who had the better case against the mobster. Larry and Jerry had been arrested, too, but stand-up guys they weren't. They'd offered to flip before the fingerprint ink was even dry on their processing papers. They were more than willing to make a deal in exchange for testimony against their old boss. So no matter which state took him, Taffy was definitely going to be convicted of something.

As for dear little Agent Veronica Springer, no one seemed to know what the feds had done with her. Loretta had asked Tarantella and Gibson about her, but they clammed right up. Maybe there was a special dungeon somewhere in the hinterland where bad feds are sent. Maybe they'd let her diet herself down until she was paper thin, then use her as a target for new recruits at the FBI training grounds at Quantico. A cautionary poster with bullet holes.

Loretta was suddenly pulled out of her ruminations by Jennifer's plaintive voice. "But, Mom, I *love* him."

Loretta's blood pressure instantly shot up. Who was she talking about?

"I don't care about love," Annette said. "He's a bum. Look at him." She pointed an accusing finger at Sammy, and Loretta sighed with relief.

Sammy's mouth fell open, and his glasses slipped down his nose. "What're you talking about, Annette? I saved your lives. You people would've been pepperoni if I hadn't shown up."

Jennifer was nodding vigorously.

But Annette was unmoved. "You're a bum, Sammy, and you always were."

Sammy grabbed Jennifer's hand, and they locked fingers. "We don't care what you say, Annette. We're getting back together. And we're gonna make it work this time."

Annette looked up to heaven as she bit the knuckle of her index finger. "Help me, God. Help me!"

Marvelli took a sip of coffee to help the cheesecake go down. "Just one problem," he said to Sammy.

"What's that?"

Marvelli speared another chunk of cheesecake. "You're wanted for a parole violation back in Jersey. Loretta and I have to take you back."

Loretta's heart started pounding. Jennifer and Sammy *had* to get back together. The thought of Jennifer single under her mother's influence filled Loretta with cold dread.

Sammy pleaded with Marvelli. "Hey, come on, man. Can't you cut me some slack here?"

"It's not up to me, Sammy," Marvelli said, his voice clogged with cheesecake. "I mean, even if we did leave you here, some skip tracer would eventually come looking for you. You're money in the bank to those cannibals."

"How will they know about me?"

"Sammy, you're in the computer. Every bounty hunter from here to Bayonne will know about you."

"Why? I didn't actually kill Rispoli. I only tried."

"Doesn't matter, Sammy. You're still a jumper. You violated the terms of your parole."

"Yeah, but I should never have gone to prison in the first place that time."

Marvelli held up his hand. "Stop! I've heard this song before. Every con I've ever picked up sings it, over and over again. 'I was framed, I didn't do it, it wasn't my fault, it was a mistake.' Please. Spare me, Sammy."

"No, it's the truth," Sammy insisted. He was a little pale, and he seemed to be having trouble getting the words out. "I . . . I never really killed anyone . . . ever. I took that rap for another wiseguy in Taffy's crew so I could get in with those guys. I wanted to get made."

Marvelli stopped eating and stared at him. "Sammy, you're Jewish. They don't make Jewish guys."

"I thought they'd make an exception."

"You mean you never really killed anybody?" Jennifer asked.

Sammy shook his head, clearly ashamed. "I made it all up. I just told everybody I'd done a couple of hits, but it's not true."

Marvelli was dumbfounded. "How could you make up stuff like that?"

Sammy shrugged. "I'm an English major. I just stole the details from books I'd read."

Marvelli just shook his head.

Annette was scowling at Sammy. "What a jerk! At least I thought you knew how to do something. You're worse than I thought."

Sammy looked to Marvelli. "So can't you get me out of the computer? Like I said, I shouldn't have been there in the first place."

"It's not that easy, Sammy. You'll have to go back to Jersey and ask the prosecutor's office to reopen the investigation. Then you'll probably have to have a retrial. It'll take years."

Sammy's chin crumpled. "But I don't wanna go back to Jersey. I want to stay here with Jennifer." A tear clung to the bottom of his horn-rimmed glasses. "Frigging computers!"

"There's nothing I can do," Marvelli said, his brows slanted back in sympathy.

Loretta was all choked up, seeing how much Sammy loved Jennifer. She wanted them to be together—*desperately* wanted them to be together.

"Maybe I can help." Alan Winslow timidly approached the table. He waited until he had everyone's attention before he continued. "I overheard what you were talking about. I mean, I couldn't help it. You people are kind of loud. Anyway, I've gotten into the New Jersey Bureau of Parole's database." He jerked his thumb at the glowing computer screen on the other side of the room. "I can delete Sammy's file if you want."

"Do it," Loretta blurted, then blushed when she heard herself.

"Yeah, do it," Sammy said.

"Please," Jennifer said.

"No!" Annette screeched.

"Wait a minute, wait a minute," Marvelli said, his voice still thick with cheesecake. "You can't tamper with those files. That's against the law."

Alan shrunk back. "Okay. I won't do it. I'll get out of there right now."

"No, wait," Loretta said quickly. "Marvelli, these two people love each other. Have a heart."

"You stay out of it," Annette barked.

"Mom!" Jennifer scolded.

"Loretta, this is against the law," Marvelli said. "We're law enforcement. We can't break the law. Remember?"

"How about *bending* the law?" she said. "You've done that before."

Jennifer gave him the doe eyes. "Please, Frankie," she begged. Her voice was barely more than a squeak.

Annette gripped Marvelli's forearm. "No, Frank," she commanded as if she were telling a dog to sit.

Yes, Loretta thought. *Say yes!*

Marvelli looked at Jennifer and let out a long sigh. "All right, do it," he finally said to Alan.

"No!" Annette yelled. "I'll turn you in. I'll turn *all* of you in."

"Mom!"

Marvelli covered Annette's hand with his. "Listen," he said softly as he pointed at Sammy. "I never believed this mook was capable of murder. I mean, look at him. He's an English major, for chrissake."

"I don't care," Annette said. "I don't want him near—"

"No, no, don't talk. Just listen to me. Sammy's like a boomerang. Even if we take him back to Jersey, eventually he'll show up here again looking for Jennifer. And if he does go back to Jersey, he'll probably go back to hanging out with his mob pals. Better to let him stay here with Jennifer and start a new life." He turned to Sammy. "You are planning on turning over a new leaf, aren't you, Sammy?"

He raised his hand as if he were swearing on the Bible. "Swear to God, Frankie. I was thinking maybe I could teach high-school English or something."

"There you go," Marvelli said.

Annette didn't seem totally convinced, but she wasn't squawking.

Loretta suddenly noticed that Alan was hovering over her. She looked up at him and saw his puppy-dog eyes gazing down on her. He obviously still had a crush on her, and she felt for him, so she stood up and gave him a hug. "Thank you for doing this," she said. Then she took him by the elbow and hustled him back toward the computer. "Come on, let's take care of Sammy's file before there's a thunderstorm or something. The weather's very unpredictable in Seattle."

"Oh, I almost forgot," Alan said, stopping short. He pulled out two diskettes from his shirt pocket. "I was doing a little hacking at home, and I got into this guy Tino's computer in New Jersey. I remembered you and Marvelli talking about him. Well, I downloaded all his files. I didn't read very much of it, but from what I saw, he seems to be in the medical-supply business."

Marvelli overhead him, and his jaw dropped. He stared at the diskettes in Alan's hand as if they were the Holy Grail. "Tino must've kept the books for Taffy. Bingo!" Marvelli was smiling like the sun.

"So do you want these?" Alan asked.

"Oh, by all means," Marvelli said, taking the diskettes. He held them like playing cards. They were his winning hand. "Say good night, Taffy."

"Alan." Loretta tugged on his sleeve.

"Hmmm?"

"Sammy's file. Come on, let's go."

"Oh, yeah." Alan lumbered back to the computer.

Loretta went with him to make sure he didn't get distracted.

Later that night, Marvelli, Annette, and Loretta were at the airport, sitting in the waiting area of their terminal, waiting for their plane to board. They were taking the red-eye, but there was going to be a forty-minute delay before takeoff. Loretta was trying to doze, but Annette's nonstop complaining and the uncomfortable molded plastic chair conspired to keep Loretta from getting any rest.

"This is ridiculous," Annette said to anyone who was listening. She was sitting in the middle between Loretta and Marvelli. "First of all, I don't know why we have to take this midnight flight. Second, I want to know why planes *always* have to be late. I mean, what's the problem now? They got a traffic jam up there?"

Marvelli mumbled something consoling, and Loretta closed her eyes, trying to tune Annette out. She wanted to tune everything out. She felt a little foolish having made a big deal about deleting Sammy's records from the Bureau of Parole's computers. Maybe she was being a little too obvious. And for what? Nothing was ever going to happen with her and Marvelli. Even without Jennifer in the mix, the cards were still stacked against them. Annette was one hurdle; the fact that they worked together was another; and then there was Marvelli himself. He wasn't interested in her, not that way. Loretta was embarrassed for ever thinking she could make something happen. Maybe she *should* go to law school in Chicago, she thought.

"These airlines should be sued when they pull this kind of crap," Annette carried on. "What do they expect us to do? Just sit here and twiddle our thumbs?"

"You know, I just thought of something," Marvelli said. "We didn't buy anything for Nina. I always get her a souvenir whenever I'm away."

"Your own daughter you forget," Annette scolded. "You ought to be ashamed."

"There's a gift shop down the corridor," Marvelli said. "Why don't you go get her something, Annette? I don't know what she likes."

"And why don't you know what she likes?"

Marvelli took a twenty-dollar bill out of his wallet. "Here. Get her something she'll like. I know I'll buy the wrong thing if I go."

Annette snatched the twenty out of his hand and struggled out of her seat. "This won't be enough," she said, waving the twenty at him.

He gave her another twenty. "Get her something nice," he said with a nod and a smile.

She sniffed at him and stalked off. Annette wasn't that big, but there was something about her walk that reminded Loretta of a mountain gorilla.

Finally I can get a little rest, she thought as she closed her eyes and propped her cheek on her fist.

"You sleeping?" Marvelli asked softly.

Loretta thought about pretending. "No," she finally said. "I'm awake."

He got out of his seat and took Annette's. His shoulder was pressing against Loretta's.

"You know, I didn't tell you the other night. You looked pretty good all dolled up."

She frowned at him. "I looked like a hooker."

"Maybe a little, but you still looked good. I was jealous."

She shifted in her seat to face him. "Jealous of what?"

"You being with Taffy."

She just looked at him. She didn't know what to say.

"I was thinking," he said, "when we get back maybe you'll let me take you out to dinner sometime. What do you think?" His eyes were so dark they were almost black. They shined like polished onyx.

He shrugged. "If you don't want to, that's okay."

"No, no. I want to." His face was less than a ruler's length from hers.

He shifted his position, turning sideways as best he could, then reached over and found her hand lying on her thigh. He ran his index finger gently down the length of hers, which relayed a parallel tingle down her spine.

A ruler, she thought. Twelve inches and closing in fast.

She swallowed hard, her breath getting ragged. She could feel his breath on her chin.

"Marvelli?" she whispered.

"What?"

"Do you think this is a good idea?"

"Yes," he said without hesitation.

Suddenly she was soaring. Her heart was a spinning gyroscope in the nose of a rocket.

He moved closer, and his nose touched hers. She closed her

eyes and parted her lips slightly. She felt limp and wired at the same time. His hand covered hers, closing over her fingers.

"Loretta, I—"

"I can't find it!"

Loretta's eyes shot open, and she abruptly jerked her head away. Annette was charging across the carpeting, coming toward them, mad again.

"There's no shop down there," she said accusingly, standing over them with her arms crossed over her chest.

Marvelli had let go of Loretta's hand as soon as they'd heard Annette's voice. Loretta's nerves were jangling, and she felt moist all over.

"I said I can't find it, Frank," Annette repeated. "What're we gonna do? We gotta get something for Nina."

"Ah . . . I'll show you where it is," Marvelli said. "Come on."

Marvelli got out of his seat, but his eyes were on Loretta as he straightened the collar of his jacket.

"Later," he mouthed silently.

Loretta watched them walk back down the corridor, the mountain gorilla and her hunky son-in-law. She grinned to herself, wishing the plane would hurry up and take them home.

Never has anyone wanted to be in New Jersey so much, she thought.

She was feeling electric, as if she'd just had a whole pot of espresso.